I0525584

Stay Hooked

SPRUCE COVE SERIES · BOOK TWO
A SPRUCE COVE NOVEL

Joy Thomas

Beach Road Publishing
South Carolina

Stay Hooked
Spruce Cove Series Book Two
ISBN (Paperback - Amazon): 979-8-990066-2-8
ISBN (Paperback – IngramSpark): 979-8-9930066-5-9
ISBN (eBook): 979-8-9930066-3-5
Instagram: Author Joy Thomas
Facebook: Joy of Fiction
TikTok: Joy of Fiction

Published by Beach Road Publishing
First edition, November 2025
For more information, visit: www.joyoffiction.com
Printed in the United States of America

Chapter 1

The courtroom buzzed with barely restrained whispers, a nervous hive of anticipation and suspicion. Ava McCormick sat in the front row, flanked by her grandmother, Esther, and Liz Walker, her best friend and co-conspirator in curiosity.

Esther sat stiffly, her spine ruler-straight, like she'd balanced a hardcover dictionary on her head all the way from the parking lot. Her hands gripping the edge of her purse like it held state secrets instead of three peppermint candies and a crumpled grocery list. Esther's lips were pursed, her eyes shadowed with worry and something that looked dangerously close to doubt. She gave Ava's wrist a small, almost absent squeeze, the kind that could mean comfort or caution. Ava couldn't tell which.

Liz had her reporter's notepad already open, pen in hand, and was chatting up the woman beside her, a middle-aged receptionist from the dental office. The one who always smelled faintly of cinnamon gum, if Ava wasn't mistaken. Liz's voice was low but practiced, her questions casual but direct. She'd already cataloged every reaction and remark, her eyes flicking from face to face with the attentiveness of someone born to stir the pot and tell the tale.

Liz leaned toward Ava, muttering, "If Beverly Klein adjusts that scarf one more time, I'm putting her down as a suspect."

The courtroom was packed, every bench filled, standing room only, and a quiet competition for who could share the juiciest scandal before catching Clerk of Court Kimberly Smith's death glare along the back wall. Word of the arraignment had rolled through town like a spring tide, pulling in locals like sea foam to rocks, inevitable, messy, and a little salty. Most had never seen anything like this here. A murder charge. Against a hometown man, no less. A girl everyone knew, and a man many had once trusted. Near the back, Coach Ellery leaned over a clipboard with Pete Branson, the pair deep in booster club talk, while Beverly Klein continued to adjust her scarf and whispered dramatically about someone parking in the pastor's reserved spot at church last Sunday.

Across the aisle sat Amelia Colburn's family.

Her mother, Delilah, wore black from head to toe with a gauzy scarf draped dramatically around her neck. Her face was stone and carefully painted. Caroline sat beside her mother, clutching Delilah's hand with quiet strength, the same steady presence she'd shown when she delivered Amelia's eulogy through trembling lips. Amelia's brother Mason, who looked lean and weathered like he was carved out of driftwood, sat on the other side of Delilah. His eyes were furious, arms crossed and his jaw tight. His gaze was locked on the front of the room. His knuckles were white. You could feel the anger radiating from him like heat off asphalt.

Beside Mason sat their younger cousin Finn, barely twenty, eyes red-rimmed, his foot bouncing uncontrollably. He wore a hooded sweatshirt under a blazer, clearly unsure of how to dress for the occasion. On his other side, Amelia's aunt clutched a tissue to her mouth like it was the only thing keeping her from screaming.

Ava glanced toward the empty jury box, which loomed like a shadowed stage. No jurors today. This was only the arraignment. She wondered how many people in this very room would be called when the trial began. Would they even be able to hold the trial in Spruce Cove? The town was too small, too tight knit. Everyone had already formed an opinion. A change of venue felt inevitable.

The heavy door at the back of the courtroom swung open.

Ava's breath caught.

Chap Fisher was led in, hands cuffed but not shackled at the ankles. He wore a plain dress shirt, blazer and a blue tie that was crooked and faded, as if someone had helped him put it on without knowing how. William would've had the knot straight, pressed sharp as a magazine ad. Chap's was crooked, stubborn, real. And it broke her heart a little.

The blazer didn't quite fit, adding to the disheveled look that made him seem more like a lost boy than a man on trial. His hair, usually tousled in a way that looked careless but charming, was flat and damp at the roots. His eyes were downcast until he crossed the threshold of the aisle and then they met Ava's.

He looked nothing like the man who'd once handed her a wrench that afternoon on the boat and told her she could fix it.

There was no easy grin, no relaxed shoulders, no trace of the man who teased her for over-salting her smoked salmon. His face was pale and drawn, eyes dark with exhaustion, fear or both. The tie made him look like a boy pretending to be a man, and the stubble lining his jaw only emphasized how out of place he was in this room.

Gasps rose around the courtroom. Liz scribbled furiously beside her. Esther sucked in a sharp breath. Ava felt the air thicken, as if everyone had forgotten how to breathe.

Deputy Ryan Hale guided Chap gently but firmly toward the defense table. Chap looked straight ahead, but Ava could tell he was aware of every pair of eyes drilling into his back. He stood still as his cuffs were removed, the tie now askew under the court's harsh lighting.

Chap turned and looked over his shoulder.

His eyes found Ava's instantly.

For a moment, the noise of the courtroom dulled. Ava's breath caught. He didn't smile. He didn't nod. But the look was unmistakable: haunted, searching for something familiar. It lasted no more than a second, but it rooted her to the bench.

Then he turned away, and the moment was gone.

"All rise," the clerk of court announced.

A collective shuffling of feet and benches followed as the entire courtroom stood. The sound of movement was accompanied by the rustle of jackets and the quiet thud of boots shifting on the wooden floor. Men removed their caps, some clutching them respectfully to their chests, others nervously wringing the brims in their hands.

The side door opened, and Judge Meredith Cleary entered. She was tall, elegant in a robe that looked newly pressed, with silver hair pulled into a low bun and horn-rimmed glasses perched at the edge of her nose. She walked with the confidence of someone who had long since stopped trying to prove herself. Her presence was commanding, a blend of civility and steel.

She seated herself and scanned the room with a look that promised decorum and swift correction if needed.

"You may be seated. This court is now in session," the clerk said.

Ava's throat tightened. The charge: first-degree murder.

Judge Cleary looked at Chap with a face that revealed nothing. "How do you plead?"

Chap's voice was quiet, strained. "Not guilty, Your Honor."

The silence that followed stretched long and tense.

The District Attorney stood, his expression grave but confident. Chief Harrow sat beside him, arms crossed, eyes locked on Chap. The charge was read, first-degree murder, and Ava already knew the rest. She'd read the indictment more times than she could count, each time feeling her chest tighten. Amelia Colburn, found in the harbor near Chap's boat. Dressed for a night out. Blunt force trauma. No defensive wounds. A burner phone. A single text sent moments before her estimated time of death: I'm here. Are you?

Mason made a guttural sound from across the aisle. Finn's head dropped. Delilah's lips trembled, but she didn't cry.

"Witnesses confirm the defendant and the victim had been seen arguing the night of and in the days prior," Harrow continued. "They had a known romantic history. There was no alibi. No explanation for the two-hour gap the night of Amelia's death."

4

Esther leaned forward slightly, like a woman bracing for an earthquake. Ava could feel her heartbeat in her throat.

The judge didn't move. Her eyes flicked between Chief Harrow, Chap, and the gallery.

The defense attorney stood, stammering something about circumstantial evidence. He cited Chap's years of service to the town, his lack of criminal history, his cooperative behavior. But the words didn't carry. They fluttered like moths against a closed window.

The judge ordered Chap remanded to the city jail pending transfer to prison. No bail.

The gavel struck. The noise was sharp, surgical. Final.

As Chap turned to be led away, his eyes met Ava's one last time. This time, there was no recognition. Only blankness. Like he had disappeared inside himself.

Ava's body stayed frozen in place, but her mind raced.

William would've told her to stay out of this. To protect her peace. He wasn't wrong. But staying away was the one thing she couldn't do.

***

Outside the courthouse, Ava paused on the steps, blinking against the cold. The fresh air did little to settle the buzz in her brain. Around her, people whispered, shifting in the shadows. Ava glanced back at the courthouse behind her, its windows like watching eyes.

"Annie's?" Liz asked, voice quiet but steady.

Ava nodded.

They crossed the street in silence.

By the time Ava and Liz stepped into Annie's, Martha was already mid-rant, waving a spatula like she was swatting flies.

"If the supplier thinks I'm paying that much for flour, they've got another thing coming. Next, they'll be charging extra for the oxygen we breathe."

A man at the counter chuckled without looking up from his crossword.

"Careful, Martha. Don't give them ideas."

Martha spotted Ava and Liz and pointed the spatula at them like an accusation.

"You're late. Your booth's been looking lonely for fifteen whole minutes."

Without waiting for an answer, she poured two mugs and slid them across the counter.

"And don't even think about asking for the good muffins. Frank already beat you to them."

Frank grinned without glancing up.

"Early bird gets the muffin."

Ava smirked.

"And the cholesterol."

They made their way to the back booth. Ava curled her fingers around the mug, letting the heat soak in. Her voice was barely above a whisper.

"Did you see his face? Right before they took him out?"

Liz nodded slowly.

"Like a man walking to his own funeral."

"Like he was in disbelief," Ava murmured. "His eyes were empty."

Ava folded and refolded the same napkin as she remembered the way his hand used to brush hers when he passed her coffee, the way he stopped asking questions when she needed quiet and how he hummed Johnny Cash like it was a language only they shared. How could this man be a killer?

Ava blinked hard.

"He didn't do it, Liz."

Liz took a long sip.

"You've only known him a few months."

"I know. But it doesn't add up. That burner phone, the text. None of it makes sense."

"They argued," Liz said gently. "And she was found near his boat. They had history."

"Everyone argues. And 'history' doesn't make you a killer. They don't have anything concrete. Just bad timing and assumptions."

"You really believe he's innocent?"

Ava nodded.

"Yeah. I do."

Liz leaned back, a wry smile tugging at her lips.

"McCormick, last week you wrote eight hundred words about the town's oldest crab pot. Now you're talking murder?"

She took another sip.

"What's next, a Pulitzer?"

Ava smirked, though her pulse ticked higher.

"You think we can figure this out?"

Liz tilted her head.

"I think you've already decided you can and you're just waiting for the rest of us to catch up."

Ava smiled, but it didn't quite reach her eyes.

Outside, the clouds pressed lower, and Spruce Cove held its breath.

Chapter 2

The scent of dark roast filled the McCormick kitchen long before the sun broke over the harbor. Ava stood at the stove, barefoot, her fingers curled tightly around her favorite chipped mug. The warmth seeped into her skin but did nothing for the cold settling in her chest. The house was too quiet, like even the floorboards were holding their breath. Yesterday had carved something out of her, left her feeling hollow in a way grief didn't quite explain.

Chap's face haunted her. That flicker of recognition when their eyes met. That second look, the blank one, like he was already halfway gone. She didn't know which one broke her more.

She'd hardly slept. Tossed and turned until the pillow was damp and the shadows had shifted on the ceiling. When the clock hit 5:47 a.m., she gave up entirely and came downstairs to chase thoughts of yesterday's arraignment in the quiet hum of the percolator.

There was something about the early hours in this house. How the light hit the salt-streaked windows just so, how the kitchen always smelled faintly of lemon oil and burnt toast. This place had been a cocoon for her once. A refuge. Now, it felt like a waiting room for a truth she wasn't ready to hear.

The quiet click of the back door snapped her out of it.

Liz Walker swept in with a gust of sea air and a white paper bag. "I come bearing pastries and judgment," she said, plopping the bag on the counter like it was evidence.

Ava raised a brow. "You brought judgment to *my* kitchen? Bold move."

"Journalistic reflex," Liz said, kicking off her boots and rolling up her sleeves. "You looked like someone who needed caffeine and a push."

She pulled out a pair of cinnamon rolls the size of saucers. Ava offered a tight smile. Liz bit into her pastry thoughtfully, then said: "Okay, I have a serious question. Are you going to *be* Ava McCormick, high school valedictorian and Yale graduate, or do we get Ava 'he's-just-misunderstood' McCormick who ignores red flags?"

Ava let out a humorless laugh. "I haven't figured that out yet. Depends on how much sugar's in that cinnamon roll."

Liz flashed a grin. "That's what I thought. This …" she waved the pastry around "… is self-care."

Ava handed her a mug. "Doctor's orders."

"Exactly." Liz set her cup down with purpose. "Now, we need a plan A?"

They settled at the table, the space between them filled with steam, sugar, and unspoken things. For a few beats, it was quiet.

"So," Liz began again, her voice lower, "we're really doing this?"

"I think we have to."

"Do we?" Liz picked at a flake of pastry. "Because what I saw yesterday wasn't just a courtroom. It was a town ready to crucify a man, which means we aren't going to be particularly popular."

Ava looked down at her coffee. "And not one of them actually *knows* what happened."

"Neither do we," Liz replied. "Which is exactly why we can't go into this with blinders on. I know you care about him."

"I don't just care," Ava said quietly. "I *know* him. Or I think I do. I hope I do."

That was the thing. She couldn't stop remembering every good deed that she had seen in her short time in Spruce Cove. She remembered the way he once offered her his raincoat without a word when she forgot hers on George's boat. How he erected a wire fence around Esther's raspberries to keep the deer from helping themselves. He'd had a quiet way of noticing, of showing up, of listening without interrupting. And now ...

"Now you're not sure what you know anymore," Liz finished for her, gently.

Ava nodded. "It's like I'm holding pieces of two different people, and I don't know which one is real."

Liz reached for her notebook but didn't open it. "You can believe in him. But you still have to ask the hard questions."

"I will," Ava said. "But I need to do this my way."

"No torch and pitchfork?" Liz teased.

"Just coffee and uncomfortable truths."

Liz leaned back in her chair, expression softening. "Alright. Then let's treat this like a real investigation. No bias. No assumptions. We look at everyone, including Chap."

Ava hesitated, then nodded. "Deal."

Esther's voice broke the moment. "You girls making deals this early in the morning?"

They both turned. Esther stood in the doorway, robe belted tightly, hair still in its nighttime braid. Her face was unreadable, but her tone held that familiar edge. Gentle but firm, like ice just beneath the surface.

"Morning, Grandma," Ava said cautiously.

Esther walked to the sink and filled the kettle, her movements smooth and practiced. "I heard you get up. Figured you'd be stewing."

"I wasn't."

"You were. You always stir your coffee clockwise when you're anxious. Counterclockwise when you're just cold."

Liz let out a soft laugh. "That's ... weirdly specific and disturbingly accurate."

Esther turned, eyes fixed on Ava. "Are you really sure this is what you want to do? Poke around in a dead girl's life?"

"She wasn't just a headline. She was someone's daughter, sister, friend."

"And Chap?" Esther asked. "Where does he fit in?"

Ava held her grandmother's gaze. "He fits where the truth puts him."

Esther studied her for a long moment, then nodded slowly. "Just remember, truth's a tricky thing. Sometimes it sets you free. Sometimes it burns everything down."

Liz straightened in her chair, sensing the undertow. "We're not looking to burn anything. Just to understand what actually happened. For Amelia, for everyone."

Esther's lips pressed into a thin line, unreadable. "You dig long enough; you always hit something. Just be sure you're ready for what comes up."

She turned toward the stove, pulling out a skillet. "Truth doesn't care what you *want* it to be. It's not a story you can rewrite. It's the law of things. Solid, sometimes brutal, always there whether you're ready or not."

Liz gave Ava a look and leaned in. "Your grandma *is* the law. Someone get this woman a robe and a bench."

Ava almost laughed and it felt like oxygen rushing in after a long dive. She stood and grabbed plates. "Let's eat. We've got work to do."

***

The shop was freezing.

Ava tugged her sleeves over her hands and kicked the space heater with her heel, trying to coax it into doing more than grumbling. The McCormick shop had once been George's sacred space, part workshop, part nautical junkyard, the walls still lined with old floats, rusted hooks, and one very suspicious anchor lamp that hadn't worked since 1993. Now, it was their war room. Their crime board. Their best shot. The wind creaked through the weather-warped wood doors, and a thin draft whispered under the eaves like a secret.

Liz stood beside the whiteboard they'd propped against the far wall, uncapping a red marker like she was about to crack open Watergate. "Alright, McCormick," she said, all business. "Let's begin with the obvious. Our victim."

She wrote "Amelia Colburn" in all caps across the center.

"Found in the harbor. No defensive wounds. Cause of death: blunt force trauma. Burner phone in her pocket, one text sent to a second burner phone that she bought at 10:39 pm, 'I'm here. Are you?'"

Ava stood next to her, arms crossed. "Estimated time of death between 10:45 and midnight. Body discovered by a dockhand at 6:12 the next morning."

Liz drew a quick circle around Amelia's name, then began webbing out lines like spokes on a wheel. Chap. Caroline. Mason. Delilah. The bar. The Colburn house. The harbor. A jagged little cluster of scribbles that already looked like a family drama crossed with a crime scene.

Liz uncapped a green marker. "Alright, should we add Wanda the librarian to the list? She once shushed Amelia for talking during silent reading hour. Motive, if you ask me."

Ava cracked a smile. "We're not adding Wanda."

"Fine. What about Tim from the marine shop? He's been mad ever since someone stole his prized bait bucket."

Ava raised an eyebrow. "Pretty sure he just misplaced it. Again."

"That's what they *want* you to think," Liz muttered, scribbling Tim's name in the corner with a question mark. "I'm just saying, the man owns five taxidermy bears. That's not nothing."

"Should we add Martha? I hear she's been hoarding blueberry muffins and unresolved grudges."

Ava stared back at Amelia's name.

"She touched everyone in this town," Ava murmured. "Even the people who say they didn't know her."

"Especially those people," Liz said. "She was magnetic in that complicated-girl kind of way. You could feel it just walking into a room with her. The kind of person who made you feel seen like she was peeling back layers you didn't know you had."

Ava winced. "She could also be cruel."

"Cruel and compelling. That's a dangerous mix."

They stood quietly for a moment, marker fumes mixing with cold air. Then Liz drew a hard underline under Chap's name.

Ava's hand hesitated near Chap's name.

"Let's talk motive. He and Amelia had history. A messy one."

"Messy doesn't mean murderous," Ava said, but her voice lacked bite.

Liz tapped the marker cap against her chin. "Okay. What about Mason? Overprotective older brother, quick temper. Didn't exactly hide his dislike for Chap. Wouldn't have been pleased if he knew she was pregnant."

"I don't think he was subtle about disliking anyone," Ava said. "And hating your sister's ex doesn't exactly rise to motive. If it did, half this town would be in handcuffs."

"True," Liz admitted. "Then there's Caroline. The golden child, the fixer. Held Delilah together at the arraignment like it was her job."

Ava uncapped a second marker and began drawing lines of her own. "If Amelia was in trouble, Caroline would've known or at least guessed."

"Unless Amelia was keeping secrets."

"She had a burner phone, Liz. She *was* keeping secrets."

They stared at the board again. Red and blue ink bleeding like veins. One line snaked from Amelia to the phrase Liz had scrawled hastily in the corner: Unknown contact.

"That's the key," Ava said softly. "Whoever she was meeting, it wasn't someone she associated with in her normal life."

"Then maybe it wasn't about love," Liz said. "Maybe it was about leverage. Money. Blackmail. A secret."

Ava pulled the sleeves of her sweatshirt tighter. "Do you think someone was threatening her?"

"I think someone wanted her quiet."

Liz said it gently, but it still settled like frost in Ava's chest.

Ava stared at the board, her jaw tightening. "We have to talk about the pregnancy."

Liz turned, surprised but not dismissive.

"It barely came up in court," Ava continued. "No one wants to touch it, but it changes everything. She was only a few weeks along. Early enough to keep quiet."

Liz nodded slowly. "Because if someone got her pregnant and she didn't want anyone to know who, that's not just a complication. That's a motive."

Ava added, "A secret relationship. A man with something to lose. Or someone who panicked when she said she was keeping the baby."

"And whoever he is," Liz said, "he may still be out there."

Liz was already two steps ahead, tapping the marker against her chin. "Maybe she didn't know who the father was. Or maybe she did and knew he wouldn't want anyone else to know."

Ava nodded slowly. "If she was seeing someone in secret, it has to be someone with something to lose."

She hesitated. "Chap was kind of in a relationship."

"Right," Liz said, catching the thread. "So maybe it wasn't about hiding Amelia. Maybe it was about hiding *himself*. Married? Involved? Someone who'd lose everything if the truth came out."

The air in the shop shifted again. This time cooler, tighter. Ava didn't speak, but her fingers tightened around the marker.

"Or older. Or powerful. Or someone close."

They exchanged a look. The kind of wordless reckoning that passes between friends who know when not to say the obvious.

"That pregnancy changes everything," Liz said finally. "If we figure out who the father is …"

"We figure out what she was hiding," Ava finished.

They both turned back to the whiteboard. Liz added a red question mark next to the word pregnancy and drew a dotted line out to the side, still unconnected.

"I keep thinking about that text," Ava whispered. "'I'm here. Are you?' It doesn't sound afraid. It sounds expectant."

"Like someone she'd met before. Someone she trusted."

Ava drew a slow breath, feeling her throat tighten. "And that narrows it down to basically everyone in town."

The space heater gave a final huff, then whirred into something vaguely resembling warmth. Ava didn't move from the board.

Liz scribbled one more line, connecting Chap and Amelia with a red arrow. "Until we can prove otherwise, everyone's a suspect."

Ava didn't answer. She was staring at a blank corner of the board. Something about the shape of the map they'd created bothered her. Not what was on it, but what was missing.

"She'd been back for months," Ava said slowly. "The dust had mostly settled. Then out of nowhere, she's dead in the harbor. What changed?"

"Maybe she found something. Or someone found her."

Ava reached for the black marker and wrote two words in the empty space.

Why now?

***

The wind off the water slapped Ava's cheeks as she stepped onto the weathered planks of the harbor dock. The tide was low, leaving boats bobbing in their slips, their lines groaning with each restless movement. Seagulls wheeled overhead, screeching like they had something urgent to report. The whole harbor smelled like fish, diesel, and old secrets.

Liz trailed behind, trying to wrangle her scarf from the wind's grip. "You know, for a town obsessed with coffee and wool, you'd think someone would've invented windproof gossip."

Ava didn't laugh. Her gaze locked onto the row of slips, most of them still, except for a few boats rocking against their bumpers like they couldn't settle either.

She stopped at Slip Nine.

Chap's slip.

Empty now. The ropes coiled neatly. No sign that the *Malahini* had ever docked there. Except Ava could still see it, clear as anything. Chap in his worn flannel, tossing a line to George. The sound of boots on wet planks. Her own laugh, rising above the water like a secret she hadn't meant to tell.

They walked further down. Ava crouched beside the cleat, fingers brushing the edge of the dock.

"This is where she was found?" Liz asked, voice quieter now. Reverent, almost.

Ava shook her head. "A few feet off. Floating just past the end of the dock. No blood. No bruising that would've meant a fight." She paused. "Blunt force trauma. That's all they could say for sure."

Liz crossed her arms against the cold, her tone sharpening. "So, either she was hit and pushed or fell and someone let her drown."

"Or someone made it look like that."

They were quiet for a moment, the wind tugging at their jackets and the smell of low tide thick in the air.

"You remember what she texted?" Ava asked.

Liz nodded. "'I'm here. Are you?'"

"It sounds so casual. Like a hookup."

"Not a warning," Liz agreed. "Not a plea. She wasn't scared."

"Or she didn't *know* she should be."

Ava rose slowly, brushing her damp hands on her jeans. "She didn't drive. No car was parked nearby. Nothing showed on the video by the gas pump. Someone picked her up or followed her here."

"Harbor night manager didn't see anything?"

"He said he heard voices. Laughter. But that was it. Thought it was just kids sneaking beers."

"Anyone ask if he recognized the laugh?"

Ava looked at her. "You want to drive over to his trailer and ask?"

16

"Tempting," Liz said. "But let's not get kicked off the docks before noon."

They moved slowly along the walkway, stopping now and then to glance into the water. The surface was calm, but shadows shifted below, and Ava couldn't stop thinking about Amelia's hair fanning out like seaweed. Her dress soaked. Her eyes open. The stories people kept whispering. *She must've slipped. Must've been drunk. Must've been in love.*

"You think she came here to meet Chap?" Liz finally asked, her voice nearly lost in the wind.

"I think she came to meet someone," Ava said. "But I'm not convinced it was him."

"She was pregnant."

Liz stopped walking. "You think she was going to tell him?"

"Maybe." Ava turned to face her. "He told me he already knew. If he did find out that night, maybe he didn't take it well."

Liz didn't respond, but her face said enough. She didn't want to believe it either. Chap had that boy-next-door veneer, the one that made you want to root for him. But even golden boys could fracture under pressure.

Ava's hands were shoved deep in her pockets. "I just, I keep going over the last time I saw her. We weren't close, but I could tell she'd changed. There was something unsettled in her."

Liz tilted her head. "Guilty?"

"No. Determined."

They walked back toward the parking lot, boots echoing softly against the wood. As they reached the edge of the dock, Ava glanced back one last time.

"It's like the water swallowed the truth," she murmured.

Liz followed her gaze. "Then we fish it out."

The Colburn house stood like it always had: too perfect, too still. The yard was manicured even after the fade of summer, and the porch swing barely moved in the breeze, like it knew better than to draw attention.

Ava hesitated at the gate. She could see Caroline through the front window, her silhouette framed in glass and calm. Inside, the house still smelled like lavender and floor polish, the way Liz said it always had during sleepovers back in middle school. Back when Amelia still wore lip gloss that tasted like cherries and Caroline kept her books in color-coded stacks.

Liz nudged her gently. "You good?"

Ava nodded, but her stomach was a knot. They weren't here as friends. Not really.

Caroline opened the door before they knocked.

"I saw you coming," she said, folding her arms across her chest. "Tea?"

Liz blinked at the abruptness, but Ava just nodded. "Sure. If it's not a bad time."

"It's always a bad time lately," Caroline said, stepping back to let them in. "But come on. It's cold out."

Inside, nothing had changed since Ava interviewed Amelia for the Salmonberry Queen story. The living room was immaculate, soft throws folded over the couch and magazines stacked in surgical symmetry. A candle burned quietly on the coffee table. Something citrus and clean. Grief, it seemed, had not disrupted the decor.

Caroline poured tea into porcelain cups like she was hosting book club instead of a conversation about her dead sister.

"How are you holding up?" Ava asked.

Caroline gave a small, polite smile. "Like anyone would. It's awful. And numbing. You don't realize how many people want a piece of your pain until it's the only thing you're allowed to offer."

Liz nodded, her notepad still tucked away. "We don't want to push. We just had some questions. Not official, just trying to understand."

Caroline sat. "You're reporters, you're not detectives. So, what are you hoping to understand?"

Ava sat beside her carefully. "We're trying to piece together who Amelia might've seen the night she died."

Caroline's jaw flexed. "You think I know?"

"We think she may have confided in you. Even just a little. You two were close."

Caroline looked down at her tea. "Amelia confided in no one. Not really. She kept things to herself, always had. Even when we were kids, she'd lie about sneaking out just so I wouldn't get in trouble too."

Liz leaned in. "But had she changed lately? Was she seeing someone new? Acting different?"

Caroline hesitated. Just long enough.

"She was restless," she said finally. "It felt like she was waiting for something. Or someone."

Ava exchanged a glance with Liz. "Do you know who?"

Caroline shook her head. "If I did, I would've told the police." She stopped, her breath catching for the first time. "She wouldn't tell me. I asked, more than once."

The room grew still. Even the candle seemed to lower its flame.

Ava took a breath. "Were you aware she was pregnant?"

Caroline didn't answer at first. Then she set her teacup down slowly, precisely. Her fingers trembled.

"I found out after," she said. "When the coroner called me. They said it was early."

Liz spoke gently. "Do you think anyone else knew?"

Caroline stared at the candle. "Maybe the father, maybe not. Amelia wasn't always careful with her heart, but she was protective of her power. If she didn't say who it was, it was because she had a reason."

Ava tried not to flinch. "Was there someone she was seeing? Someone involved with someone else?"

Caroline's lips parted, then closed again. "Chap was involved." She didn't say more, just glanced meaningfully at Ava.

The room seemed to shrink.

Ava blinked, but didn't look away. Her throat tightened. There was no accusation in Caroline's tone, just fact wrapped in restraint. Still, it stung like being handed a betrayal she hadn't asked for.

Liz shifted beside her but said nothing.

"You think Amelia would've gone there anyway?" she asked finally, her voice lower.

Caroline nodded slowly. "She didn't always make safe choices. And Chap, he never fully closed that door."

Ava looked down at her tea, suddenly cold in her hands. Her fingers tightened around the cup, but she didn't drink.

Finally, Caroline stood. "I think that's all I can say."

Ava rose with her. "Thank you. Really."

Caroline gave a small nod. "I want her to have peace. Even if it means shaking things loose."

As they stepped back into the cold, Liz exhaled hard. "Well. That felt like a polite slap."

"Did you catch the pause? When I mentioned the pregnancy?" Ava asked.

"Yeah, like she knew more than she wanted to admit."

Ava glanced back at the house. The porch swing moved now, ever so slightly. Not from wind. From something else.

She pulled her coat tighter, jaw set.

"Peace doesn't come from silence," she said. "It comes from truth."

Chapter 3

The McCormick house smelled like nutmeg and legacy.

Esther had been up since dawn, orchestrating Thanksgiving dinner with the precision of a five-star general. She moved through the kitchen in wool socks and her ancient "Butterball Commander" apron, muttering like the turkey could hear her.

"Roast, not incinerate," she hissed at the oven. "This is not a Christmas ham."

Ava stood at the counter, chopping celery with more force than necessary. Her hands moved automatically, but her mind was elsewhere. Looping through images of Chap in that courtroom, the way he'd looked at her like she was the last familiar thing in a foreign world.

Her thoughts were interrupted by a loud cheer from the living room. "Defense just ran it back for six!" George bellowed, a fist raised from his recliner. His mug of cider nearly toppled.

Esther didn't flinch. "Every year, same game, same cheer. He won't remember the score tomorrow, but he'll tell people my stuffing changed his life."

Ava smirked faintly. "Start signing autographs now. You'll be a legend by dessert."

Before Esther could reply, the front door flung open and Liz stomped in, cheeks flushed from the cold rain. A bottle of wine in one hand and a half-tamed grin on her face.

"I come bearing alcohol and a sparking personality," she declared. "Mostly alcohol."

Trailing behind her was Mabel in a red fleece cape, cradling a leopard-print cat carrier like it contained royalty. Which, of course it did.

"Princess said there's unresolved tension here. Probably between the cranberry sauce and whoever's pretending to like it."

Esther side-eyed the carrier. "She better not scratch the furniture."

"She wouldn't dare," Mabel said with indignation. "She's a registered emotional support oracle."

Liz raised an eyebrow. "I thought that was just your Etsy store tagline."

Mabel gave her a long look, then proudly lifted the foil off the dish she was carrying. "I brought my famous Harvest Delight," she said proudly.

Liz squinted. "Is that shredded carrots? In Jell-O?"

"With raisins," Mabel beamed.

"That's not a side dish," Liz muttered. "That's a cry for help in gelatin."

"It's a recipe from a *church lady*," Mabel snapped.

"Was she excommunicated after serving it?"

Esther intervened before it turned into a casserole-based duel. "Set it on the end, next to the rolls. Far end."

Ava couldn't stop herself from picturing the other Thanksgiving she was supposed to be at. By now, she and William would have been sitting at his parents' mahogany table as man and wife. China plates gleaming under a chandelier, everyone passing dishes like they were auditioning for a Norman Rockwell painting. Instead, she was here at Esther and George's, where the mashed potatoes were served in a chipped ceramic bowl and the gravy boat listed slightly to one side. Two different versions of her life, and she wasn't sure which one she was supposed to want anymore.

Dinner came together like it always did. Slightly behind schedule, plated with love and fraying nerves. The table was a glorious mess of mismatched China and old silver. Candles flickered in jelly jar holders. The cranberry sauce quivered in that unsettling, factory-made way. George had been forced into a button-down, but his tie hung loose and proud.

The conversation flowed. George regaled them with the time he deep-fried a turkey in the yard and singed off his eyebrows. Liz reenacted a newsroom meltdown involving a broken fax machine, a caffeine crash, and a story about feral chickens. Mabel read Princess's aura with a crystal on a string.

"Your energy is very purple today," she told George.

"That the good purple or the senile purple?" he asked.

"Bit of both," she replied.

Laughter filled the room, but Ava felt its echo more than its warmth. She pushed peas around her plate while everyone else refilled their glasses.

Then Mabel struck.

"Princess says Chap didn't do it," she announced, fork poised midair. "She had a vision."

The room stilled.

Esther's hand froze on the gravy boat. George's fork clinked softly against his plate.

"We're not talking about this on Thanksgiving," George said, voice low, firm.

Mabel blinked. "Princess disagrees. She says…"

"She's a cat," he cut in.

"She's a *seer*," Mabel corrected. "And she's deeply concerned about local injustice."

Esther cleared her throat. "Gravy's getting cold."

The tension broke, but the air felt heavier. Liz didn't meet Ava's eyes. No one did.

Ava stabbed a slice of turkey with more force than necessary. Chap should have been here. Should've had seconds, teased Liz, and coaxed a reluctant smile out of Esther. Instead, he was behind bars, probably eating reheated turkey loaf under fluorescent lights.

She could feel the guilt rising like steam off the mashed potatoes.

Later, as the pie cooled and Mabel tried to teach Princess to high-five for leftovers, Ava found Liz alone in the kitchen, sipping wine straight from the bottle.

"I need to see him," Ava said softly.

Liz nodded. "I figured. Let's bring pie. It's a holiday."

***

The rain had turned to sleet by the time Ava and Liz reached the sheriff's station. Spruce Cove didn't decorate much for the holidays, but someone had taped a lopsided paper turkey to the front window. It looked like it had seen some things.

Ava shifted the covered pie tin in her hands and exhaled slowly. "Are we really going to jail on Thanksgiving?"

Liz pulled open the door. "Too late to back out now. Besides, even the wrongly accused deserved carbs on a holiday."

Inside, the office was warm and mostly empty. Deputy Hale sat behind the front desk, chewing what looked like a turkey sandwich from the gas station deli. He wore a wrinkled flannel jacket over his uniform and the kind of expression reserved for men who'd drawn the short straw on holiday duty.

He glanced up as the door swung shut behind them. "Well, well," he said, voice deadpan. "If it isn't investigative journalism and moral ambiguity, coming to brighten my shift."

Liz leaned on the counter, chin resting in her hand. "Happy Thanksgiving, Ryan."

He eyed the pie tin suspiciously. "That what I think it is?"

"Esther's pumpkin pie," Ava said. "With real whipped cream. Bourbon-infused."

Ryan sniffed the air. "Bribery smells better than usual."

Liz smirked. "Consider it a goodwill offering."

He leaned back in his chair, arms crossed. "What do you want?"

Ava hesitated. "Just ten minutes. With Chap. He doesn't know we're coming."

Ryan arched a brow. "And I'm supposed to break jail protocol for a pastry?"

Liz smiled sweetly. "Not just any pastry. This one came from Esther McCormick's oven and nearly cost Ava her left eyebrow when she tried to help brown the top."

Ava cleared her throat. "Please. Just a few minutes. I'll bring a slice of pie in, nothing more."

Ryan studied her, his expression softening just slightly. "Cell block's empty. He's the only one back there. Just, don't touch anything and I'll pretend I didn't see it."

Liz winked. "We knew you had a heart under all that lawful neutrality."

He handed Ava a keycard. "Last cell on the left. Don't slam the door, it sticks."

Ava nodded, thanked him, and followed the corridor down the hall, her boots echoing on the cold linoleum. The pie was warm through the paper towel, and her hands gripped it like an offering.

When she reached the cell, she paused at the bars.

***

Chap was sitting on the edge of his cot, arms resting on his knees, head bowed. His hair was slightly damp, as though he'd just rinsed off in the tiny sink. The orange jumpsuit made his skin look paler than she remembered. But it was still him.

He looked up and the second his eyes met hers, something shifted.

His whole face softened, like someone had cracked a window in a sealed room.

"Ava," he said, quiet. Disbelieving.

She stepped closer. "I come bearing contraband."

A smile tugged at the corner of his mouth. "Tell me it's not carrots in Jell-O."

"Esther would disown me. It's pumpkin. Still warm."

Chap stood and crossed to the bars. His eyes searched her face like he was looking for something he'd lost. "You didn't have to come."

"Maybe not," she said, carefully unwrapping the pie. "But you're stuck in here and I had leftovers. And Liz is currently seducing Ryan, so we've got a solid ten minutes."

He let out a quiet laugh that faded almost immediately.

Ava slid the pie through the bars. He sat back on the cot and took a bite like it was the first real food he'd had in days.

He closed his eyes. "This tastes like freedom."

"It tastes like bourbon and guilt, which is pretty much the McCormick brand."

He opened his eyes again, and they were less tired. "You look different."

"Post-turkey bloat and family dysfunction. It's seasonal."

"No," he said. "Not that. You look more like you."

That stopped her cold. "What's that supposed to mean?"

He set the pie down slowly. "Just that when I first met you, back on the dock, you looked like you were holding your breath. You don't anymore."

Ava blinked. Her throat tightened.

He looked down. "You shouldn't be here. Not because I don't want you to be. But because this place doesn't deserve you."

"Maybe not," she said. "But you're here. And someone needs to remind you you're not forgotten."

He stared at her like he didn't know what to say to that.

So, she did what she always did when silence got too loud.

She made a joke.

"You know," she said, folding her arms, "it's deeply disturbing how good you look in orange."

Chap raised an eyebrow. "Disturbing how?"

"Like I might need to examine some of my life choices."

He chuckled again, this time more freely.

Behind them, a door buzzed. Liz's voice floated down the corridor. Half flirty, half exasperated.

"Ryan, if you start listing football stats, I'm walking out of here."

Ava looked back at Chap, who'd gone quiet again. His hand still rested lightly on the empty plate.

"Happy Thanksgiving," she said softly.

"Thanks," he said. "For the pie. And for showing up."

Ava didn't move. Neither did he.

The air between them hummed. Not loud, not chaotic, but charged.

"You really didn't think I'd come?" she asked.

"Nope," he said. "You're smart and beautiful. You shouldn't waste your time."

Ava's fingers brushed the bar again. "You think this is a waste?"

"No," he said quickly. "I think it's the only good thing that's happened to me in days."

She swallowed hard, the words sticking in her throat like dry pie crust.

"I haven't really known what to do since Amelia died," she said quietly. "Everyone keeps looking at me like I'm supposed to know the story. And I don't. I just know something's off."

Chap nodded, stepping closer. "It is off. All of it."

"I keep thinking. What if I'm wrong about you?" Her voice cracked. "What if I believe in you and it makes everything worse?"

He didn't answer right away. Then he said, "Then at least I'll have had one person who believed in me, even when it cost her something."

She looked at him, really looked. Not just at the jumpsuit or the bruise near his collarbone or the way his hands were still callused from dock work, but at the person underneath.

And maybe that's when it happened. When she realized she wasn't coming to see Chap out of pity.

She came because something in her trusted him more than she trusted everyone else.

He stepped closer to the bars again, one hand wrapping around the cold metal, the other still brushing the edge of the pie tin.

"You keep doing that," he said, eyes locked on hers.

"What?"

"Knocking the wind out of me."

She swallowed. "You're in jail, Chap."

He tilted his head. "And you're the one who looks trapped."

That landed like a stone in her gut. She opened her mouth, then shut it. Looked away. Looked back.

"I don't know what I'm doing," she admitted.

"Neither do I," he said. "But I know what I want to do."

The buzz of fluorescent lights filled the silence between them.

Ava pressed her hand to the bars. Not quite a touch. Just close enough.

Chap mirrored her, his palm facing hers, just an inch of air and rusting iron between skin.

She whispered, "Tell me you didn't do it."

"I didn't do it," he said without hesitation.

And just like that, she believed him.

Ava leaned forward. Close. Close enough to feel the warmth of his breath. "Good," she said. "Because I'm getting really tired of not knowing what to believe in this town. But for some reason, I believe in *you*."

Chap looked at her like he might shatter if she disappeared.

"Come here," he murmured.

She moved to the narrow space where the bars split slightly wider, probably to allow handcuffs or paperwork through. It was barely a gap, but it was enough.

He bent slightly. She angled up.

And they kissed. Quick, desperate, and full of everything they hadn't said.

The metal bars were cold against her arms. His mouth was warm, and a little rough, and tasted faintly like bourbon whipped cream and grief.

It only lasted a breath. But it changed everything.

When they broke apart, both stayed still, like any movement might undo the moment.

"Well, add that to the list of things I'll overthink tonight."

"Yeah," he said. "I want another one."

Ava gave a soft laugh and stepped back, dizzy in a way that had nothing to do with the heat of the room.

"Next time, no bars," she said.

"Next time, no murder charges," he replied.

Another buzz sounded from the hall. Liz again, this time with a sharper edge to her voice.

"Ava? Wrap it up. Ryan's starting to tell me about his high school wrestling records."

Ava turned, heart thudding, emotions jumbled into something hot and dangerous and oddly bright.

Chap reached for her hand again but stopped himself.

"Be careful," he said. "Whatever you're about to do."

She nodded. "You too."

And then she left, the pie tin still warm, the kiss still burning.

***

The jail door buzzed behind her, and Ava stepped back into the warmth of the front office like she was waking up from something. Her cheeks were flushed. Her heart was still doing acrobatics.

Liz sat on the edge of Ryan's desk, nursing a second cup of vending-machine coffee. She raised her eyebrows when she saw Ava's face.

"You kissed him, didn't you?"

Ava blinked. "How?"

"You've got that dazed look," Liz said. "Like you just discovered carbs and pheromones can coexist."

Ava didn't answer.

Ryan leaned against the wall, arms crossed. "Nothing illegal happened, right?"

"Not unless flirting now counts as a misdemeanor," Ava said.

He shrugged. "Depends who you ask."

Ava and Liz stepped outside a minute later. The cold slapped Ava's face like reality reminding her who was still behind bars.

The sleet had slowed, but everything glistened under a thin sheen of ice. The kind of weather Spruce Cove always seemed to conjure for the holidays. Not a postcard winter, but something messier. Realer.

They walked in silence for a bit, boots crunching on the salted sidewalk.

"Well?" Liz finally asked. "Was it worth it?"

Ava exhaled. "It wasn't just about the pie."

Liz gave her a sidelong glance. "It never is."

Ava stopped near the curb, eyes fixed on the shimmer of ice under the streetlight. "He didn't do it."

"You sure?"

"Yes."

"Because he's charming? Or because you believe him?"

"Both," Ava said. "And because I know what guilt looks like. I've lived with it. Chap isn't carrying that."

Liz went quiet for a moment. "Then we better figure out who did it."

Ava nodded. "Yeah. We really do."

"Even if it means digging into stuff people in this town want to stay buried?"

"Yes," Ava said again. "Because if we don't find the truth, Chap rots in there. And I ..." She stopped, swiping at her eyes. "I won't let that happen."

Liz pulled her keys from her coat pocket and clicked them without looking. "Then let's start back at it tomorrow."

Ava turned to her. "You're still in?"

Liz grinned. "You kissed a murder suspect on Thanksgiving. I'm not letting you solve this without supervision."

They climbed into the car. The heater wheezed to life, spewing out air that smelled faintly of old coffee and pine-scented air freshener.

Ava looked out the window, watching sleet paint silver lines across the windshield.

Tomorrow, they'd begin asking questions no one wanted answered. But tonight, she let herself sit in the stillness.

The pie was gone. The kiss had happened. And everything was about to change.

***

Ava didn't go straight home after dropping off Liz.

She drove the long way, past the harbor, where the trollers were docked in a lazy row, hulls slick with rain and salt. Their ropes creaked gently in the wind, a low and familiar sound that tugged at something old in her chest.

She pulled over and killed the engine.

The sleet had finally stopped, but the air was sharp. The kind of cold that cut straight through wool and bone. Still, she rolled down the window a few inches. Let it in.

Chap's kiss was still warm on her lips.

She touched her mouth absently, not smiling, but not frowning either. It hadn't been romantic, not in the usual sense. It had been something else. Urgent. Lonely. Real.

She didn't know what it meant. Or what it would become. But it felt like a beginning. Or maybe the middle of something she hadn't admitted was starting.

Her phone buzzed. A text from Liz:

YOU IN LOVE WITH THE INMATE OR JUST HORNY?

Ava smiled, thumbs poised to type back.

Then paused.

She wasn't in love. She didn't know what she was. All she knew was that Chap didn't belong behind bars. And someone did.

She typed: *Tomorrow, we dig. No more guessing. No more lies.*

Then she sat in the silence, watching the boats rock, listening to the water slap against the pilings.

Spruce Cove had always been a place of routine. Same faces. Same gossip. Same seasonal casseroles.

But something was different now. The surface still looked smooth, but Ava knew better. There were ripples under it. Cracks forming.

And she was going to follow them.

All the way to the truth.

Chapter 4

The Gaff Hook hadn't changed. Same warped floorboards, same fryer grease and beer ground into the wood, same neon signs blinking like they were too tired to keep up. But Ava had.

The last time she'd walked through this door, she'd thought Spruce Cove was the kind of place where people had your back. Where a song on karaoke night and a few rounds of drinks meant you belonged. Then Chap was accused of murder, and she watched those same smiling faces shift in an instant. Neighbors turning on him with whispers and sidelong glances, as if loyalty had an expiration date.

Now, coming back felt different. She kept her gaze steady, ignoring the microphone in the corner, refusing to remember the night they'd begged her to sing *Jolene* and how she'd let herself believe the applause was friendship. She knew better now. In Spruce Cove, kindness came with edges, and people could cut you loose the moment it suited them.

She couldn't help but remember the moment Amelia had slid onto the stool beside her uninvited, confident, as if she owned the room. Amelia didn't stay long; she didn't need to. Her presence, her easy way of drawing eyes, was enough to make Ava feel like an extra in her own story.

And later, when Ava had watched her slip into that dim building across the street, the unease had settled in deep. She'd let it go at the time. But now? Now that memory scratched at her like something half-buried, just waiting to surface. That had been weeks ago. Before the arrest. Before

Amelia's body turned up in the water. Before every memory had a new weight.

Ava followed behind Liz, who made a beeline for a high-top table near the dartboard, like they were just here for a drink and not digging into someone's death.

"Different vibe tonight," Liz murmured as she slid onto the stool, her reporter's instincts already sparking behind narrowed eyes.

Ava nodded. The bar was quieter, a low hum of murmured conversation and clinking glasses. No karaoke. No laughter. Just the uneasy static of a town that didn't know where to look now that one of their own was in jail for murder.

They slipped into their seats. The bartender gave them a nod. Same guy from before, barrel-chested with a gray-flecked beard. Friendly enough. But his eyes lingered on Ava a moment longer than she liked, like she was wearing the front page across her forehead.

She wrapped her hands around the pint Liz had ordered, an Alaska IPA that tasted like pine needles. She let her eyes roam the room. There was a poker game in the back. A couple of dockhands hunched over the bar, their faces scrubbed pink from wind and cheap whiskey. Everything looked the same, but the air felt different. Like the moment right before a storm, when the sky goes still and even the regulars start watching each other a little too closely.

Ava leaned in toward Liz. "Last time I was here, I thought singing Dolly Parton would be the most embarrassing moment of my month."

Liz chuckled. "You're underselling it. It was bad. Brave, but bad."

Ava cracked a smile, just barely. "Braver than this?"

Liz tilted her beer toward her. "This time we're not here to impress anyone. We're hunting for the truth."

Ava looked around at the half-familiar faces, the wary glances, the silence undercutting every word. She could feel it. The weight of suspicion. Not just toward Chap. Toward anyone who dared to defend him.

"Well," she said softly, her voice almost lost under the buzz of the lights, "let's see who's willing to tell it."

**

It didn't take long for the room to notice her. Not just notice, register. Ava could feel the shift in the air as clearly as if someone had changed the music. The card game in the back grew quieter. One of the dockhands gave her a once-over that wasn't quite unfriendly, but definitely assessing. Even the bartender, who'd gone back to wiping down pint glasses, snuck glances every few minutes. As if trying to place her not just in the bar, but in the story everyone had been whispering about.

Chap's story.

Liz, unfazed, pulled a notebook from her coat pocket and flipped it open casually, like she was jotting a grocery list and not about to dig into a potential homicide. She scanned the room with the cool precision of someone used to being underestimated, then leaned toward Ava.

"We need someone who drinks just enough to talk, but not enough to slur."

Ava glanced around. "That narrows it down to exactly no one in this room."

Liz smirked. "You don't know Spruce Cove as well as you think."

Just then, a man in a faded Sitka hoodie and a trucker hat limped past them, nodding in Liz's direction. He smelled like salt and fish guts and maybe a little regret. Liz lit up like she'd spotted a source.

"Doug," she called. "You still playing trivia at O'Malley's or did they finally ban you for being too smart?"

Doug chuckled, slow and raspy. "They banned me for bein' too good-lookin'. Can't help that either."

He slid onto the stool beside her with a grunt, tipping an invisible hat toward Ava. "Don't think we've met."

"This is Ava," Liz said. "She's Chap's …"

Ava jumped in. "Friend."

Doug blinked. "Sure. Friend. Heard about the mess. Sorry it shook out like this."

He didn't say whether he thought Chap had done it. He didn't have to. The unspoken stretched between them like rope, frayed and fragile.

"You were in here that week, right?" Liz asked, her voice light. "You see Amelia around?"

Doug scratched at the back of his neck, looking up toward the ceiling as if the answer might be etched in the wood. "Yeah. She came in once or twice. Wasn't drinking. Sat over there." He pointed to a booth along the far wall. "Just stared at the door."

Ava's stomach twisted.

"Someone meeting her?"

Doug shrugged. "Maybe. Or maybe she was waiting for someone who didn't show."

He took a sip of his beer, the glass trembling slightly in his hand. "She looked nervous. That's what I remember. Like a kid about to lie to her mom."

Ava leaned in a little. "Nervous how?"

Doug didn't answer right away. He watched the foam settle in his glass, then gave a slow shrug.

"Not jumpy, exactly. Just off. Like she was trying real hard to act normal. But you could tell something was eating at her."

Liz scribbled in her notebook, her shorthand quick and neat. Ava stayed quiet, letting the silence coax Doug into filling it.

He did.

"She asked if I'd ever felt like someone was watching me," he said, then gave a dry chuckle. "Told her I was too ugly to be worth spying on. She didn't laugh. Just nodded, real serious, like she already knew who it was and was just looking for someone to say she wasn't crazy."

Ava felt a chill crawl along the back of her neck.

"Did she say who?" Liz asked.

Doug shook his head. "No names. But she kept checking her phone. Not texting. Just checking. Over and over. I told her the signal in here's garbage, but she said she wasn't expecting a call. Just wanted to see if anything changed."

Ava exchanged a glance with Liz.

Before they could ask more, another voice broke in.

"Amelia was always dramatic."

The woman who spoke leaned against the jukebox, arms crossed. Shoulder-length gray-blonde hair, sharp cheekbones, and a look that said she'd seen it all and didn't buy most of it. Ava didn't recognize her, but Liz gave her a nod.

"Evening, Mary."

Mary arched an eyebrow. "You're stirring things up again, Liz?"

"Just asking questions," Liz said. "Trying to understand what happened."

Mary sipped her whiskey. "Well, I saw Amelia in here that week too. Thursday, I think. She came in late, alone. Sat at the end of the bar, wouldn't meet anyone's eye. Guy next to her tried to flirt. It was Stan, I think. She shut it down fast."

Doug grunted. "Said she had a boyfriend. Wouldn't say who, though. Stan thought she was lying."

"She wasn't," Mary said flatly. "She was scared. Not of Stan. Of something else."

She held Ava's gaze a beat too long.

"And if I had to guess, I'd say it was someone close. Real close."

Ava's voice came out before she could think. "Why didn't she just say who it was?"

Mary's gaze sharpened. "Maybe she couldn't."

And just like that, Ava was back in that moment outside the bar. Watching Amelia disappear into the darkened building, her posture tight, her steps too quick. She hadn't been sneaking off for fun. She'd been slipping away like someone carrying something heavy.

Something she wasn't supposed to have.

***

The hum of the bar faded beneath the weight of Mary's words. Ava felt them settle like stones in her stomach. Not because she believed it was Chap, not yet, but because she could feel the room leaning in. Listening without listening.

Many folks had decided it was Chap. That theory had already bloomed all over town when he was arrested. Like mildew in a wet basement: quiet, stubborn, spreading.

Hearing people speculate about who it was here, in this bar, with someone who actually saw Amelia that week? It hit different.

Doug stood, glass in hand. "Pool table's calling. At least it doesn't talk back," he mumbled, already halfway to the back.

Mary didn't move. She stared into her drink like it might offer more answers than Ava ever could.

"What do you think she was afraid of?" Ava asked, her voice quieter than before.

Mary shrugged. "Hard to say. Could've been someone leaning on her for something she knew. Could've been something she was mixed up in that went sideways." She looked at Ava again. "Or someone she thought cared about her until they didn't."

The words stung. Not just because of what they implied but because Ava had asked herself the same question in the darkest corners of her doubt.

Liz cut in, her voice cool but probing. "You said she wouldn't say who she was seeing. Did she ever come in with anyone?"

Mary shook her head. "Not once. Always alone. Always watching the door like she expected someone who never showed."

Ava's thoughts jumped to that night again. Amelia slipping into the dark building across the street. She remembered the way her steps had quickened, the way she hadn't looked back.

"She went into that building across from here," Ava said, more to herself than anyone.

Mary's brow furrowed. "The old red one? That place?"
She made a face.

"It's half-empty these days. Used to be a travel agency, I think. Now there's a bookkeeper in one office. Denise Ellery, maybe? And someone doing massage therapy or reiki or something weird upstairs. Place is a hodgepodge."

Ava filed that away, her pulse ticking. That didn't make anything clearer. If anything, it made it worse. Amelia could have met anyone. For anything.

Mary sipped her whiskey. "I wouldn't read too much into it. Unless you think she was getting her taxes done after midnight."

A man two stools down gave a pointed cough and looked away when Ava met his eyes. The message was clear: tread lightly. People here had long memories and short patience.

Liz closed her notebook. "We're done here."

They stood, the weight of too many almost-truths hanging in the air behind them. As they made their way toward the door, Ava felt it again. The stares, the silence that seemed to follow them out like a tide.

Opening the door, the cool night wrapped around her like a blanket freshly shaken out, bracing and a little too real.

Ava looked back once.

Mary was still at the bar, her drink untouched, her gaze on the door like she was waiting for someone who wouldn't come.

***

The door of The Gaff Hook shut behind them with a tired creak, and for a moment, Ava just stood there on the sidewalk, breathing in the cold night air like it might rinse her clean.

The street was mostly empty. A few trucks parked haphazardly along the curb, the yellow glow of the bar's windows casting long shadows behind them. Across the street, the red building stood squat and silent, like a secret daring someone to ask the right question.

39

Liz wrapped her scarf tighter around her neck. "Well. That clears that up."

Ava shook her head. "That wasn't clarity. That was smoke."

They started walking, boots crunching over old salt. Spruce Cove didn't sleep early, but it didn't exactly stay up either. The town simmered at night, quiet gossip drifting between lit windows and cracked doors.

"You think she went there often?" Ava asked.

Liz shrugged. "Depends on who was inside. If it was Chap, she wouldn't have had to sneak."

Ava winced. "That's not …"

"I'm just saying," Liz said gently. "She was clearly hiding something. Maybe someone."

They passed the red building. It looked harmless now, almost forgettable. But Ava couldn't forget the way Amelia had moved that night, like she was walking into something she didn't want to be seen entering. Not romantic. Not casual. Something with stakes.

"There's something off about it," Ava muttered.

Liz stopped, turned to face it. "Want to poke around?"

Ava blinked. "Now?"

Liz grinned. "You never know what you find behind a locked door."

They crossed the street. The building's front entrance had a narrow awning and a faded directory behind glass with half the names scratched out or covered with paper. One office was listed as "D. Ellery, CPA." Another just said, "Wellness Suite – By Appointment Only." A third, lower down, was labeled "Storage."

"I'd kill for a floor plan," Liz whispered.

Ava squinted at the door. A thin strip of light glowed beneath it, even though the windows above were dark.

"Someone's inside," she said.

Liz raised an eyebrow. "Or forgot to turn something off."

They waited a second longer, watching. No movement. No sounds.

"Let's not get arrested tonight," Ava said finally, though her voice lacked conviction.

They turned away, but Ava's mind didn't. She kept picturing Amelia's face that night. That look that wasn't fear exactly, but something close. Hesitation. Uncertainty.

Or guilt.

***

The drive back to Liz's cottage was quiet, broken only by the soft swish of the windshield wipers and the occasional rattle of gravel beneath the tires. Liz didn't push, which Ava appreciated. Her thoughts were too knotted to unravel out loud.

They passed dark storefronts, shuttered shacks, and mailboxes decorated with carved ravens. It was late. That kind of late where everything feels a little softer, a little more haunted.

"She really did seem off," Ava said finally. "Amelia."

Liz kept her eyes on the road. "Yeah. Like something was weighing on her. Not surprising I guess if she was pregnant."

Ava nodded slowly. "Not scared, exactly. Just preoccupied. Like her brain was somewhere else and she couldn't catch up."

Liz didn't respond right away. The road curved along the edge of the harbor, black water glinting behind tangled grass.

"You think it had to do with the person she was meeting?"

Ava looked out the window. "If she was meeting anyone. She could've just been watching. Waiting."

"For what?"

Ava didn't answer.

She didn't want to say the name out loud. Not just because it felt dangerous, but because part of her still didn't believe it could be true.

Chap wasn't perfect, far from it. But he wasn't cold. He wasn't manipulative. He didn't orchestrate secret meetings behind bars or pressure girls into silence. Did he?

When they pulled into the gravel drive, Liz turned off the ignition but didn't move to get out.

"I'll follow up on the building," she said. "See who actually rents space there. Maybe we'll get lucky."

Ava nodded, but her stomach twisted. If they did get lucky, if they found out who Amelia was meeting that night, what then? What if it was someone Ava had trusted? Someone she still wasn't ready to question?

They got out of the car and Ava looked up at the cottage. The porch light that Liz insisted on keeping on cast a golden glow over the steps. It made the place look warmer than it felt.

"You okay?" Liz asked, locking the car behind them.

Ava hesitated on the top step. "No. But I'm getting closer."

Liz gave her a look. Not pity, just understanding, and stepped inside.

Ava lingered on the porch for a moment, arms wrapped around herself. The night air bit at her cheeks, but it cleared her head too.

She looked out across the dark water in the distance, barely visible beyond the trees. Spruce Cove had always seemed quiet. Safe.

But now? It felt like something was coming loose.

Just then, her phone buzzed in her coat pocket. She almost didn't check it. Then she saw the name on the screen.

William: *Still thinking about you. Hope you're okay.*

No question mark. Just a statement. Simple. Soft.

She stared at the message for a long second, her thumb hovering.

She hadn't answered his last text. Or the one before that.

Not because she didn't care.

Because she did.

And because she still didn't know how to reconcile the man who made her feel seen with the one who kept a life hidden from her for months.

Secrets. They were everywhere, including this town. In texts unsent, buildings unmarked, voices lowered at bars.

Spruce Cove was full of people protecting something: reputations, affairs, old pain. And it was starting to dawn on her that trust here wasn't just fragile. It was rare.

She slipped the phone back into her pocket, heart thudding in quiet rhythm.

How would you know who to believe when everyone had a reason to lie?

Chapter 5

Annie's Café was half-full with regulars that morning, the kind of sleepy Tuesday crowd that preferred gossip over cream in their coffee. The windows fogged slightly from the steam of fresh cinnamon rolls, and the hiss of the espresso machine gave the room a heartbeat.

Ava sat across from Liz in their usual booth, her untouched scone growing stale beside a rapidly cooling latte. She watched the front counter like it might give her a reason to breathe deeper.

Liz, meanwhile, had her eyes fixed on Martha, the café's manager and unofficial keeper of everybody's business. Martha could recall birthdays from a decade ago and knew everyone's coffee order and marital history with unsettling accuracy.

"So," Liz said casually, stirring her coffee as Martha approached to clear a nearby table, "busy weekend?"

Martha sighed, pausing mid-wipe. "Spruce Cove busy? Please. Unless you count the four guys who got kicked out of The Gaff Hook for arguing about halibut quotas. Or the rumor mill working overtime on Chap's case."

Ava stiffened. Liz's eyes sharpened just slightly. "What rumor mill?"

Martha lowered her voice. "Someone saw Chap and Earl Jasper going at it outside the bar the night Amelia died. Loud. Public. Said Chap was yelling. Hit Earl and he hit back.

Ava blinked. "Are you sure?"

"Pretty sure. It was Sheila from the bookstore who saw it. And you know Sheila doesn't drink or exaggerate."

Liz leaned in. "Did Sheila say what started it?"

Martha glanced over her shoulder, then lowered her voice further. "Only that Chap looked off. Not drunk, but close. Earl was red in the face. Chap said something about 'keeping your mouth shut about her.' Then Amelia showed up. That's when Sheila left. She said the tension was like wet dynamite."

Ava's stomach twisted. "Amelia was there?"

Martha gave a pointed nod. "Walked right into it. Sheila said she barely spoke, but the look on her face could've iced over the harbor. She was mad, that much was obvious."

"Did anyone else see this?" Liz asked.

"Probably. But no one's saying. Everyone's clammed up since the arrest. People are scared. Or tired of being dragged into it."

Ava's fingers wrapped tighter around her mug. "What time was this?"

"About ten-thirty, give or take."

That was right in the middle of the two-hour gap the police kept circling.

Liz scribbled a note on a napkin. Ava's mind was already spinning.

The longer Ava turned it over, the more it gnawed at her. Chap said he'd blacked out, but had he really? Or was he skipping over what he didn't want to say? If that timeline held, Amelia's confrontation with him might have been one of the last things she experienced.

"Thanks, Martha," Liz said, sliding a twenty under her coffee cup. "This is helpful."

"You never heard anything from me," Martha replied with a wink before disappearing into the kitchen.

Small towns didn't keep secrets well. They just learned to whisper loud enough that the truth could hide behind the gossip.

For a long moment, neither of them spoke.

The café buzzed around them: cutlery clinking, someone softly arguing over crossword clues at the counter, the faint whir of the blender churning a smoothie for someone far too cheerful for a murder-town morning. But Ava's ears buzzed with only one thing: the echo of Martha's words.

He was yelling. Amelia was there.

Liz looked up. "You think the fight was about the pregnancy?"

"I don't know. But if she confronted him that night, and he didn't tell me, why?"

Liz sipped her coffee, giving Ava time to sort her thoughts. "Could be he was too drunk. Could be shame. Could be trauma. Could be he didn't want to involve you."

"Or he's hiding something," Ava said softly. She hated the way her own voice cracked.

"You're allowed to be upset," Liz said, her tone gentler now. "This doesn't have to be clean. You care about him and you're allowed to be mad that he might've lied."

"I just, I thought I knew him."

Liz reached across the table and squeezed her hand briefly. "Maybe you still do. But we won't know unless we dig."

Ava nodded, but her heart wasn't in it. A splinter of betrayal had lodged deep, subtle and sharp.

***

Outside, two fishermen loaded crab pots onto a flatbed, their breath fogging in the cold morning air. One of them looked over his shoulder at the café, his eyes lingering a little too long before turning away.

"People are watching," Ava muttered.

"They always were," Liz said. "Now they just have a reason to whisper."

"If one more person says, 'He always seemed so normal,' I'm going to lose it," Liz muttered into her mug. "Normal's just what you call someone before the documentary comes out."

Ava smirked. "Spruce Cove: where every man's either 'just quiet' or 'a definite serial killer.'"

"Both drink coffee black and wear flannel, so good luck sorting them out."

Ava looked past her to the door, where Martha chatted with a couple of customers in line. Even here, surrounded by people who'd once treated her like the prodigal granddaughter, she felt like an outsider. Like she was borrowing a life that didn't quite fit.

"So what now?"

"Now," Liz said, tapping her pen against the napkin, "we talk to Earl. Find out what the fight was really about. Get the truth from the source."

Ava nodded slowly. But unease twisted through her.

There was something about Earl. And something told her he wasn't the type to give up secrets without making someone bleed for them.

Outside, the chill hit them like a slap. Ava pulled her scarf tighter, trying to shake off the tension that had burrowed into her spine. The sun hung low and pale, more suggestion than warmth. A pair of dogs barked somewhere down the dock, the sound carrying through the stillness of a town holding its breath.

They walked side by side down the weather-worn boardwalk, the scent of salt, old rope, and fish gut weaving through the air.

"You ever think," Ava said, her voice low, "about the last time we saw her?"

Liz didn't answer right away. "She was laughing," she finally said. "At that god-awful trivia night. She beat everyone, even Chap."

"She knew every maritime regulation by heart," Ava murmured, half-smiling. "And made sure everyone knew it."

They paused at the edge of the dock, watching a gull rip into a bag of forgotten fries.

"Sheila said she looked furious the night she died," Liz said. "Not scared. Not panicked."

"That's what's bothering me." Ava glanced down at the water. "If she was afraid of Chap, she wouldn't have walked straight into a fight. She wasn't afraid."

"Then something else happened after," Liz finished.

Ava nodded. "Something we haven't found yet."

They turned toward the pier where *Tanglewood* bobbed, tethered and weathered.

"You sure you're up for Earl?" Liz asked.

"No," Ava said. "But I'm not walking away."

They stepped onto the dock, the boards creaking underfoot like a warning.

***

The *Tanglewood* sat slouched in the water like she was nursing a hangover. Peeling paint flaked from her hull, and the faint reek of diesel mixed with fish guts lingered on the breeze.

Ava stepped aboard first, her boots thudding against the weathered deck. Liz followed, knocking twice on the cabin's metal siding.

"Earl!" she called. "We brought caffeine and uncomfortable questions."

From below came a low groan and the scuff of boots on metal. The cabin door creaked open, revealing Earl Jasper in all his glory. Rumpled flannel shirt half-buttoned, his beard gray-streaked and unruly, and eyes bleary with sleep or whiskey.

"Well, hell," he muttered. "Didn't think I rated a social call."

"Don't flatter yourself," Liz said, handing him a to-go cup. "Martha made the coffee."

Earl sniffed it, then took a long sip. "She still burns it. But it'll do."

He motioned toward two upside-down buckets lashed to the deck. "Sit. Say what you came to say."

Ava sat, Liz remained standing. The boat rocked gently beneath them.

"We heard you and Chap had a fight the night Amelia died," Ava said.

Earl sighed. "If you're sniffing for scandal, you're late. But yeah. We had words."

"Start from the beginning," Liz said. "Please."

Earl leaned back against the cabin doorframe, rubbing a hand down his face.

"She was at The Gaff Hook that night. Alone. Looked tense, but not fragile. I pulled up a stool. We talked."

Ava felt a flicker of something. Surprise, jealousy, confusion.

"About what?" Liz asked.

Earl gave a small shrug. "Nothing that mattered. She didn't want to talk much. Said she had things on her mind. That wasn't unusual. Amelia could shut down faster than a bar at last call. I asked if she was alright. She brushed it off."

He paused, gaze drifting to the harbor.

"I've tried to talk to her before. Always the same wall. She was polite, but never gave me much. Guess I wasn't her type."

"You were interested in her?" Ava asked, trying to keep her tone neutral.

Earl shrugged. "Sure. Couple years back. Thought maybe she'd give me a shot. She didn't. Always found a reason not to. I got used to it."

"What happened next?" Liz asked.

"Chap showed up. Had some words with someone outside. Then he saw us at the bar. Didn't like it. Pulled me outside, said he needed to talk. He was on a roll that night."

"And?" Ava asked.

Earl's jaw tightened. "He was drunk. I wasn't sober either, I'll admit it. We weren't yelling, not yet. But he was tense. We took it outside. He said Amelia was going through something and needed space. I asked him

49

what he meant, and he got cagey. Said she was 'in a way.' Didn't say pregnant, just that she needed people to back off."

Ava's heart dropped.

"That's when I lost my temper," Earl continued. "I told him if he didn't want anyone near her, maybe he should've thought of that before whatever happened between them. I might've shoved him a little. He shoved back."

"You two fought?" Liz clarified.

"Pushed each other. Maybe a punch or two. Nothing serious. More pride than fists. I walked away before it got dumb."

"And Amelia?" Ava asked. "Did she see it?"

"She didn't come out while we were talking. But when I went back inside to grab my coat, I passed her near the jukebox. Told her that I wasn't interested anymore. That she had enough on her plate."

Ava flinched. "Why did you say that?"

Earl looked ashamed. "Because I'm an idiot. And I was drunk. I thought I was being clever. She just looked at me like I wasn't even worth the air."

"And after that?" Liz pressed.

"I left. Walked out. But before I even hit the sidewalk, I heard her yelling at Chap. Amelia was really yelling. The kind of yelling that burns bridges. She was pissed. Hurt, maybe. I didn't stick around to listen."

"Did you see them after that?" Ava asked.

Earl shook his head. "That was the last I saw either of them that night."

Silence settled between them, heavy and unsatisfying.

"You think Chap killed her?" Liz asked finally.

Earl took a long sip from the cup, then stared into it like it held the answer. "I think something broke that night. In both of them. Doesn't mean he killed her. He doesn't seem like the type. But I think he's not telling the whole truth."

Ava stood slowly, her limbs stiff. "Thank you."

"I didn't say it to help," Earl muttered. "Just said it because it's what happened."

She nodded, but her throat tightened. The truth hurt more than lies sometimes.

As they stepped off the boat and onto the dock, Ava glanced back. Earl remained in the doorway, staring out at the gray sky, coffee in hand, a man who had seen the worst of people and kept his own regrets close.

There was something about Earl, something that lingered in the way he avoided saying her name.

***

Ava and Liz didn't speak as they left the dock.

The harbor was quiet, almost too quiet, the kind of hush that came just before a storm or after one had done its damage. The tide was creeping back in, swallowing the muddy flats in slow, deliberate inches.

Ava wrapped her arms around herself as they walked toward the truck.

Liz didn't push. Not yet.

It wasn't until they reached the edge of Main Street that Ava finally exhaled.

"He was lying," she said, without looking at Liz.

"Not outright," Liz said gently. "But holding back? Maybe."

"He was defensive. Evasive. He wanted to be the good guy, but you could tell something about that night didn't sit right with him. Something he's trying to forget, or rewrite."

Liz unlocked the car and climbed in. "People remember things differently when they're scared. And men like Earl? Pride comes before truth."

They drove through town in silence, storefronts passing by like washed-out snapshots. The hardware store, bookstore, the old firehouse turned the marine repair shop. Familiar. Ordinary. But every corner held whispers now.

George's woodshop came into view, tucked between the diner and the post office. Ava felt her jaw tighten.

"Let's get to work," she said.

"War room it is," Liz replied.

***

George's woodshop smelled like cedar, varnish, and home. The back room, once filled with dusty filing cabinets and discarded tackle boxes, had been repurposed into what Liz jokingly called their "war room." Maps of Spruce Cove were pinned along the back wall, crime scene printouts fanned across a card table, and a whiteboard leaned against the shelves, cluttered with names and motives written in Liz's messy scrawl.

Ava tossed her coat onto a stool and flopped into the rolling chair with a groan.

"That man makes my blood boil," she muttered, reaching for the printout labeled *Earl Jasper: Harbor Records & Incident Reports.*

Liz leaned against the table, arms crossed. "You mean the one who willingly told us he shoved Chap, admitted to being drunk, and still walked away?"

"Yes."

"You know he didn't actually hurt her."

"He humiliated her," Ava said, sitting up straighter. "He said something awful right before she died. Maybe he didn't kill her with his hands, but he still left a mark."

Liz raised an eyebrow. "Okay, but do we think he has an actual motive? A real one? Wanting a date with someone who never gave him the time of day doesn't exactly scream murder."

Ava stared at the whiteboard. "It was the way he said it. That he wasn't interested *now*. He made it sound like she was damaged goods."

"Still not motive."

"Maybe not alone," Ava snapped. "But what if he was involved in something bigger? What if she knew something about him?"

"You're reaching."

"I'm exploring possibilities."

"You're protecting Chap," Liz said, bluntly.

Ava's head whipped around. "Excuse me?"

"You're not being objective," Liz said calmly. "I get it. I do. But you're not analyzing this like a journalist. You're looking for someone else to blame because you've already decided Chap's innocent."

Ava opened her mouth, then shut it again. Her pulse throbbed at her temples. She hated that Liz was saying it and hated more that she wasn't entirely wrong.

Liz gave Ava a look. "Truce?"

Ava exhaled. "Truce. But I still think Earl knows more than he's saying."

"I don't disagree," Liz said. "I just think we should keep the net wide."

They started tidying the table, pushing papers into neat stacks, sliding push pins back into the corkboard.

Ava's phone buzzed.

She glanced at the screen, expecting a weather alert or a text from Esther.

Incoming Call: Spruce Cove Police

Her breath caught.

She answered. "Hello?"

"Ava."

His voice was gravel, low and unsteady. But it was him.

"Chap," she breathed. "Are you okay?"

Another pause, longer this time.

"I think so," he said. "It's quiet here. Too quiet. Like everyone's watching, even when they're not."

"You're still here. Good."

"Until the transfer, yeah. There's one other guy in the cell block. Sleeps most of the day. But the walls, they hum. And it's worse at night."

"I'm glad you called."

Another silence. Then: "Ryan heard you talked to Earl."

"Yes."

"I remember I pushed him. Outside the bar. I didn't like him talking to her. I don't know why I snapped. I'd been drinking. Maybe I just lost it."

"You were angry," Ava said softly.

"I was scared."

He sounded small, like the confident, teasing man she'd known was buried beneath layers of grief and confusion.

"I told him she was pregnant," he said. "Did he tell you that?"

"He did."

"I didn't mean to say it. She trusted me and I failed her."

Ava closed her eyes, throat tight.

"I didn't kill her," he said. "I swear. But I don't remember everything. That night's blurry. Like it's underwater and I can't reach it."

"It's okay," she whispered. "We'll find the truth."

"Even if it's not me?"

She opened her eyes. "Especially then."

A click signaled the end of their time. The line went dead.

Ava stared at her reflection in the dark screen of her phone. She didn't know if he remembered what mattered. But she did.

And she would remember for both of them.

***

The phone slipped from Ava's hand and landed softly on the workbench. The room felt smaller, like the walls were inching in. Liz hadn't said a word during the call. She'd just quietly organized a stack of Amelia's high school yearbooks they'd pulled earlier.

A knock sounded on the frame of the door, followed by George's voice.

"Esther says supper's on, and she's not reheating it twice. You two planning to eat, or just live off murder and coffee?"

Ava offered a tired smile. "We'll be right there."

George lingered a moment, his gaze drifting across the cluttered room. The whiteboard, the crime scene map, the silence heavy between them. Then he gave Ava a nod and left.

Liz stood, brushing her hands off. "Come on. Let's eat before Esther decides we're not hungry after all."

But Ava didn't move right away.

She stared down at the open notebook in front of her, the name *Chap Fisher* circled three times in red ink.

"He was the only one she told," Ava said, almost to herself.

Liz turned back, her brow lifting.

"I don't think she told Caroline. Or her mother. Just him."

She looked up, her eyes hollow.

"She trusted him. With the biggest news of her life. And now, he's sitting behind bars as the prime suspect in her death."

The heater clicked on, stirring the scent of sawdust and old varnish. The war room was quiet again.

Liz moved beside her. "Trust and truth aren't always the same."

Ava nodded slowly, standing. "But they should be."

Together, they walked out, the shadows of the workshop stretching long behind them.

Chapter 6

It had been seven days since Ava last saw Chap Fisher.

Not that she was counting. Except she was, in the quiet, compulsive way people count grief. In sleep-starved mornings and too-long showers. In the space between headlines and half-eaten toast.

She told herself it wasn't about him. That this visit was about clarity, about piecing together what had happened the night Amelia died. But part of her, the part that still remembered the way he used to smile like it cost him nothing, was terrified.

Terrified he'd be a stranger.

Terrified he wouldn't be.

The Spruce Cove jail didn't pretend to be anything more than it was: gray concrete, black metal bars, the smell of overbleached floors and cold resignation.

Ava walked beside Liz in silence until they reached the sign-in desk. Liz slowed, scanning the hallway with casual disinterest so performative it might as well have been on a résumé.

"If Ryan's on shift," she murmured, smoothing a nonexistent wrinkle from her sleeve, "remind me to act only vaguely amused by his entire existence."

Ava didn't look up. "Is that before or after the part where you make intense eye contact and mention your firm boundaries?"

Liz grinned. "Exactly. Confuse him. Keep the upper hand."

"Right," Ava muttered, pressing her name into the logbook with more force than necessary.

Deputy Hale stepped out from behind the door with a raised eyebrow. "Ladies."

"Officer," Liz said, suddenly all sunny smiles.

He barely blinked. "Ava, Chap's in the back already. Walker, you wait in the front."

"What, no jailhouse charm from Ryan today?" she teased.

"He's off. Try again next misdemeanor."

Ava followed Deputy Hale down a hallway lined with faded PSA posters and scuffed paint. Her heart pounded as they approached the small visiting room.

Chap sat behind the glass divider, elbows braced on the counter, staring at a fixed point on the wall. He looked thinner and paler. Like he was dissolving from the inside out.

When she stepped in, he didn't look at her.

She sat, picked up the phone. He waited a moment before lifting his.

"Didn't think you'd come," he said.

"I was hoping this nightmare would be over by now," she answered honestly.

They sat in silence for a moment, the hum of the overhead light pulsing between them.

"You look terrible," she finally said.

He smirked faintly. "Feels worse than it looks."

"I was hoping maybe something's come back to you. From that night."

"Bits," he said. "Nothing that makes sense. It's like watching TV with the sound off. Amelia's there. She's mad. I'm angry? Loud. It's like I'm watching myself screw it all up in slow motion."

Ava leaned in. "Do you remember what the fight was about?"

He winced, rubbed at his eyes. "I remember her crying. I remember shouting. But the words? Gone."

"You said it might've been about the pregnancy."

"Probably." He looked exhausted by the idea. "But why would I argue with her about that? Why would I even care?"

He paused. Then shrugged bitterly.

"I mean it wasn't my problem," he said, more to the air than to her.

Then he laughed, low and bitter. "That's ironic. I thought it wasn't my problem. And now? It's the only problem I've got."

"I keep waiting for the damned DNA test. Hoping maybe that will help. My lawyer says the lab is understaffed and the scientist who runs the DNA tests for the State quit," he said.

"She was spiraling. Panicking. And I couldn't deal." He shook his head, jaw clenched. "All I could think was, here we go again. Same chaos, same pressure. I didn't have the energy to play the calm one. I just wanted out of it."

Chap stared ahead, jaw tight. "I remember how I felt. I remember being pissed off and concerned. Like everything was closing in and I couldn't breathe."

He rubbed his eyes with the heel of his hand. "I can't believe I piece this together. I was so drunk, I don't even know if I said anything that made sense."

Ava stayed silent, her hands cold against the plastic phone receiver.

"That's the worst part," he muttered. "That I might've said something I can't take back and not even know it."

He looked down, his voice breaking. "Not that I could apologize. She's gone."

He looked up, finally meeting her eyes. "Do you know what it feels like to doubt your own memory?"

"I've questioned everything in my life. Made it my full-time job since arriving," she said. "But I always knew what I said. What I did. That's different."

"Yes it is," he said.

Ava stared at the lines in his face. They were deeper than she remembered. He looked older. Fragile in a way that scared her.

"You should stop coming," he said suddenly.

"What?"

"You've got your life. A job. People who still look at you like you're not guilty of something. Don't waste time on me."

"That's not your choice to make."

"It's not loyalty, Ava. It's grief, guilt. I get it. But I'm not your problem either."

She stood then, the chair scraping back loudly.

"Don't pretend like you know what this is for me."

"I know it's eating you alive," he said.

"Then maybe you should start fighting like you want to live."

She got up to leave before the truth got mean, or worse, honest.

***

When Ava stepped back into the lobby, the fluorescent lights felt too bright, the air too still. She blinked, adjusting to the shift from claustrophobic pain to whatever this was.

Liz sat on the edge of the front desk, twirling a pen like it was a prop. Ryan stood across from her, arms folded, a faint smirk on his face.

"You're avoiding the question," Liz said.

"I'm not," Ryan replied. "I'm just choosing not to answer."

"Which is basically a yes."

"I'm a cop," he said, deadpan. "Avoidance is a skill set."

Ava cleared her throat. Neither of them jumped, but Liz did shift off the desk like a kid caught doing something vaguely inappropriate in the school library.

"There you are," Liz said. "How'd it go?"

Ava hesitated.

Ryan took one look at her expression and the air around him shifted. "He's shutting down."

"He's not just shutting down," she said, biting her lip. "He's disappearing."

59

Ryan's jaw tightened. "He's in a bad spot. Too proud to show it, too scared to admit it. But he's not lost. Not yet."

Liz looked between them, quiet for once.

"Don't give up on him, Ava," Ryan said gently. "People drown when no one sees them sinking."

She nodded once, slow. "It's hard to watch."

She followed Liz outside into the too-bright afternoon, the words still echoing behind her like footsteps in an empty hallway.

***

The Gaff Hook didn't get better with repeat visits, just more familiar in a way that felt vaguely shameful.

"I swear," Liz said as they pushed open the scarred door, "if we come here any more often, the town's gonna start a GoFundMe for our liver transplants."

Ava raised an eyebrow. "We could call it 'Wine & Regret.' Make it a podcast."

"I'd listen to that," Liz said, scanning the bar. "Twice divorced, emotionally repressed, and sipping whiskey at noon? The brand writes itself."

"Speaking of twice divorced," Ava murmured.

Ruby was behind the bar, leaning against the cooler. Torn jeans, faded tank top with a stain that might've been grease or something more interesting. Tattoos ran the length of both arms with bold lines and ink that looked like it had stories. The kind that came with restraining orders.

Her hair was piled into a messy knot, chopsticks jammed through like she'd been mid-rant and got distracted.

She looked up and clocked them in one sweep. "Well, well," she said flatly. "Back again. What is this, a study on poor coping mechanisms?"

Liz blinked. "Wow. That's your opening?"

Ruby snorted. "Trust me, sweetheart, that's my friendly setting."

Ava stepped forward, careful. "We're here to cause just a little bit of trouble."

"That's what people usually say before they get 86'd."

"We're just …" Ava glanced at Liz, who was already halfway to the barstool. "… curious."

Ruby set down a glass she hadn't been cleaning and eyed them with something between suspicion and mild amusement. "Curious gets you punched around here. Or worse, invited to karaoke."

Liz leaned in. "You sing?"

"I hit a guy with a pool cue during Shania Twain once," Ruby said. "He took the mic after me and butchered the key change."

A moment passed. Ava laughed, quick and involuntary.

Ruby's gaze lingered on her. "I heard you've been asking about Amelia."

Ava nodded. "Yeah."

Ruby sighed, pulled two beers without asking. "Fine. Sit. But if you're looking for some big reveal, I hope you aren't holding your breath. I'm not a fountain of secrets."

"We're just trying to understand," Ava said quietly.

Ruby handed them the beers. "Then you're already in better shape than most people who ask."

The bar settled into a rhythm around them. Someone dropped coins into the jukebox, boots thudded on sticky floors, and a man in a flannel three sizes too big shouted at a basketball game no one else was watching. It was the kind of place where everything felt suspended in time, like nothing here could get worse because it had already bottomed out.

Ruby asked what brought Ava to town. Liz deflected with something charming and vague. Ava said nothing. She was too busy studying Ruby. The way she moved, like someone always ready for a fight or a smoke break.

It wasn't until their second drink and a slew of divorce war stories (Liz holding her own) that the pool cue came out. Ruby offered a game like a dare, not a gesture of friendship.

"Don't embarrass yourselves," she warned.

They played, Liz trash-talked and missed everything, and Ava held her own just enough to make Ruby raise an eyebrow.

Halfway through the third rack, Ruby leaned on her cue and said, "You know, the night Amelia died, she had a meltdown in the bathroom."

The words dropped like chalk dust on the table.

"Was she okay?" Liz asked, suddenly sober.

Ruby shrugged. "Crying like the world ended. Wouldn't tell me what set her off. Just kept saying the same thing, *It's not his problem. He told me to take care of it.*' Over and over."

Ava's cue slipped. Just slightly.

Ruby didn't notice. Or pretended not to. "I figured it was about a baby. What else would she be talking about?"

Liz frowned. "She didn't say?"

"I asked. Told her I'd knock his ass to next Sunday. Meant it, too." Ruby sank her last ball without looking. "But she just shook her head. Wouldn't out him. Still protecting the guy, even then."

Ava stared at the felt. The weight of that phrase hung there like smoke.

She didn't say anything. Not to Ruby, not to Liz. Not yet.

***

They stepped out of the bar and straight into twinkle lights and cider steam.

Ava blinked. "Did we just leave the Gaff Hook and enter a Hallmark movie?"

Downtown was lit up like it had something to prove. Strings of white lights draped from every storefront, carolers clustered in front of Annie's, and kids sprinting with candy canes and parents trailing behind.

"I forgot the community tree lighting was tonight," Liz muttered, zipping up her coat. "Great. Now we're the drunks who wandered into Christmas."

Ava sniffed her sleeve. "We reek."

A frantic twenty-something with a handmade press badge darted past them, nearly tripping over a power cord.

"Excuse me! I need a quote about intergenerational community bonding!"

"No, thank you," Liz said, physically pivoting Ava away from the intern like they were dodging a plague.

"Run," Ava whispered, and they bee-lined toward the sidewalk.

The chilly air sharpened the buzz of the bar into something more manageable. Ava pulled her scarf up to her nose and tried to forget the weight of what Ruby had said. *Not his problem.* The words echoed louder now under fairy lights and paper cups of hot cocoa.

***

They made their way back to George's shop. It was warm, lit by overheads and the glow of an old banker's lamp.

George's shop always smelled like old paper and sharper truths. The kind you didn't want to look directly at.

He had been staring at the cluster of sticky notes and red string on the whiteboard when they came in. "You smell like my mid-twenties."

"We bring gifts," Liz said. "Bar gossip and emotional distress."

Ava took a seat near the space heater and let the warmth uncoil something in her spine. "We talked to Ruby."

George turned, curious now. "The bartender with the tattoos who once broke a guy's nose with a cue stick?"

"That's the one," Liz said proudly.

"She said Amelia had a breakdown in the bathroom the night she died," Ava added. "Was crying. I guess the guy said it wasn't his problem and told her to take care of it. Not that we know for sure what 'it' was."

George's face shifted, not surprise exactly but interest sharpening like a lens.

"She assumed Amelia meant the baby," Liz said. "That the guy told her to get rid of it."

"And she wouldn't say who it was," Ava said. "Ruby tried."

George nodded slowly and walked over to the whiteboard. On it, he'd scrawled the timeline from Earl's account: *Amelia running out, phone call, Chap following, yelling about 'not being dragged into this.'*

He tapped the words. "This lines up."

Ava stared at the phrase. Her stomach turned.

"I haven't told you everything," she said softly.

Liz stopped mid-sip of her coffee. "Please don't say you're pregnant."

"I'm serious."

George turned.

Ava hesitated. "At the jail, Chap said something. He couldn't remember the fight, couldn't remember what he said. But he remembered how he felt. That he was angry. Frustrated. He said he thought it wasn't his problem."

Liz's coffee mug hit the desk louder than it needed to.

Ava winced. "He didn't say he said it to her. He doesn't remember. But he said those exact words to me."

Silence filled the room.

George stepped back, expression unreadable.

Liz was quiet, then shook her head. "Jesus, Ava."

"I know."

"No, you don't. You're still clinging to this version of him in your head. The one who could never say something like that. But what if he did?"

"I'm not!"

"You are," Liz said. Not unkind. Just clear. "You want him to be innocent so badly that you're ignoring what's right in front of you."

Ava looked down.

"I'm not saying he killed her," Liz went on. "But we can't solve this if you keep filtering the evidence through who you wish he was. You have to be willing to see the truth even when it's ugly."

Ava felt the heat rise in her throat. "You think I don't want the truth?"

"I think you want it to hurt less than it does."

That landed hard. Because it was true.

She nodded once. "Okay."

George quietly reached for another marker and wrote *'Not my problem'* in big, capital letters under the word *Motive?*

Ava stared at it, pulse thudding.

They were closer now. But every step forward made the fall seem steeper.

***

They left George's shop just past ten, stepping into the crisp night air.

Ava and George's walk back to the cabin was short, gravel crunching beneath their feet, the air sharp with pine and woodsmoke. Quiet wrapped around them like a weighted blanket, comforting but heavy in the chest.

By the time they reached the porch, Ava felt the fatigue of the day settling deep in her bones. The questions. The half-answers. The way every new piece of the puzzle made the picture harder to recognize.

Inside, Esther sat on the worn couch, wrapped in a cardigan that looked hand-knitted by a woman with too many stories and not enough time.

She looked up as they entered. "You look like the bottom half of a coffee filter."

"We've been worse," George said, toeing off his boots.

Esther smiled tentatively. Ava's hand rose to her temple. "I have a headache. Think I'll call it early."

"Want tea?" Esther asked.

"No. Just quiet. And a bed that doesn't ask questions."

Esther pressed a light hand on Ava's shoulder, then Ava vanished down the hall without another word.

***

Ava closed her bedroom door and leaned against it for a moment. The warmth from the main room faded behind her, replaced by the low hum of the baseboard heater and the occasional groan of old wood settling.

She didn't bother turning on the light. Moonlight poured through the window, soft and silvery, washing the space in the kind of quiet that made reflection feel inevitable.

It wasn't just the case that kept her up at night. It was the weight of wondering who Chap really was.

But when she closed her eyes, all she saw was the way he'd looked at her that night walking home, the slight shift of his jacket toward her, the way he noticed the goosebumps on her arms without making her feel foolish. That kind of attentiveness wasn't something you faked.

She sat on the edge of the bed, pulled her knees up, and rested her chin there.

But what if Liz was right?

Maybe she didn't want to see the real Chap. Not the version weighed down by his own damage. Maybe she'd been looking for proof he hadn't changed at all, just so she could believe it wasn't her heart that had changed instead.

Just like she'd done with William.

She'd known, somewhere deep, that he wasn't trying to change her. Not really. But the more she twisted herself to fit into his carefully arranged life, the more invisible she'd felt. Until she left not because he asked her to disappear, but because she already had.

And now, maybe she was doing the same thing. Refusing to look. Refusing to admit her part in the undoing.

Her phone buzzed, face down on the nightstand.

She hesitated, then picked it up.

William: *Maybe I wasn't asking you to give up being the real you. Maybe I just didn't know how to make room for someone who finally saw me.*

Ava's breath caught.

The timing was uncanny. Painfully perfect. Like he'd somehow heard her reckoning through the walls of time and pride and silence.

She read it twice. Then again. Not ready to answer but no longer ready to ignore it either.

She set the phone down and stared out the window, the dark trees swaying in the wind like they, too, had things they'd rather not admit.

Chapter 7

She didn't move.

The door creaked open anyway.

"I could be a murderer," Liz announced, stepping inside.

"I was hoping for burglar," Ava said without looking up from her tea.

Liz dropped her bag on the table with flair. "Sorry, just me. But I brought a plot twist."

Ava blinked. "Does it involve caffeine?"

"Better," Liz said, holding up her phone. "Caroline Colburn texted me. She wants to talk. To both of us."

Ava sat up straighter. "Seriously? Again?"

Liz nodded. "Wants to keep it quiet. Says she'll explain why when we get there. Something about her parents. Apparently, they're squarely Team Chap-is-Guilty."

Ava sighed, rubbing at her temple. "Yeah. Delilah seems like she would appreciate a tidy villain."

"She wants to meet behind the old cannery."

Ava paused. "That's basically high school code for I'm betraying my family and I brought receipts."

"Exactly," Liz said, already heading for the door. "Put on real pants. If anyone has breadcrumbs that lead somewhere, it's Caroline."

Ava stood, grabbed her coat. "Real pants are a lot to ask before noon."

"You'll survive," Liz called back. "Also, maybe run a brush through that situation on your head."

Ava rolled her eyes but followed her out into the cold, the air biting but sharper somehow. Like the day had just changed direction.

***

They had parked two blocks from the cannery and ducked into the brush, following an overgrown footpath that wound around the hill. It used to be an unofficial make-out trail for Spruce Cove High's students. Now it felt more like the set of a true crime reenactment.

Liz stepped over a root and grumbled, "If I run into a patch of wild celery, I swear."

She stopped mid-sentence as she walked straight into a tangle of tall, stalky plants.

She froze. "Oh, come on."

Ava smirked. "Congratulations. You just threatened Mother Nature and she called your bluff."

Liz backed out slowly, inspecting her arm. "Unbelievable. Of all the things to get ambushed by, it had to be a stupid plant with a personal vendetta."

"Try not to rub it. It only gets worse," Ava said, already pulling a bottle of hand sanitizer from her coat pocket. "Fieldwork isn't always glamorous."

They emerged from the woods still muttering when they spotted Caroline waiting near the cove.

She stood alone by the water's edge, her coat buttoned up to her throat, arms wrapped around herself like she was trying to keep from unraveling. Her hair was pulled into a tidy braid, but the ends frayed with the wind.

"Hey," she said, her voice barely carrying over the waves. "Thanks for coming."

Ava nodded, her concern rising. "Are you okay?"

69

Caroline glanced over her shoulder at the trail. "I will be. Just couldn't talk at home. Not right now."

"They still think Chap's guilty?" Liz asked, stepping up beside Ava.

Caroline let out a slow breath. "It's not even a question to them. My mom won't rest until the trial is done. My dad has already talked to a contractor about converting Amelia's room."

Ava blinked. "Seriously?"

"They think it's closure," Caroline said. "I think it's denial in real estate form."

She shifted with her hands tucked tighter under her arms. "I should have said this before, but I wasn't ready to talk. I've been thinking about something Amelia said. A few days before, you know. She was off. Not like she was scared, just stressed. Closed off. Like she was holding something in."

Ava stepped closer. "What did she say?"

Caroline hesitated. Then, quietly:

"She said, she needed to 'limit the fallout' and that I would 'know soon enough.'"

"She made it sound like things were in motion. Like she was trying to keep the damage from spreading. She was trying to control things."

Liz's brow furrowed. "Did she say who she was seeing?"

Caroline shook her head. "She wouldn't name names. And I didn't want to push. But it didn't feel like she was blaming anyone. It felt like she was protecting someone."

Ava's stomach tightened. "Not Chap?"

"It couldn't have been Chap. If it was, she would've said so. Amelia wasn't scared of him. If anything, she made a sport out of putting him in his place. She didn't tiptoe around Chap. Not ever."

Liz crossed her arms. "So, you believe she was in trouble. But not because of him."

Caroline nodded. "I don't know what scares me more. That my sister's killer is still out there, or that Chap's rotting in jail for something he didn't do. Either way, I can't just sit with either of those truths."

Ava glanced around. "Does anyone know we're here?"

Caroline hesitated, then said quietly, "I've gone through her room a dozen times, and I still don't know what I'm looking for. The police aren't looking anymore. Maybe I need another set of eyes. I'm not seeing straight."

She glanced toward the house. "My parents are at lunch with the Morrises, and Mason's off playing basketball."

"I can take you to Amelia's room. Just ... if anyone asks, you were never there."

Liz nodded solemnly. "We don't exist. But if we did, we'd leave fabulous footprints."

They followed the curve of the cove, wind cutting low across the water. Caroline walked ahead, focused, while Liz trailed just a little behind fidgeting.

At first, Ava thought Liz was just adjusting her scarf. Then her glove. Then her beanie. But the subtle rubbing grew increasingly less subtle.

"Are those blisters?" Ava whispered, leaning close.

Liz hissed through her teeth. "I think I'm dying."

"You've got a rash, don't you?"

"Don't look at me."

Ava turned. "It's on your face."

Liz froze, hands hovering near her jaw. "Please tell me I don't look like a cautionary tale from WebMD."

Before Ava could answer, Caroline suddenly stopped and turned around.

"Are you okay?" she asked, eyes narrowing. "You're kind of blotchy."

Liz dropped her hands and attempted something between a smile and a grimace. "I am fully composed and absolutely not reacting to wild celery."

Caroline blinked. "You got it on you?"

"She walked into it," Ava muttered.

Caroline sighed, then pulled a small balm tin from her coat. "Here. This might help. You're lucky you didn't brush your eyes."

Liz took it with the reverence usually reserved for ancient artifacts. "If I survive this, I owe you a drink. And possibly a kidney."

"You're fine," Caroline said, handing over the balm. "Nature just doesn't vibe with your skincare routine."

They kept walking, Caroline leading them toward the house's back trail while Liz dabbed ointment with one finger and cursed wild celery like it was a private religion.

By the time they reached the edge of the yard, Ava felt the shift in the air. It was heavier now, like the closer they got to Amelia's room, the more real this all became. Not just theories and timelines. But pieces of a girl's life. And death.

Caroline turned to face them. "They don't know you're here. So, if anyone shows up, especially Mason, just follow my lead."

Liz raised the balm tin. "In exchange, I'll try not to go full tomato before we find a clue."

Caroline didn't smile, but there was a flicker of something. Trust, maybe.

"Let's go," she said. "Before I change my mind."

***

Caroline slipped the back door open with a practiced hand and motioned them inside. The hallway was dim and quiet, with creaking floorboards and the faint scent of old wood, dust, and dried lavender. It smelled like time settling in.

Framed school portraits dotted the wall. There were pictures of Amelia through the years: baby teeth, braces, a bold pixie cut in eighth grade. Ava paused in front of the fifth-grade photo of Amelia grinning wide, cheeks full, hair pulled back with butterfly clips.

Caroline noticed. "She hated that one. Said it made her look like she had too many teeth."

Ava smiled faintly. "She did. But she made it work."

They kept moving, their footsteps soft on the runner rug. Caroline led them upstairs, past closed doors and a stack of laundry half-folded on the landing. At the end of the hall, she paused.

Caroline glanced back down the hall, voice low. "We don't have much time before they get back. Come on. We need to move fast."

Liz raised an eyebrow. "Great. Nothing like speed-snooping under pressure."

Caroline didn't laugh and opened the door without ceremony.

The room felt like someone had pressed pause. Amelia's duvet was neatly pulled, her desk tidy but not curated. It wasn't a shrine; it was just hers. A mug still held a few dried-out pens. There was a scarf half-folded on the chair. The scent here was different too. Hints of old shampoo, vanilla lip balm, and something floral that had faded over time.

Ava stepped in slowly, like her presence might jostle something loose.

"I've looked through everything," Caroline said from the doorway. "Drawers, closet, under the bed. I thought maybe you'd see something I didn't."

Liz was already crouched near a low bookshelf. "We'll be gentle. Mostly."

Ava moved to the desk and opened a drawer. Neat rows of gel pens. A few receipts. A stack of old birthday cards with scribbled notes.

Liz, meanwhile, opened a small wooden jewelry box. Most of it was everyday stuff. Tangled hoops, enamel studs, a lone bobby pin.

She paused, holding up a single earring, a delicate teardrop with a deep blue stone set in gold. "Okay, this one doesn't belong with the rest," she said. "It's fancier. Definitely not cheap."

Ava looked up. "There's only one?"

Liz sifted through the rest of the box. "Yep. No match. Just this."

Caroline leaned in for a better look. "That's not her style. She liked big, bold stuff. This is subtle, more grown-up."

Ava glanced between them. "Do you mind if we hold onto it? Just until we figure out where it came from?"

Caroline hesitated, then nodded. "If you think it matters, take it."

Ava gave Liz a look. "Carefully."

Liz nodded and wrapped the earring in a tissue. "Always. But it is an odd thing to keep, especially solo."

Ava turned back to the desk and checked the bottom drawer. Inside, under a half-used notepad and a pair of sunglasses, was a slim, worn leather journal. Her breath caught.

"Found it," she said softly.

Caroline crossed to her. "I haven't read it all. It felt wrong. But maybe you'll find something I missed."

Ava took it gently, running her fingers over the worn binding. "We'll take care of it."

Before Caroline could respond, sharp footsteps echoed on gravel outside. They froze.

Caroline's face went pale. "Mason."

Panic hit like a jolt.

"He comes in through the side," she hissed. "You need to go. Now!"

Liz was already moving. "Window?"

"Onto the shed roof," Caroline whispered, rushing to the window. "It's low. You'll be fine. Just go!"

Ava tucked the journal under her coat and followed Liz. They climbed out fast, landing with twin thuds on the shed roof, then scrambled down and ducked behind the hedge, adrenaline spiking.

Ava's boot hit a branch. Liz nearly slipped in the wet grass. But within seconds, they were out the gate and around the corner, lungs heaving.

Back at the car, Liz pulled out the tissue with the earring and stared at it.

"Well, that was casual. Totally invisible. No one noticed a thing."

Ava clutched the journal, her heart still racing.

"She was with someone," Ava said quietly. "The question is, who and was it choice or trap?"

***

The newspaper office was quiet when they stepped inside. Just the low hum of computers and the whir of a dusty space heater near the desk. Ava slid the journal into her purse as casually as she could, heart still thudding from their near-miss at the Colburn house.

Liz yanked the door shut behind them, her voice low. "Okay, what are the odds Mason has some secret twin brother who just happens to be a brooding hallway lurker too?"

But before Ava could respond, a deep voice interrupted.

"You two have a second?"

They both jumped.

Chief Harrow stood near Liz's desk, arms folded, his bulk filling the small room like a threat you couldn't ignore. His uniform was crisp, his expression anything but.

"How'd you get in here?" Liz asked, setting her bag down slowly.

"Door was open," he replied, not bothering to sound apologetic. "Figured I'd wait."

Ava felt her pulse quicken. "Something you needed, Chief?"

He looked between them, unreadable. "I've heard rumors about you two asking questions. Stirring up things that don't need stirring."

Liz leaned against the desk, all casual confidence. "You'll have to be more specific. We ask a lot of questions. It's our job."

Harrow's eyes narrowed. "This isn't a game, Walker. And it sure as hell isn't some cozy little mystery column."

He turned his gaze to Ava. "Spruce Cove's been through enough. The people here deserve peace, not more chaos. Not more headlines. What they don't need is two outsiders peeling scabs off wounds that are trying to heal."

Ava swallowed. "We're trying to help."

"No, you're trying to interfere." His voice dropped. "Let the system do its job. Chap Fisher is behind bars where he belongs. Poking holes in a case that's already solid doesn't help anyone. It just drags out the pain."

"We're not dragging anything out," Liz said, stepping forward. "We're just not pretending everything's fine when it's not."

"You keep pushing," Harrow said, "and you'll find yourselves in the middle of something you can't control. And if I catch wind of you tampering with evidence, or witnesses, or anything else that might compromise this investigation I'll shut you down. Legally or otherwise."

Ava met his stare. "Is that a threat?"

"No," he said. "It's a promise."

Then he turned, walking out without another word.

The silence he left behind was heavier than the door that clicked shut.

Liz let out a breath. "Well. That was subtle. Almost didn't notice the part where he threatened us."

Ava reached into her purse, fingers brushing the leather cover of Amelia's journal.

She didn't say anything.

She didn't need to.

***

The cold nipped at their coats as Ava and Liz stepped out of the office, both unusually quiet.

They didn't speak until they reached Liz's car.

"You read it first," Liz said, nodding at the journal peeking from Ava's purse.

"You're the one who keeps showing up and demanding that we figure this out. That counts for something," Liz said gently.

Ava hesitated. "We'll both read it. Separately. I want your take. Not just a co-sign on mine."

Liz smirked faintly. "A double-blind emotional autopsy. How very us."

Ava smiled, but it didn't quite land. "Let's meet in the morning."

"Bright and way-too-early," Liz promised.

Ava nodded and turned toward the cabin, the journal feeling heavier with every step.

***

The door creaked as she stepped into the warmth of home. The smell of baked bread and cedar hit her first, comforting and familiar. But something was off.

Esther stood at the kitchen counter, one hand gripping a tea towel like it was an anchor. She didn't look up at first.

"You were gone awhile."

Ava shrugged out of her coat.

"Stopped by the paper."

Esther finally turned. Her expression was controlled but tight in the way it got when she was mad but trying not to be.

"I got a call," she said. "From Chief Harrow."

Ava's stomach dipped, same sick drop she got when she heard her mom's "young lady" voice from across the house.

Esther set the towel down with precision. "He's not thrilled with you and Liz poking around. Said you're making things harder for everyone. And putting yourselves in the middle of something you don't understand."

Ava dropped her bag near the door. "We're trying to understand. That's the whole point."

Esther's eyes softened, but her voice stayed steady. "Honey, you think I don't want the truth? Of course I do. But Harrow's not wrong about one thing. This town is wounded. And when you go poking around in open wounds, don't be surprised when people start to bleed."

"I'm not afraid of the mess," Ava said.

"You should be afraid of the cost," Esther said, her voice low. "Not just for what it might stir up but for what it might do to you."

Ava looked down. Her fingers were brushing the journal in her purse.

Esther turned back to her tea, but her shoulders stayed tense. "I don't like that Harrow's upset. And I like even less the thought of you walking into something that might not be safe."

"I'll be careful," Ava said softly.

"Promise me that's not just something you say to make me stop worrying."

Ava didn't answer. Because she wasn't sure it wasn't.

Chapter 8

The rain had turned to mist by the time Ava pulled the throw blanket around her shoulders and settled on the edge of her bed. The journal waited on her nightstand like it knew things she didn't: patient, silent, accusing.

She hadn't opened it since Caroline handed it over.

It was time.

The cabin had gone still: the crackle of the wood stove in the next room, the faint patter of rain hitting the trees, her grandparents breathing slow and steady in the back bedroom. It all faded beneath the buzz building in her chest. Her lamp cast the room in a soft, amber glow, and the edges of shadows curled like old secrets waiting to speak.

She picked up the journal, its worn leather cool beneath her palms. No name, no decoration. It was just like Amelia. Striking without needing to try, veiled even when she seemed laid bare.

Ava opened to the first page.

No "Dear Diary." No date. Just a voice.

"I've spent too long pretending confidence is the same thing as stability. Turns out they're not even close. Lately, I feel like I'm wearing my life like a rented dress. Fits well enough from a distance, but one wrong move and everything falls apart."

Ava's breath snagged.

"I don't want to be the loudest voice in the room anymore. I want to be someone with more to say. Someone who doesn't have to spin every wound into a punchline."

"I want to be someone different. And I think he sees that. Or maybe just sees me."

Ava closed her eyes for a second.

She hadn't known what to expect. Cold detachment? Vague melodrama? But this? This was sharp and human and desperate in all the ways Ava understood too well.

She turned the page.

"It started with an argument. He pushed. I pushed back. Nothing big, but it cracked something open. Like pressure behind glass. Then he kissed me."

"Not soft, not careful. Like lightning."

"I didn't know I could want someone like that. Not again. Not really."

Ava blinked. Her stomach dropped.

She stared at the page, heart racing. She saw it like a film reel she couldn't turn off. She imagined Chap pressing Amelia against a wall, mouths clashing, hands tangled in hair.

She hated it, the way you hate a mirror that's a little too honest.

And then, as if summoned by instinct, she remembered the Fireweed Festival. Their first kiss.

The summer night, the music and bonfires, the sound of fiddles and waves, how Chap's hand had found hers and pulled her toward the makeshift dance floor.

It had been sweet. Intentional. Careful in a way that made her feel cherished instead of claimed. A promise, not a challenge. The kind of kiss that didn't just start something; it rooted it.

Ava looked back at the page in her lap, read the line again.

"Like lightning."

It sounded like a secret she wasn't supposed to hear.

She turned the page, hands trembling.

"He asked me what I'd do if I could start over. I told him I'd leave. Burn it all down and leave the ashes."

"He said he sees me. Not the girl from the stories. Not the mess. Just me."

"I didn't know what to say. No one's ever seen me without the noise before."

Ava drew her knees up to her chest.

The page pulsed like a wound. This wasn't just a fling. Whoever he was, Amelia had believed him. Had let him in.

She turned the page again.

"I took the test. Twice. There's no more maybe."

"I didn't tell my mom. Or Caroline."

"I told him."

"He froze."

"Then he reached for my hand. Said we'd figure it out. That he was just shocked. That it didn't mean he was walking away."

"I believed him."

Ava exhaled, sharp and shallow. She didn't realize she was crying until her vision blurred.

This wasn't a crush. This wasn't drama.

This was real.

"He kissed my forehead. Said we were a team."

"I started to picture it. A small place, a baby in the other room. Us figuring things out."

"I think I wanted that more than I knew."

Ava swiped at her eyes, throat thick. A few pages later, Amelia's love story began to fall apart.

"Saw him at the rec league game tonight. He didn't even look at me."

"I dropped my phone. I laughed too loud. I sat two rows behind. Nothing."

"He smiled at everyone but me."

"It was like watching someone forget your name on purpose."

"I left before the third quarter. Left my scarf on the seat. Wonder if he noticed."

The ache in Ava's chest spread wider.

Who was he?

She flipped forward.

"He showed up at the lookout. No warning. Just him, holding a small box."

"The earrings were beautiful. Subtle. Expensive."

"I asked where he got them, and he said, 'Not everything has to be loud to be special.'"

"They were a peace offering. But not the kind I needed."

"He said this is too complicated. That he had other obligations to take care of."

"He asked me to get rid of it."

"I asked if he'd still be here if I did."

"He didn't answer."

"I told him I needed to think. But I already knew."

Ava's hand clenched around the journal.

This wasn't about recklessness. This wasn't some tragic girl playing with fire.

This was someone trying to build something that kept falling apart in her hands.

"Chap and I had an epic blowout on the dock today. People watched. Like it was entertainment."

"He told me I chase chaos. That I like it. That I can't sit still without creating smoke."

"He doesn't know what it's like to live under everyone's microscope. To be loud and still never be heard."

"I walked away first. I had to."

Ava read that one twice.

She remembered that fight. Everyone did. It had been the final flashpoint, the scene people gossiped about at the grocery store and at the diner. And now, here it was. Quiet and raw on the page.

Not rage.

Not guilt.

Just hurt.

"Ava sat next to me today."

"She asked about my mom. Then she actually listened."

"I wanted to hate her. The way she fits into rooms I have to fight my way into. I hate the way Chap looks at her."

"But she looked at me like she saw something."

"Maybe we could've been friends."

Ava stared at the journal, as if focus could steady her pulse.

She turned to the last page.

"It's over. I know it now."

"He made it clear. This baby is not what he wants."
"But I do. Even if I'm terrified."
"I need to get out of Spruce Cove. I need to stop hoping he'll change."
"This town doesn't want the truth. They want the story that hurts the least."
"I'm leaving, but I'm not going to disappear. Not quietly."
Ava closed the journal slowly, her hands shaking.
This wasn't just a tragedy.
It was a map of a girl unraveling.
It was a warning.
And a promise.

***

The next day, the newsroom was still shaking off its slumber. The kettle whistled weakly in the breakroom. A dusty shaft of light cut across the carpet, catching on a dried fern no one had watered since May.

Ava perched at her desk, elbows on knees, trying not to look at Liz who was curled on the couch across from her with Amelia's journal on her lap, one ankle resting on the opposite knee like she had all the time in the world. She didn't. Not really. But Liz moved like someone in no rush to resurface.

Every few minutes, Liz sighed. Not a dramatic sigh. A thoughtful one. Occasionally she reached for the pen tucked into her messy bun and scribbled something on the notepad beside her.

Ava sipped coffee that had gone cold twenty minutes ago. She had no idea what Liz was writing. She hadn't dared ask. But her eyes kept drifting over, like they were magnetized.

Liz turned a page slowly, lips pursed.

Ava cleared her throat. "So?"

Liz didn't look up. "Give me another second."

"That's what you said twenty minutes ago."

Liz made a noncommittal sound, still reading. Still scribbling. One knee jiggled gently.

Ava stood, crossed to the kitchenette, poured her cold coffee down the sink. She didn't need caffeine. She needed air. Distance. Something to keep her from blurting out: *Do you think it was him? Do you think she meant Chap?*

When she turned back, Liz had flipped the journal shut.

And just sat with it. One hand resting on the soft leather cover like she wasn't quite ready to let go.

"Well?" Ava asked again, quieter this time.

Liz looked up. Her eyes were tired, and her usual quips weren't waiting at the surface. That more than anything made Ava's stomach twist.

"It's not a journal," Liz said finally. "It's a slow-motion unraveling."

Ava nodded once. That's exactly what it had felt like.

"She was scared," Liz added. "But I don't think it was Chap. She was scared of what came next. Of what the baby meant. Of being left."

Ava folded her arms. "Did it sound like him to you?"

Liz was quiet for a beat. "It could be."

Ava raised a brow. "But?"

Liz met her eyes. "But it also doesn't quite sound like him."

Ava didn't say anything.

Liz leaned forward, elbows on her knees. "I mean, Chap's got his faults. He bottles things up, he deflects with jokes and disappears when things get messy. But buying expensive jewelry? Asking someone to … " She paused, lowered her voice. "To get rid of a baby? That's not the guy I know."

She looked back at the journal. The entry about the earrings. That line. "Not everything has to be loud to be special." It *sounded* like him. It *felt* like something he'd say.

And still.

Would Chap ever ask someone to end a pregnancy?

Ava's stomach churned.

She wasn't sure anymore.

"People surprise us."

"Sure," Liz said. "But don't you think it's strange that if it *was* Chap, Amelia never wrote his name? Not even once?"

Ava dropped into her chair. "It could be because she was trying to protect him."

"Or," Liz countered, "because she didn't trust herself enough to name him. Like naming it made it more real. Or dangerous."

They sat with that for a moment.

Ava reached out, slid the journal toward her, opened it to a page near the middle. "This line," she said, pointing. "She says he looked right through her. Like she was just another face in the crowd." She tapped the page. "That doesn't sound like someone who was just scared. That sounds like heartbreak."

Ava's throat tightened. The kind of silence Amelia described being made invisible by someone who once saw everything. It rang too loud to ignore.

Liz leaned over, read the line again, then blew out a breath. "Yeah. That's a gut punch."

Ava traced the edge of the page. "She thought they had a shot. That they could do it together. And then he just …"

"Vanished."

Outside, the fog hadn't lifted. The bay was still wrapped in a blanket of white, the docks barely visible from the newsroom windows.

Liz tapped the journal. "There's something we're missing. A piece that hasn't been flipped over yet."

Ava looked up. "The earrings?"

"Maybe. We need to figure out who gave them to her. We find that, we find *him*."

Silence settled again. Not heavy. Just full.

Liz reached for her coffee, took a sip, grimaced. "This town needs to invest in better beans."

"You bought that coffee."

Liz smirked faintly. "Then I need to make better investment decisions."

Ava closed the journal gently. "We'll find him."

Liz nodded. "And when we do?"

Ava didn't hesitate. "We tell the truth. All of it."

Even if it wrecked someone.

Even if it wrecked her.

She exhaled, exhausted. "We can't do this alone. Not anymore."

"We need help. Like real, actual, badge-carrying help. Not just us playing Nancy Drew in yoga pants."

***

The door to George's shop creaked open with its usual reluctant groan.

Deputy Ryan Hale stepped in, eyes immediately locking onto the makeshift war room they'd assembled. His steps slowed as he took it all in, the whiteboard overtaken by color-coded scrawl, the walls littered with sticky notes and grainy photocopies, timelines snaking from table to floor to shelf. Three half-empty coffee cups sat like forgotten relics among the chaos.

He paused. "Either you're solving a mystery or preparing to overthrow the town council."

Liz, standing on a stool with a marker in hand, waved dramatically. "Welcome to the epicenter of our collective unraveling."

Ryan walked farther in, lips twitching with something dangerously close to amusement. "You've got a string board and a white board? That's commitment."

"We don't do things halfway," Ava said from where she sat, legs crossed on a sagging plaid armchair. She looked tired. Sharper than usual. "Also, we ran out of yarn."

Liz hopped down and gestured toward the board. "We've got motives, we've got timelines, we've got a suspiciously fancy earring and a whole mess of secrets. What we don't have is jurisdiction. Or, you know, a badge."

Ryan studied the board for a long moment, then set his coffee on the table and picked up a dry erase marker. "All right. What are we looking at?"

Ava lifted a brow. "Didn't even flinch. Impressive."

He shrugged. "I didn't say I wasn't going to regret it."

Liz beamed. "He's in."

"We're out of our league," Ava said simply. "We need someone who can see what we can't."

Ryan circled something on the board. "And someone who can request evidence without using sparkly stickers on the envelope."

"That was one time," Liz muttered.

They worked for a while, piecing through threads, debating contradictions, arguing over timelines. Ryan took notes with the same focus he probably gave to real case files. Liz kept throwing him teasing glances that bounced right off his professionalism. Ava stayed quiet, watching, measuring, the weight of the journal still thick in her chest.

At one point, Ryan paused mid-scribble. "There's something here. Between Amelia's last few days and the moment she went off the map. A shift."

"She stopped hoping," Ava said, voice low.

Ryan looked at her. "What do you mean?"

"She was scared," Ava said. "But she was also done. Not with life. With waiting for someone to choose her. To fight for her. I think she knew that wasn't going to happen."

Silence stretched between them.

Then Ryan nodded. "Okay. Let's keep going."

They stayed until the sky began to dim and George's clock ticked toward closing. Liz stretched, cracking her neck. "All right, brain's tapped. I'm going to go pretend I'm capable of eating a vegetable."

Ava pushed to her feet. "I'll catch you later."

As Liz wandered off, Ryan stayed behind, gathering his notes. He glanced at Ava, then reached into his coat pocket.

Ava took it slowly. Her name was written in firm, familiar handwriting.

Chap's.

"He asked me to give it to you. Said it wasn't urgent. Just overdue."

Ava held the letter like it might shatter.

"Thanks," she said, her voice quieter than she meant it to be.

Ryan nodded and stepped back. "Let me know if you find something in there."

He left without waiting for an answer.

Ava stood in the quiet shop, letter trembling slightly in her hands.

And then, with careful fingers, she opened it.

***

The porch swing creaked as Ava leaned back. The night had settled around the cabin like a hush, thick with pine and sea salt, stars peeking through the trees in cautious handfuls.

In her hands: an envelope.

Cream-colored. Crisp. Her name scrawled across the front in Chap's unmistakable handwriting, messy, familiar, infuriating.

Just her name. No return address. No explanations.

She hadn't opened it. Not yet. Not since Ryan passed it to her with a look that said nothing and everything.

Ava let the corner of the envelope trace the edge of her thumb. She could almost hear Chap's voice, cocky and soft all at once. It had always been his trick: saying something with a smirk and meaning it with his whole damn heart.

She took a breath. Then opened the letter.

Ava,

I didn't know if I should write. Hell, I don't even know if this will make it to you. But Ryan said he'd try, and I figured if anyone could get a piece of mail into working, it'd be him.

So. Here we are.

First: I'm sorry. For that last conversation. For every time I made you doubt yourself, or me. I was scared. Not of you, never of you. Just of what it meant to want someone like I wanted you. To need something that badly. You have this way of seeing people, really seeing them, and I didn't know how to stand still under that kind of light.

But I miss you.

God, Ava. I miss you so much it makes everything else feel smaller.

I don't know how this ends. I don't know what you've learned. What you think of me now or if you're still trying to put all the broken pieces together. I hope you are. Because the truth deserves that. Amelia deserves that.

Whatever you find, whatever comes next, I believe in you.

I believe we'll see each other again. Outside of this place.

Yours,

Chap

***

Ava let the letter fall open in her lap, the words glowing faintly under the porch light. Her chest ached, tight and stubborn.

She should've felt relief. Or closure. Or anger.

Instead, she felt everything too much and not enough.

The swing rocked gently. Somewhere, an owl called once, then went silent.

Ava leaned her head against the porch post and whispered into the dark.

"I'm still looking, Chap. I'm not done yet."

And this time, she meant it.

Chapter 9

Spruce Cove High hadn't changed much in the last twenty years. Same worn industrial carpet with soda stains, same cork bulletin boards overloaded with curled flyers, same trophy case featuring decade-old team photos no one had dusted since Y2K. Sunlight filtered through tall, drafty windows, illuminating every floating speck of dust in the quiet air. There were banners hanging above the lockers, faded red and gold ones proclaiming past championship wins in volleyball and cross-country. There was a handmade paper sign taped to the wall that read *Welcome, Seniors!* in slightly smudged bubble letters.

Ava McCormick adjusted her canvas tote and walked slower than necessary, glancing at the flyers pinned to the hallway bulletin board: car wash fundraisers, SAT prep sessions, a blood drive hosted by the science club. It was the kind of place where the water fountains still buzzed when used and the lockers rattled like they remembered better days.

She hadn't been inside this building since she grabbed a quick photo at a student art show. Today, she was on assignment. Liz had asked her to write a spotlight on Karen Doyle, the long-standing history teacher recently nominated for a state teaching award. The kind of feel-good piece that gave the Gazette some breathing room between heavier headlines.

Ava found the classroom easily. Room 108 was marked with a crooked brass plaque. The door was open. Inside, Karen Doyle stood at the whiteboard, wiping off stray marker smudges and humming to herself.

"Ms. Doyle?" Ava asked, knocking gently on the doorframe.

Karen turned with a smile, her silver-streaked hair pulled into a low bun and sleeves rolled up to her elbows. "You must be Ava."

"That obvious?"

"Your mom was one of my students," she said. "You have her walk."

Ava smiled. "Hoping that's a compliment."

Karen laughed. "Come on in. Want the desk chair or the squeaky stool?"

"I'll risk the squeak," Ava said, settling next to a front-row desk.

The room smelled faintly of dry-erase markers, hand sanitizer, and floor polish. A smell Ava hadn't registered since her own school days but that immediately tugged at some tucked-away memory.

Karen sat across from her, propping one knee over the other with easy confidence. She was one of those teachers who clearly loved her job. Not in a performative way, but in the way that made kids feel seen.

They talked for nearly twenty minutes. Karen answered all of Ava's questions without sounding like she was giving a speech. She talked about curriculum, the evolving attention spans of Gen Z, the importance of teaching kids to spot propaganda, and how she'd incorporated oral histories from local veterans into her American history unit.

Ava had just finished scribbling a quote when Karen leaned back and exhaled, not dramatically, just the kind of sigh that carried weight. She glanced out the window, where the winter light looked tired before noon.

Karen shifted in her chair, gaze drifting toward the window where winter sunlight pooled like it was running late.

"This year started heavy," she said, almost like she was talking to herself.

Ava glanced up. "Because ...?"

Karen's mouth tightened, like she was weighing whether to say the name out loud. "Amelia Colburn."

Ava's heart skipped a beat.

"She started volunteering here last spring," Karen continued. "Girls' basketball mostly, but it turned into more. She was helping decorate for dances, sitting with kids who didn't have anyone else. She just kept helping. Not for credit, not for applause. Just showed up."

She paused, then added, "The kids adored her. We all did."

Ava's pen stilled.

"She helped with the basketball team. Sat on the bleachers during practice. Organized snacks for the kids who forgot lunch. She was there for all of it: the fundraisers, the hallway decorating, the pep rallies. And the thing is, she wasn't doing it for attention. If anything, it seemed like she was finally grounding herself. Finding a version of life that didn't feel so temporary."

Karen looked back at Ava, her face lined with something close to regret. "And then one day, she was just gone."

Ava blinked. "I hadn't heard that."

Karen nodded. "She never made a show of it. That was the thing. She wasn't trying to be impressive. She just seemed like she wanted to matter. Like she wanted to be here."

There was a pause. Ava's fingers hovered over her notebook.

"She seemed happy," Karen went on. "For a few months, I thought maybe she'd figured something out. I had watched her grow up and waited for that moment."

"But?"

Karen's lips thinned. "She started pulling away right before she died. Not all at once, just gradually. She missed a couple of team events. Looked pale, distracted. One day I caught her just standing in the hallway after the final bell, staring out the window like she didn't know where else to go."

Ava's throat tightened. "Did she talk to you?"

"Only once," Karen said, quieter now. "She said, 'I thought I was getting somewhere. But I think I just circled back.'"

Ava thought to herself this was a teacher who'd noticed. Who'd cared. And who, like everyone else, hadn't known what to do with the pieces Amelia left behind.

"I wish I'd pushed more," Karen said. "Asked the hard questions. But you know how it is in a town like this. Everyone assumes they've already heard the worst."

Ava nodded, her chest tight. "Do you think anyone knew what was really going on?"

Karen hesitated. "I think someone did. Or should have."

She offered Ava a soft, sad smile and walked her to the door.

"If you figure out what happened to her," she said, "don't let them twist it into something neat. She wasn't neat. She was messy and angry and luminous. She deserves more than a cautionary tale."

"I'll do my best," Ava said.

Ava thanked Karen after wrapping up the interview that ended up focusing mostly on Amelia, pocketed her notebook, and stepped back into the chilly hallway. She had a story to write, the kind Liz would call "clean copy with a conscience." But there was another story tugging at her heart. One with pieces that still didn't fit.

She headed back to the office, hoping a change of scenery might help her write both.

***

The Gazette office was unusually quiet for a Wednesday morning. No ringing phones, no humming printers, just the occasional creak of the old radiator sputtering heat like it was doing Ava a personal favor. She was at her desk with a mug of cold coffee and a legal pad full of half-sentences, trying to untangle the feel-good profile from the thread of something heavier that wouldn't let go.

The door opened behind her.

"Knock, knock," came Ryan Hale's voice, casual, low, the kind of tone people used when pretending they weren't nervous.

Ava turned. He stood in the doorway holding two coffees and wearing a soft, well-worn flannel and an expression that said he wasn't entirely sure this was a good idea.

"Liz isn't in yet," Ava said, hiding a smirk.

Ryan scanned the room once more just in case, then shrugged. "Figured. But I brought offerings."

He walked over and set one of the coffees on her desk. Ava raised an eyebrow. "Coffee before small talk? You're skipping steps, Ryan."

"I'm evolving," he said, dragging the extra chair over like he'd done it before. "Small-town charm and caffeine. Irresistible combo."

Ava sipped. Black. No sugar.

"Thanks," she said, a little surprised at how good it was. "You were hoping to see Liz."

He didn't even pretend. "Maybe."

Ava leaned back. "She'll be flattered. She likes being a little bit of trouble."

Ryan grinned. "She always has."

They were quiet for a beat. Ava tapped her pen against the pad, flipping to a blank page.

"So," she said, "what were you and Chap like as kids?"

Ryan laughed softly, shaking his head. "Disasters. Creative disasters. One summer we tried to adopt a bear."

Ava blinked. "You what?"

"Cub wandered close to the edge of town. Chap was convinced it had 'chosen' us. Like we were family. So, we built it a little den behind his dad's workshop and started sneaking it food."

Ava stared at him. "Please tell me this ended before anyone lost a limb."

"We got caught before it got that far. Chap's mom found a trail of apple cores and a backpack full of hot dogs. I still remember the look on her face. Pure rage, wrapped in disbelief."

Ava laughed, hand over her mouth. "That's insane. How old were you?"

"Ten. Maybe eleven. We were gonna name it Murphy."

She was still smiling when the door opened again and Liz walked in, windblown and clutching a tote bag overflowing with folders.

"Did I miss something good?" she asked.

"Only Ryan and Chap's failed attempt at bear adoption," Ava said, gesturing at him.

"Oh, I've heard the stories," Liz said, dropping her bag with a thud. "Remember the time you got your foot stuck in the fence at the marina?"

Ryan groaned. "Why is *that* the one everyone remembers?"

"Because you screamed like a baby," Liz said, deadpan. "Chap had to bribe you with ice cream to keep you from crying."

"I was six!"

"You were nine."

Ryan raised both hands. "I come here to share a coffee and a laugh, and this is the abuse I get?"

Ava chuckled, but something in her chest tugged sideways. It was so easy to picture Chap and Ryan as boys, Liz tagging along, all sharp elbows and summer cuts. It made Chap feel more real and more impossible at the same time. He had a history here. A life before her.

And maybe part of her wanted to belong in that picture too.

"Don't act surprised," Liz said, pulling her chair around backward and straddling it. "You and Chap were literal chaos magnets. I once caught you both trying to sled down Cemetery Hill on a plastic kiddie pool. In July."

Ryan winced. "Oh God, I'd blocked that one out."

"You hit a fire hydrant. Chap sprained his wrist, and you cried because your mom said you weren't allowed to play dead anymore."

"I wasn't crying," Ryan muttered. "I was calculating trauma."

Liz smirked. "Sure, you were."

Ava was laughing now, full and unguarded. It felt good. Strange, but good, to be part of something this silly, this harmless. Like maybe healing didn't always have to feel like surgery.

She looked at the two of them, these people who had roots in every sidewalk crack of Spruce Cove, and for the first time, she didn't feel like she was just passing through.

She belonged at least a little.

And maybe that was enough for today.

***

The newsroom had quieted to a hum. Just the occasional clack of keys, the creak of chairs, and the distant shuffle of Liz rustling through a pile of edits with the dedication of someone trying to win a fight against semicolons.

Ava had her head down, fingers flying, shaping her school notes into something clean. The kind of story Liz called "soft with a spine."

It was about a fundraiser for new uniforms, updated sports gear, that sort of thing, but it had heart. Kids organizing, parents surprising themselves with how much they cared, teachers pulling double-duty because that's what they always did. If she was lucky, she'd sneak in a line about Amelia. How her absence lingered, not like a shadow, but like a hum beneath the floorboards. Quiet, steady and inescapable.

Across the room, Liz had vanished into her corner office with a bag of kettle chips and a red pen. Ryan stuck around, half-leaning against a desk, tossing out gentle barbs and teasing Liz whenever she emerged to grab another file.

"You've got a very intimidating editing face," he said once. "If I didn't know better, I'd assume someone just wrote 'your' instead of 'you're.'"

Liz didn't look up. "They did. Twice. I'm still recovering."

Ava smiled behind her screen.

By seven-thirty, her back ached and her eyes were dry. She hit save, closed her laptop, and stretched.

The back exit led through the kitchen and out to the gravel lot. She crossed quietly, grabbing her coat and paused.

Voices carried.

Liz's office door had drifted open an inch.

"So dinner?" Ryan said, voice low and casual.

A beat passed.

Liz's laugh followed, surprised and warm. "That your way of asking me out?"

"Subtle's never been my thing," Ryan said. "But yeah. I figured if I'm gonna get mocked for middle school bear bonding, I might as well get fed afterward."

Another laugh. "Sure. Why not?"

Ava turned, pulling her coat on with more force than necessary.

She wasn't jealous. Not of Liz or Ryan. Just the ease, of the rhythm that seemed to click into place for everyone but her. Like she'd been dropped into a dance mid-song and couldn't quite find the beat.

Outside, the cold kissed her cheeks. The stars were brilliant, sharp and clear, like someone had polished the sky just for her.

She stood still for a moment.

Then walked toward the cabin, hands tucked deep in her pockets, the day settling in her chest like a stone she wasn't quite ready to let go of.

***

Ava walked slowly, gravel crunching beneath her boots, stars overhead like they'd been hung with extra care. But her mind wasn't on constellations.

It was on Amelia Colburn.

Unsuspecting bake-sale enthusiast. Booster club mascot. Spruce Cove High's most enthusiastic supporter?

With no kid of her own.

Why? Why now? Why had Amelia, of all people, suddenly decided to plant herself at Spruce Cove High? Host fundraisers. Take photos at games. Bake for booster clubs. That wasn't the girl Caroline used to describe in flippant anecdotes and unfinished sentences. That wasn't the Amelia who had always seemed allergic to permanence.

It didn't track.

Was it guilt? Nostalgia? Or something, someone, that kept pulling her back into the building?

By the time Ava reached the cabin, the chill had seeped through her sleeves, and her thoughts were circling each other like tired dogs.

She stepped inside and saw her grandfather in his recliner, reading the same Louis L'Amour paperback he'd read ten times already. Her grandmother sat on the couch with a mug of tea and a full face of cold cream, knitting something bright and unwearable.

"Home before midnight," her grandfather said without looking up. "I owe your grandma five bucks."

"Technically," her grandmother said, "you owe me ten. You said she wouldn't be home till *tomorrow.*"

Ava smiled, unwinding her scarf. "You two bet on when I will get home?"

"Only because you've started acting like a real McCormick," her grandfather said. "Staying out late, chasing stories, forgetting to eat."

"Sorry I'm late. Got stuck at the paper finishing my story. Then Ryan started in on some middle school saga about him and Chap trying to adopt a bear."

Her grandmother raised an eyebrow. "A *bear?*"

Her grandfather snorted. "That tracks."

They made room for her on the couch. Her grandmother tucked a blanket over Ava's lap, unasked, like she used to when Ava was a kid, watching old movies and pretending not to cry during the sad parts.

For ten sweet minutes, they talked about nothing. Recipes they'd ruined. A neighbor who got a drone and immediately flew it into a pine tree. Whether Ava's grandfather was losing at poker on purpose so her grandmother would feel superior.

The moment was comforting, like the feeling of your favorite sweatshirt after a long day, not fancy, not new, but exactly what you needed.

Later, in bed, the fire in the stove dying down to coals, Ava reached for the journal. She hadn't touched it since Liz returned it with quiet eyes and too many unspoken questions.

She flipped back to the beginning. Read the first entry again. Then the one about the kiss. Then the one where Amelia said he saw her, *really* saw her.

Ava frowned, thumbing the corner of the next page.

What had made Amelia change course? From chaos to school volunteer?

And how had it all unraveled so quickly?

Ava laid back on her pillow, the journal open across her chest, the room settling around her like a secret.

Tomorrow, she'd press harder. Ask more questions. Follow the thread.

But tonight, she let the words wrap around her like a tide coming in, gentle, relentless, inescapable.

***

She curled under the covers, the journal still beside her but closed for now. The fire in the stove had burned down to embers, and the only sounds were the ticking of the old clock in the hall and her grandfather's faint snore down the hallway.

She reached for her phone, mostly out of habit but maybe a little out of hope.

William's last message still sat there.

Hey. Just checking in. No pressure. Hope you're okay.

Her thumb hovered, then tapped out a reply.

Hey. I'm okay. Just a lot of life happening all at once. Finally horizontal, hoping my brain gets the memo.

A moment later, the screen lit up.

Quieting brains is my specialty. Should I start listing random facts about sea cucumbers again?

Ava grinned.

Only if you're prepared to be blocked.

Bold talk from someone still afraid of crab rolls.

They have legs. That's not dinner. That's a warning.

So do chickens, Ava.

Yeah, and I don't trust them either.

She chuckled softly, then tucked the phone close to her chest for a beat before setting it back on the nightstand.

It wasn't passion. It wasn't mystery.

But it was something gentle, familiar. A hand reaching out in the dark.

Chapter 10

Snow came in sideways off the cove, the kind that couldn't decide whether it wanted to rain or snow and so did both, dampening Ava's hair and spotting George's coat. The church glowed at the end of the street, its stained-glass windows lit from within, casting swatches of blue and red onto the snowbanks outside. Someone had strung a line of mismatched Christmas lights along the rail, their colors flickering in the wind like they were holding on out of sheer stubbornness.

Esther tucked her arm through Ava's, her other hand tucked into her coat pocket like it was hiding state secrets. George walked just ahead, boots crunching on the salt and gravel scattered over the icy walkway. At the steps, people stomped snow from their XtraTufs, their laughter rising into the cold air before they ducked inside.

"Don't slip," Esther warned, which in grandmother translated to "I still remember your toddler skull meeting our front steps."

"I've got her," George said, one hand steady on Ava's elbow despite the fact that he was the person most likely to wipe out on black ice. He wore his good wool coat and the salmon tie he saved for weddings and funerals, which said a lot about how Spruce Cove treated Christmas Eve.

Inside, the vestibule felt like the town had poured itself into a single room: parkas shedding, mittens slapping against radiators, toddlers in velvet stomping their patent-leather Mary Janes. The air smelled like damp wool and evergreen. A teenager in a white robe that looked like it had been borrowed from the church's "one size fits none" collection handed them candles, thin white tapers with paper collars that promised to catch the drips and never did.

"Silent Night later," he whispered, with the seriousness of a boy entrusted with the nuclear codes.

They squeezed into a pew halfway up on the right. It was McCormick territory, Esther said, because apparently pews came with invisible nameplates. All around them: familiar heads in unfamiliar hats. Mrs. Leland, who ran the post office like a benevolent dictatorship, waved from across the aisle. Earl nodded once, the closest he ever got to festive. Liz wasn't with them. She'd texted she'd meet them "inside the Jesus zone," which Ava took to mean she'd slide in late like a repentant chorus girl.

"Look at Princess," Esther whispered, and it took Ava a second to realize she meant Mabel's cat, who was tucked into a camouflage sling on her owner's chest like a furry contraband hot water bottle. The collar jingled once, then went mercifully still.

The choir launched into "O Come, All Ye Faithful," the organ wheezing in that charming, slightly asthmatic way that suggested it was old enough to vote twice. The priest proceeded down the center aisle, incense swinging like a tiny, smoky planet. Ava watched the smoke rise and thought about how faith is mostly that, something you can't hold and curling into the air.

When the readings began, she let the words wash over her like a radio station half a degree off. Isaiah, light and darkness, a people who walked and all that. She knew the cadence even if she didn't remember the chapter and verse. Her mom's Christmases had been more tree-lot than church, but she'd gone on the years Ava asked. "We can sit in a pew and hum," her mom had said. "God likes humming."

The priest's homily was short, which made the faithful love him more than doctrine ever could. He talked about waiting, which felt apt. Not just Advent, but the other kind. The kind where you sit in a hospital corridor or a kitchen chair at 2 a.m. He spoke about empty chairs at holiday tables and how the story of Christmas had room for grief right alongside joy. "We're a small town," he said, his voice going soft at the edges. "We know how to carry one another. We've had to this year."

No one said Amelia's name, but the congregation tilted the way people do when a wave comes in. Ava felt it hit and recede, leaving behind a glimmer of shame for how relief could live next door to sorrow. She wasn't sure what she believed most days, but she believed in rooms like this with people shifting to make room for one more body on the end of a pew, sadness folded into the hymn.

"The peace of the Lord be with you always," Father Matthias said, his voice carrying easily over the creak of the pews.

"And with your spirit," the congregation answered, a low, familiar rumble.

"Let us offer each other the sign of peace."

Esther leaned in and kissed Ava's cheek, the faint scent of rose lipstick clinging to her skin. George clasped her hand, two quick squeezes. Their code for I love you. Around them, handshakes, hugs, the half-second evaluation that happens when you greet someone you only ever see in the frozen aisle at Thorne's General. Peace be with you. Also, I have thoughts about your new haircut.

"Peace," Liz whispered, finally sliding into the pew and bumping Ava's hip. She wore a black turtleneck and a grin that said she was about to whisper a story wildly inappropriate for church. She didn't. Maybe the candles held her in check.

After communion, the lights dimmed until the sanctuary was mostly velvet and breath. The acolytes moved down the aisles, touching flame to wick, fire hopping pew to pew like gossip with better manners. Esther tipped her candle to Ava's, sheltering the flame with her palm the way she used to shelter Ava's lunch money from the wind.

"Careful," George murmured. "Don't set your hair on fire."

"That was one time," Esther hissed, which, if accurate, was not reassuring.

The first notes of "Silent Night" unspooled, and the church loosened. Shoulders fell an inch. A baby hiccuped somewhere in the back and was shushed by soft voices. Ava sang quietly, the way you sing when the words feel borrowed but true. Her flame wobbled, then steadied. She thought of her mother. Their last Christmas in Seattle. An apartment that smelled like burnt sugar cookies and fresh laundry, a cheap pine candle doing the Lord's work. "You can always start over," her mom had said, and it had sounded like a dare.

By the last verse, the candles turned every face beautiful. Even Earl-from-the-docks glowed like an advertisement for redemption.

The final blessing was brisk; the church emptied like a jar of marbles, everyone bumping into everyone else and apologizing with their eyebrows. Out in the aisle, the town reassembled into gossiping knots. Ava stood with Esther and George and accepted the season like a series of surprises in tissue paper.

"Ava! You're looking well," Mrs. Leland said, which in small-town dialect meant I have a dossier on your life and I'm being gentle. "Back for good?"

"For a while," Ava said, the answer she'd learned to give when the truth was complicated.

"Tell your grandmother my fudge beat hers blind this year," said Mr. Cotter, who had two hearing aids and a vendetta. Esther smiled like a woman who would die defending her cocoa ratios.

Ryan made his way up the aisle, uniform jacket dusted with snow. His eyes did their usual sweep of the crowd, but when they landed on Liz, his mouth twitched into the kind of smile you try to hide in uniform. He gave Ava a nod, polite but warmer than the all-business version he used on everyone else. The glance lingered a moment longer before he moved on.

And then there was Coach Ellery. He worked the crowd like a politician at a pancake breakfast, smile prepped and hand already extended. He was handsome in the way that made women apologize to themselves for noticing: tall, easy shoulders under a dark coat, jawline you could shelve books on. His tie was festive in a restrained, expensive way. His wife trailed half a step behind him, one hand on their son's shoulder, her mouth set in a line that said she was one more conversation away from switching to bourbon.

"George," the coach boomed, clasping her grandfather's hand with both of his. "Esther." He turned to Ava and delivered that eye contact. Direct and generous, the kind you feel obliged to return.

"Ava. Haven't had you sticking a recorder under my chin in a while."

"It's been a few," she said, matching his smile with one that didn't quite reach her eyes.

"Too long," he replied, his voice smooth in that way it always was when his wife wasn't within arm's reach. "Guess I'll have to watch what I say again."

"You always should've," Ava said with a half smile.

He chuckled, and for a moment it was just like the sideline interviews. Except now, his wife was standing five feet away, smiling with the strained precision of someone who could hear every word.

"Hope we'll see you around," he added, letting the words land in a place that felt like an invitation you couldn't RSVP to without a chaperone.

Denise Ellery's smile didn't move. Up close, the tension coming off her felt like power lines in winter. Humming, dangerous if you got too close. She drew their son in until he was nearly tucked behind her coat.

"Lovely service," she said to Esther, which was the kind of conversational decoy women tossed one another when the real sentence was don't.

"Mm," Esther said, returning a grandmotherly smile that, if translated, would have read: I see you seeing us. Move along.

They did, the coach's palm landing lightly on his wife's back like punctuation. Liz leaned in the instant they were out of earshot. "He's got the social confidence of a golden retriever who's been elected mayor," she murmured. "And she looks like she's thinking about witness protection."

Ava didn't answer. The charm was the point; it made people feel rude for stepping back. She thought of Amelia, the last night Ava saw her at The Gaff Hook, the way she slid onto the barstool. The memory nudged at her like a stone in her boot.

They shuffled toward the door, candles long blown out, the paper collars wilting in the heat of the crowd. Outside, the cold wrapped around them with both arms. The luminaries guttered in the wind, small defiant suns.

"Home," George said, clapping his hands together once as if to summon the truck from thin air.

"Home," Esther echoed, then peered at Ava's face, the way only grandmothers can. Like it's a book they've read a hundred times and can still find new meaning in. "You okay, honey?"

Ava tried on a smile and checked the fit. "Yeah. It's just …" She looked back at the church, its windows spilling color onto the snow. Inside, people were still hugging, still finding their coats, still pretending they couldn't hear the undertow of a town deciding things about one another.

"… a lot," she finished.

Esther slipped her arm through Ava's again, tugging her close as they stepped into the crunch and squeak of the path. "It always is," she said. "That's why God invented pie."

"Pretty sure that was Esther McCormick," George said, opening the truck door with a gallant little bow that made Ava grin despite herself.

They climbed in, breath fogging the windows as George coaxed the engine awake. As they pulled away, Ava watched the church grow smaller in the rearview, a bright, humming box in a dark, indifferent night. She pressed her gloved fingers to the antique mirror of the side window and imagined the flame from her Midnight Mass candle, small and stubborn.

Faith could be that, she decided. Not certainty. Just a decision to keep your hand around a thing that flickers and try to keep it from going out.

The house smelled like pine from the bull pine George had chopped down himself a week ago. Its branches sagged under the weight of ornaments collected over decades, from the glass fishing float Esther swore was lucky to the macaroni wreath Ava had made in second grade.

When they came in from Midnight Mass, George went straight to stoking the woodstove while Esther fussed in the kitchen, humming "O Holy Night" under her breath. Ava climbed the stairs, peeled off her boots, and stood at her bedroom window for a moment, watching the snow drift in the yellow glow of the streetlamp.

She could still feel the warmth of the candle in her palm, the low hum of the hymn in her chest. But beneath it was something sharper. She thought about the way Denise Ellery's eyes had assessed her, the coach's too-familiar smile, Ryan's subtle glance at Liz. Spruce Cove might be small, but its undercurrents ran deep.

She went to bed with the sound of the tide brushing against the pilings, and woke to a quieter world. The kind of hush only a heavy snow could bring.

***

The next morning, the smell of coffee and the Christmas tree pulled her toward the living room, where the tree lights glowed against the morning gray and the stockings bulged like they'd been holding secrets all night.

George was already in his plaid flannel, Esther in her quilted robe and red holiday socks with most of the puff balls long gone. They started with the usual presents. Esther's practical magic (fleece-lined gloves, a jar of spruce tip jelly "to keep you honest"), George's handiwork (a birdhouse carved to look like the McCormick cabin, slightly off-kilter but charming), and Liz's contribution, wrapped in an old Anchorage Daily News with a headline about a moose problem on a golf course.

107

Then Esther handed Ava a slim, carefully wrapped box addressed in William's unmistakable blocky handwriting.

Inside was an antique silver hand mirror, its scrollwork handle worn smooth from decades of use. Beneath it, a note on thick cream stationery:

Ava,

I hope this year is about you finding yourself. I've been doing the same. I'm sorry for the ways I've failed us, but I believe in the person you are and the life you'll build.
- W

She read it twice. The first time, it sounded like an apology. The second, like permission. She set the mirror down gently, its weight somehow heavier than its size, and reached for another gift before either grandparent could ask how she felt about it.

The last package under the tree was for Ava. It was a thick, leather-bound novel, the wrapping plain but neat. The tag had Ryan's name, but when she opened the cover, she found a short inscription in Chap's blocky handwriting:

Ava, Merry Christmas. Thought you could use a reminder. - Chap

It was *The Old Man and the Sea.* They'd once argued about it over coffee at Annie's. Chap claimed it wasn't about fishing at all. Ava insisted every good fishing story was about something more.

Beneath the title page, he had underlined a passage in deliberate strokes:

"A man can be destroyed but not defeated."

Her fingers lingered on the page, smoothing the edge as if it were something fragile. The words pressed against something in her chest, not quite hope and not quite ache. She wondered how many times he'd read them before deciding to send them to her.

Esther glanced over but didn't ask. George cleared his throat and headed for the kitchen. Ava closed the book gently and set it on the coffee table, its weight still warm in her hands.

"Prime rib's not going to season itself," Esther said, standing. But her voice was softer, and Ava could tell she'd noticed more than she let on.

***

By late afternoon, the McCormick kitchen smelled like sizzling prime rib, garlic, and the briny sweetness of Dungeness crab. George was in his element, carving the roast with the precision of a man filleting halibut, pausing only to shoo Ava away from the cutting board with a mock glare.

Esther moved between the stove and the counter in her holiday apron, sliding crab melts under the broiler and stirring smoked salmon dip in a green Pyrex bowl older than Ava. The air was warm and damp from the steam, and the windows fogged so thoroughly that the world outside had disappeared.

Liz arrived with a bottle of wine she claimed was "Christmas-appropriate" because the label had holly on it. She kicked off her boots, shook the snow from her hair, and immediately zeroed in on the appetizers. "You've outdone yourself, Esther. Which means I'll eat enough to roll home."

They gathered around the table, plates piled high, conversation moving in loops. Fishing stories from George, small-town gossip from Liz, gentle steering from Esther when a topic veered toward anything sharp-edged. Ava listened more than she spoke, watching the easy rhythm of her grandparents together. George topping off Esther's glass without asking. Esther sliding the platter closer to him when he didn't notice he'd run out of potatoes.

For a moment, the heaviness in her chest loosened. She let herself be pulled into Liz's retelling of the year the harbor froze solid and someone tried to ice-skate to the cannery. George laughed so hard he had to put down his fork.

By the time the plates were scraped clean and the roast had been reduced to a few stubborn bones, the warmth in the room felt like something living. It was not just heat from the stove, but something made between the four of them. Ava caught herself wishing it could be bottled, tucked away for the days when the cove felt colder in other ways.

When the plates were cleared and George had retreated to his chair by the woodstove, Liz tugged on her boots. "Come on," she said, her tone light but her eyes already telling Ava where they were headed.

Esther didn't ask. She just pressed Ava's scarf into her hands and said, "Don't stay too long."

Outside, the cold caught them quick, slipping through the seams of their coats. Snowflakes drifted sideways in the wind coming off the cove, settling in Liz's hair as they walked. The streets were nearly empty, the holiday hush wrapping the town in something close to stillness.

Ryan was alone at the front desk when they walked in, coffee in hand, boots kicked out in front of him.

"Hey stranger," Liz said.

"Perks of being the low man on the totem pole," Ryan said with a grin. "Holidays, nights, and any other shift nobody else wants." He stood and buzzed Ava through without another word. "Five minutes," he added, but Ava caught the way he didn't look at the clock.

Chap was already on his feet when she reached the bars. He stepped closer, fingers wrapping around the cold steel.

"Merry Christmas," she said.

His eyes swept over her like he was trying to memorize something. "It is now."

"I didn't get you anything." She felt ridiculous the second the words left her mouth.

Chap leaned in just enough that she could see the faint shadow of stubble on his jaw. "You showed up. That's better than anything I'd unwrap."

Heat curled low in her stomach. She tried to smile it off, but it stuck in her throat. "I liked the book."

"I'm glad you got it." His fingers tightened briefly on the bars. "You get me, Ava. That's something."

Her pulse kicked. "You chose the right quote."

"Fits, doesn't it?"

"It does."

Somewhere down the hall, a chair scraped. Ava gave his fingers a quick squeeze before she could think better of it and stepped back.

When she pushed through the door into the office, Ryan was leaning across his desk, hands braced on either side of Liz, his head bent toward hers. They broke apart when they saw Ava, but not fast enough to hide Liz's flushed cheeks.

"Really?" Ava said, tugging her scarf into place. "At the jail?"

Liz grinned, unbothered. "It was a convenient location."

Snow crunched under their boots as they headed toward home. Ava couldn't stop thinking about how this Christmas was supposed to be different. She should have been celebrating her first married Christmas with William. Chap should have been at George and Esther's table, teasing George about overcooking the prime rib. Instead, she was walking home from the jail with Liz, who was clearly moving forward while Ava felt stuck, caught between two men she couldn't be with.

Not yet.

Chapter 11

Caroline's text arrived like it had worn a disguise to get there.

Can we meet? Not at my house. Not anywhere obvious. 20 minutes. Behind the cannery. Come alone (Liz can come too).

"If she's asking us to go back through that wild celery, I'm out. My shins still look like I fought a feral salad bar."

They cut through the brush the way Liz had in high school when "cutting through the brush" meant sneaking to Make-Out Point and not to rendezvous with a grief-stricken informant. The path was still half-swallowed by a tangle of green that snagged at their jeans like it had opinions.

"Deja vu," Liz muttered, swatting at a stalk. "I swear this plant remembers me."

"It does," Ava said. "You called it vindictive celery last time."

"It *is* vindictive celery."

They popped out at the back of the cannery, where the wind pushed ocean air up the hill and the siding still wore a permanent coat of salt. A seagull eyed them from a rusted beam like it had seniority. The only other sign of life was a faded PRIVATE PARKING sign screwed into a post with the long-suffering air of a boundary habitually ignored.

"Code word?" Liz asked, deadpan. "If this goes sideways?"

"Harvest Delight," Ava said. "If I yell that, it means run."

"Perfect. Nothing strikes terror like raisins in Jell-O."

A shadow detached from the cannery wall. Caroline stepped into view wearing a black puffer, a baseball cap tugged low, and (God bless her) oversized sunglasses in a town with twelve minutes of sunlight today.

"Is that a disguise?" Liz whispered.

Caroline didn't smile. "I had to get out of the house without my mother asking why I suddenly like long walks. I told her I was meeting Rachel about youth group."

"Good to see you too," Ava said gently.

Caroline exhaled, a thin cloud in the cold. She glanced behind them, then at the cannery's rear door, then at the gull, which absolutely did not care. "If Mason finds out I'm talking to you, he'll blow his top, and my mother will finally use it as an excuse for the nervous breakdown she's been saving for a special occasion."

"Big moment for everyone," Liz said.

Caroline finally managed a small, brittle smile. "This will be quick." She slid a manila envelope from inside her jacket like she was smuggling state secrets and not flouting the ethical gray area of someone else's Facebook.

Ava took it, feeling the slickness of laser-printed paper through the folder. "What is it?"

"Messages," Caroline said. "Screenshots. Amelia and someone saved as 'C.' in her Facebook. The DMs are not nice."

Liz leaned closer. "Not nice like 'you owe me an apology' or not nice like 'I know what you did last summer'?"

"Firm," Caroline said. "Aggressive. Short. Who uses periods anymore in texts? 'C' does."

"'C, as in?" Ava let the question hang.

"I don't know," Caroline said quickly. "I tried to. I went through every 'C' in her contacts and it's useless. There are a hundred. It could be anyone. Cam, Carl, Coach Ell—" She stopped herself like the word burned. "I don't know. I truly don't."

Ava slid the first sheet free. The screenshots were crisp, time stamps intact, the way only a sister who color-codes her spice rack would deliver evidence.

C.: *Don't do anything stupid. 10:06 p.m.*

Amelia: *I'm done being careful. 10:07 p.m.*

C.: *You're not listening. 10:08 p.m.*

C.: *We agreed on discretion. 10:09 p.m.*

Ava's stomach shifted. Liz's pen was already out, the cap between her teeth like a starter pistol.

"Where did you get these?" Liz asked.

"I guessed her password," Caroline said, almost apologetically. "Took me a couple of months and a lot of wine. Tried her locker number, her prom date's birthday, even that dumb nickname Mason gave her in eighth grade. Then it hit me, MrsFisher with an exclamation point. She wanted to be Mrs. Fisher when we were in high school. She never changed her password." Caroline gave a small, guilty shrug. "I know I shouldn't have gone in, but the police aren't investigating, and there's something there." She swallowed. "You'll be careful with it?"

Caroline shoved her hands deep in her pockets like she had to keep from grabbing the envelope back. "There's more. Not in there, in my head. The night before she died, Amelia left the bar and cut across to that old red building. You know the one."

Ava and Liz exchanged a glance. "We saw her do that once," Ava said. "Weeks before."

"She did it that last week too," Caroline said. "She told me she 'had to pick up a file' and laughed when I asked what kind of file you can only get after 10 p.m. I thought she meant from a friend, not an office. I didn't push. I should've pushed."

"Do you know who she was seeing in there?" Liz asked.

Caroline shook her head. "I only know she changed before she left. Different lipstick. Hair down. Not like a date. Like armor."

Wind rattled a loose sheet of tin; the gull flapped to a new vantage point, offended.

"Caroline," Ava said, "why do we keep meeting like this?"

"Because I can't be seen helping you," she said, and there it was, the raw center. "My mother thinks Chap killed her. Mason wants to kill Chap himself. If I look like I'm defending him, I won't just lose what's left of my family, I'll rip apart the story they've built to survive. The one where Amelia was perfect, and Chap was the monster. The one that makes sense."

"People don't make sense," Liz said softly. "They make choices."

"And secrets," Caroline said. "She kept so many. I can't keep this one for her."

Ava slid the envelope into her tote. "We'll keep you out of it."

"Please do," Caroline said.

"Understood," Liz said. "On a scale of one to perjury, where are we?"

Caroline took a step back, already angling her body like she could reverse into anonymity. "I have to go. If anyone asks, we discussed the scone inventory and the pastor's parking spot."

"Strong cover," Liz said gravely. "Martha would approve."

Caroline hesitated, then reached into her pocket and produced one more item. A single, folded Post-it. "I found this in one of her coats. It's probably nothing. But it was in the same pocket as her lip balm and a receipt from The Gaff Hook. I keep thinking about the timing."

Ava unfolded the paper. Four numbers, then a star. No name, no explanation.

"What is this?" Liz asked.

Caroline's gaze flicked past them toward the parking lot. "Just keep it. You'll figure it out. I believe in you!"

She pivoted toward the brush, paused, and looked back. In the dim light, the sunglasses finally tipped up, and there was Caroline the girl who used to label her notebooks, iron her jeans and hold Amelia's hair back after bad decisions, trying to do the right thing in a town that treated truth like contraband.

"Keep me posted," she said to Ava. "And don't be stupid."

115

"Never. Well, almost never," Liz said, already stupidly pocketing a blackberry thorn.

Caroline disappeared into the green, the branches swallowing her like a secret.

Liz blew out a breath. "It's like she dropped a grenade in the middle of brunch."

Ava stared at the Post-it and the envelope, the gull, the sign that said PASTOR'S SPOT like there was a moral to all of this if you parked in the right place.

"Rear stairs," she said. "After."

Liz tipped her head toward town. "Red building?"

"Red building," Ava agreed.

"And we are absolutely not stupid."

"We are absolutely going to be careful," Ava said.

"Same thing," Liz said, already moving.

They cut back through the brush, twigs grabbing at their sleeves like the town itself didn't want to let them pass.

***

They didn't say much on the walk back. The only sounds were the crunch of their boots and the snap of a flag in the wind. Inside the newsroom, the door clicked shut behind them, sealing out the cold. Ava exhaled, letting the familiar mix of burnt coffee and printer toner wrap around her like a blanket.

She spread Caroline's envelope across her desk, careful not to smudge the pages. Liz perched on the edge, one foot swinging, reading over her shoulder.

The Facebook messages were short, blunt, and a little menacing.

C: *You're making a mistake.*

Amelia: *I don't care.*

C: *This won't end well.*

Amelia: *Not your call.*

116

Liz frowned. "That's not romantic banter."

"Could be Chap," Ava said, though it tasted wrong coming out.

Liz shook her head. "Chap uses punctuation, yes. But I don't know, he's more of a slow-burn angry. This feels …" She tapped the page "… pushy. Impatient. Like someone used to getting their way fast."

Ava traced the ink with her finger. "Still. Caroline thought it was important enough to risk meeting us."

"She also thought my coat wouldn't survive that shortcut," Liz said. "And she wasn't wrong."

They went quiet for a second, the hum of the mini-fridge filling the space. Ava hated how much the messages didn't fit. If Chap didn't send them then who did? And why use just an initial?

Liz finally pushed off the desk. "We need air. And possibly snacks."

"Air first," Ava said, grabbing her coat.

***

The red building sat at the far end of Main Street, its clapboard siding weathered to a dull, almost pinkish red in spots, the white trim around the narrow upstairs windows gone gray from years of salt air. Two stories tall but narrow, it looked like it had been cobbled together from whatever lumber and nails were left over after the cannery was built.

"This is where she went," Ava said, slowing as they approached.

"After leaving the bar," Liz confirmed. "Twenty minutes inside, and nobody saw her come back out."

They moved along the side, peeking in the ground-floor windows. Most were fogged over from condensation or blocked with curling flyers. Through one, Ava caught a glimpse of a desk stacked with paperwork, a jar of pens with more chewed caps than usable ink, and a coffeemaker that looked like it had brewed its last pot sometime before the last tourist season.

Another window offered a view into a space that had clearly once been a waiting room. A couple of plastic chairs, a faded poster about charter boat safety regulations.

"Charter office," Liz said. She pointed farther down the row of doors, ticking off the businesses: "Taxidermy. Massage therapy. Bookkeeping, Denise Ellery."

Ava's gaze lingered on the sign. "D. Ellery, CPA."

They kept moving, rounding the back of the building. The lot was quiet except for a coil of thick rope piled near the siding and a dented metal trash can without a lid. A narrow metal staircase clung to the wall, leading to a second-floor door.

Liz slowed. "Electronic lock." The keypad blinked green in the dim light.

"Seems fancy for a building with taxidermy," Ava murmured.

Liz tapped the metal casing lightly. "Maybe the fish are classified."

They turned to leave and Ava froze mid-step.

One of the upstairs windows glowed faintly. A woman stood just behind the glass, short hair framing a pale face, eyes locked on them.

The curtain twitched once, then dropped into place.

"Was that?" Liz whispered.

"Denise Ellery," Ava said, her stomach tightening.

Neither of them spoke again. They just walked, briskly, toward the street.

***

They'd made it halfway back to the office when Liz stopped short.

"We should go back."

Ava followed her gaze down the street. "Now?"

"If we wait, she'll have time to come up with answers. Or a restraining order. We need to catch her while she's still wondering what we were doing outside her building."

Ava frowned. "And your plan is?"

118

"Easy," Liz said, already turning toward the newsroom. "I'm here to hire a bookkeeper. You're my emotional support animal. But first, I need to grab something."

Inside the newsroom, Liz went straight for the metal filing cabinet under her desk and yanked open the bottom drawer. She pulled out a battered manila envelope, bulging with a mix of receipts, menus, a crumpled tide chart, and something that might have once been a sticky note but now resembled an ancient fossil.

Ava raised an eyebrow. "This is what's going to convince her you're a legitimate client?"

"Absolutely," Liz said, stuffing a couple more loose receipts from her jacket pocket into the envelope. "Messy finances are disarming. Nobody suspects the woman who can't find her W-2 from 2019."

She slung her bag over her shoulder. "Let's go."

***

They pushed open the narrow glass door marked D. Ellery, CPA in peeling gold vinyl. A small brass bell gave a polite jingle.

The office was tidy, but in the kind of way that felt frantic, like someone had done a sweep minutes before they arrived. A stack of unopened mail sat on the corner of the desk, an overwatered Christmas cactus drooping, a calculator, and the air smelled faintly of coffee and paper.

Behind the desk, Denise Ellery looked up from her computer. Short hair, neatly cut, but the color had grown out at the roots. She wore a cream cardigan and a silver chain necklace that she twisted once around her finger before letting go.

"Can I help you?" she asked.

"Yes," Liz said, dropping into the nearest chair without waiting for an invitation. "I'm here to hire you before the IRS decides to make an example out of me. This is Ava. She works at the paper."

Ava sat more slowly, trying to read Denise's face.

"Well," Denise said, smoothing her cardigan. "We're accepting new clients. What sort of bookkeeping do you need?"

Liz reached into her bag and plopped the thick, crumpled envelope onto the desk. "This is my 2024 so far."

Denise blinked. "These are all your records?"

"And my drink card from The Gaff Hook," Liz said. "Can't lose that."

Ava bit back a smile, letting Liz fill the air.

Denise opened the envelope, flipping through receipts. "Charter trips, gas, groceries." She frowned faintly. "This is eclectic."

"I'm eclectic," Liz said. "What's your turnaround time? I'm hoping for someone who won't judge me too hard if my business expenses include two cartons of ice cream and an inflatable moose head."

Denise's mouth quirked, almost a smile, before she tucked it away. "I can get you an estimate by the end of the week."

Liz leaned back, looking around the office like she was deciding whether it met her highly arbitrary standards. Her gaze landed on a corkboard by the filing cabinet. It was crowded with appointment reminders, bank statements, and a few personal photos. A child in a Halloween costume, a man in a baseball cap holding up a king salmon, and, tucked in the corner, a clipped newspaper photo of the Spruce Cove High booster club at a fundraiser table.

Ava's stomach gave a small twist. Even in the grainy newsprint, Amelia was unmistakable. Standing at the edge of the group, hair loose, smiling faintly at someone just out of frame.

"Busy summer?" Liz asked casually, nodding toward the board.

Denise followed her gaze, and her whole body seemed to still. "That was the booster club's raffle booth. We raised a lot for my first year." She stepped over, plucked the clipping from the board, and slipped it into a drawer with careful precision.

Ava kept her expression neutral, though her mind was already spinning.

Liz glanced at Ava, then back to Denise. "Booster club, huh? My sister runs one in Kodiak. Between the bake sales and the gossip chain, she knows more about her neighbors than the CIA. I'm guessing it's the same here?"

"Small town," Denise said shortly, closing the drawer. "Is there anything else you need from me today?"

Liz hesitated, clearly tempted to keep pushing, but Ava caught her eye and gave the smallest shake of her head.

"Nope," Liz said brightly, standing. "That's plenty. I'll bring you more receipts when I find the other shoebox."

Denise walked them to the door. "End of the week for the estimate," she said.

Outside, the wind had picked up, flinging bits of grit across the boardwalk. Liz pulled her jacket tighter. "She's hiding something."

Ava stared at the door, the image of Amelia in that grainy photo still burned into her mind. "Yeah," she said quietly. "She is."

They walked in step until they reached the corner where the boardwalk split one way toward the newsroom, the other toward George and Esther's cabin.

"I've got to get back and type up the harbor commission thing before it leaks out of my brain completely," Liz said. "You going home?"

Ava nodded. "Yeah. I'll see you tomorrow."

"Don't do anything reckless without me." Liz gave her a look that was equal parts warning and challenge, then turned toward Main Street.

***

Ava continued along the waterfront, the sound of Liz's boots fading behind her. She was halfway to her street when she heard boots again, heavier, slower.

"Ms. McCormick."

She turned to see Chief Harrow, hands buried in the pockets of his dark jacket, gaze flat as the bay at low tide.

"Chief," she said carefully.

He stopped a step away. "Figure it out yet?"

Ava frowned. "Figure what out?"

"That your boyfriend's guilty." The words were delivered like the weather report.

Her pulse kicked, but she kept her voice even. "He's not my boyfriend."

"Doesn't change the facts." Harrow's eyes didn't leave hers. "Some people don't want to see what's in front of them. That's how they get blindsided."

He tipped his chin toward the street and walked past her, the smell of coffee and cold air trailing in his wake.

Ava stood there a moment longer, the harbor wind pressing at her back. "We'll see," she murmured, before heading for home.

Chapter 12

Ava had been expecting a quiet kitchen, maybe half a sandwich if George hadn't beaten her to the leftover ham. If he had, she'd be left with a questionable pickle spear and a smear of mustard on some bread.

She certainly hadn't expected the wall of noise that greeted her the moment she stepped inside.

The cabin's usual hum of the woodstove and radio had been replaced by a racket that sounded part casino, part barnyard. Dice rattled against tabletops, voices overlapped in a jumble of boasts and good-natured threats, and over it all came Mabel's triumphant bellow: "Bunco!"

The word cracked through the air like a starting gun, the kind of shout you made when you'd just hit the jackpot and needed to claim it before anyone double-checked the numbers.

Ava had the absurd thought that if someone walked past outside, they'd assume this was a speakeasy for retirees.

The dining table had been transformed into something between a gaming arena and a bake sale, its usual stacks of mail and coffee rings replaced by felt pads laid with military precision.

Each spot had its own scorecard and a stubby pencil sharpened to a point it could be used for surgery. Mugs of coffee balanced precariously near elbows, their contents sloshing every time someone laughed or thumped the table. In the center sat a plate of cookies: chocolate chip, oatmeal raisin, and something that looked suspiciously like it might contain coconut. They were already half demolished in the crossfire between rounds.

At the head of the table, Esther presided like a seasoned general, her "game sweater," the blue one with yarn fuzz on the elbows, marking her as both leader and long-time veteran of whatever strategic maneuvering Bunco actually required. She leaned forward in her chair with the intensity of someone brokering a ceasefire. Mabel, cheeks pink with either victory or caffeine, scooped up her dice for the next round as if she might sprint off with them. Ida sat primly, arms folded in mock disdain, her lips pursed in what could have been judgment or focus. Ruth hunched over her scorecard, scribbling numbers with the seriousness of a woman writing the next great American novel, her pencil moving so fast it threatened to set the paper on fire.

From the recliner in the living room, George was providing what could loosely be described as "color commentary," though it was more like a steady stream of sarcastic heckles. He didn't bother turning his head from the fishing show, some slow-moving program where bearded men in parkas muttered about salmon runs. His voice carried effortlessly over the clatter of dice.

"You'd think you ladies were playing for free groceries for a year," he announced. "And not the boring stuff, I'm talking the good cheese."

"That's because you've never seen the prize for winning," Mabel shot back without looking at him.

"What is it this week?" George asked. "A frozen meatloaf and bragging rights?"

"It's banana bread, and don't knock it," Esther called from the kitchen. "It's better than anything you've caught this season."

"Ha!" George barked, slapping the armrest. "Low blow, woman. My fish can't hear you, but my pride sure can."

Ava couldn't help it. She smiled. The sound of George sparring with the women was as much a part of the scene as the smell of coffee or the dice clattering on the table.

Ava hung her coat over the back of an empty chair, shaking off a few stubborn flakes of snow that had clung to her shoulders. The smell of coffee, strong, slightly burnt, and comforting in the way only cabin coffee could be, mingled with the faint tang of woodsmoke from the stove. She couldn't fight the wave of amusement. This was peak Spruce Cove domestic life: coffee cups leaving rings on the table, dice games treated like Olympic events, and gossip so pervasive it seeped into every available crack like the draft through an old window.

"You're just in time," Esther said, spotting her with the hawk-eye precision of a woman who could identify a good cribbage partner from fifty paces. She was already pushing back from the table. "Sit in for me while I check the bread."

"I …" Ava started, but Esther was halfway to the kitchen before she could protest.

"You'll be fine," Esther tossed over her shoulder. "You've got hands, don't you? And a competitive streak a mile wide."

Ava looked at the dice like they might explode. "I don't even know the rules."

"Then you can't break them," George called helpfully from the recliner.

"You roll dice and shout when the numbers match," Esther said, already halfway to the kitchen. "It's the most fun you can have sitting down and it doesn't involve cable TV."

From the recliner, George snorted. "Couldn't possibly be better than *Alaskan Catch Legends*. Last week some guy pulled a thirty-pounder out of the bay with a twelve-pound test. Said he found the line in his glove box under a Pop-Tart wrapper."

"Your goal," Mabel said, sliding the cookie plate toward her like she was closing a shady deal, "is to yell louder than Ruth when you win. Otherwise, she'll think you're not taking it seriously."

"I'm not sure yelling is my style," Ava said, eyeing the cookies. Half of them were missing, which in Mabel's world meant they'd either been shared or strategically deployed as distractions.

"Neither is losing," Ida murmured, marking her score with delicate precision. "You'll adjust."

"Some people clap when they win," Ruth said, rolling her eyes. "Some people, like me, simply radiate triumph."

"Some people," George called from the living room, "sound like they're announcing a natural disaster."

"That was one time," Ruth shot back. "And the tsunami siren test was poorly timed."

Ava took a cookie just to end the argument, biting into it while she wondered how yelling volume had somehow become a legitimate competitive category. She was starting to realize Bunco had less to do with dice and more to do with personality warfare.

Ava picked up the dice, their edges worn smooth from years of being clutched in hands like hers. Uncertain, maybe a little sweaty, but determined not to embarrass themselves. She gave them a tentative shake.

"Too gentle," Mabel warned, like Ava was cradling a baby instead of cubes of plastic. "They can smell fear."

Ava rolled her eyes but gave the dice a firmer shake this time, sending them clattering across the felt. They landed with a mismatched scatter.

"Not bad," Ruth said, leaning in to mark the score. "Could be worse. You could have rolled like Ida's first round."

"I was distracted," Ida said primly. "The coffee was cold."

"That's your excuse for everything," George called. "Missed a shot? Coffee was cold. Missed your anniversary? Coffee was cold."

"I've never missed an anniversary," Ida said without looking up. "Coffee has nothing to do with that."

The game rolled on, literally, with the table bouncing between laughter, mock complaints, and the occasional serious moment of counting dots. Ava quickly learned that Bunco had no real strategy, but that didn't stop Mabel from whispering, "You should really go for the sixes next round," as if that were an actual choice.

Between rounds, the conversation spun in the same unpredictable way the dice did, drifting from who'd had the best pie at the church pie sale on the 4th of July ("Definitely the apple crumble, fight me on it," Ruth declared) to whether the grocery store's new freezer section was too close to the produce aisle ("Destroying lettuce is a crime," Ida said).

Ava found herself laughing more than she'd expected, but each time she reached for her coffee, she caught herself scanning the room the way she did when she was on assignment. Noting who leaned in to whisper, who hesitated before answering a question, who seemed a little too interested in changing the subject. Bunco, she realized, was as much about reading the people as it was about rolling the dice.

They played the next few rounds in a blur of rolling, cheering, and mock groaning. Mabel teased Ida about her "competitive resting face," Ruth bragged about her "beginner's luck" even though she'd been playing for a decade, and George heckled all of them with the precision of a man who'd been doing it for years.

"Ida, if you roll any slower, those dice will qualify for Medicare," he called.

"You're like the armchair quarterback of Bunco, minus the arm strength," Ida shot back.

The fire popped in the woodstove, the smell of fresh bread drifting in from the kitchen. Outside, snowflakes drifted past the window. The kind that looked like postcards but clung to everything. For a few minutes, Ava let herself relax into the noise and warmth.

By the time Esther returned with a towel-wrapped loaf, Ava had survived two full rounds and had even earned a "Nice roll" from Ruth. Esther set the bread on the counter and leaned over her shoulder to watch.

"Not bad," she said. "Though you're holding the dice like they're going to bite you."

"I was trying to show respect," Ava said.

"Save that for your editor," Esther replied. "This is Bunco."

The dice clattered across the felt, stopping just short of a coffee cup that was in dangerous proximity to the edge of the table.

"Ha! Bunco!" Mabel shouted again, clapping her hands like she'd just sunk a three-pointer.

"You're going to scare the bread into falling," Esther said, sliding back into her chair.

"I'm scaring Ava into realizing she's outmatched," Mabel replied.

"I didn't realize Bunco required intimidation tactics," Ava said.

"Oh, everything requires intimidation tactics," Ida said. "It's just most people won't admit it."

George's voice floated from the recliner. "Or they use pie instead of threats. Same effect."

They'd just started a new round when Mabel threw her dice with a little too much enthusiasm, sending one skittering across the table and almost into the cookie plate.

"Careful," Ruth warned. "That's the good plate. I don't want dice in the cookies."

"I get excited," Mabel said with a shrug, then leaned in, her voice dropping to that conspiratorial pitch Ava had learned was the prelude to something worth listening to. "Speaking of excitement ... my niece in Juneau says there was a whole situation before the Ellerys moved here."

Esther glanced up suddenly interested. "What kind of situation?"

"The kind where the high school coach gets 'too friendly' with one of the senior girls," Mabel said, eyebrows lifting just enough to make the point. "Rumor was the school didn't renew his contract. And poof, here they are in Spruce Cove."

Ida stopped mid-roll. "Our Coach Ellery?"

"That's the rumor," Mabel confirmed, rolling again like she'd just casually dropped a grocery list.

Esther frowned, but it wasn't disbelief. More like calculation. "I don't understand how Denise would have stayed with him after something like that."

"Well," Ruth cut in, "I heard she talked to Carter Haines a few months ago."

"Smart to snatch up the only attorney in town before he does," Esther said.

Ruth nodded, lowering her voice as if Carter himself might be listening. "But nothing seems to have come of it. Maybe it was just about the property line. Or maybe it wasn't true at all."

"Nothing ever comes of it until it does," George called from the recliner. "Small towns don't bury secrets; they just pickle."

The table chuckled, but Ava didn't. She felt that familiar flicker of annoyance like when a chin hair appeared, thin but impossible to ignore. If the rumor was true, this wasn't just a story about a coach's bad judgment. It was about a man who might have been shuffled out of one community before anyone could hold him accountable and quietly installed in another.

She'd always thought Coach Ellery was a little too smooth for his own good, the kind of man who smiled at you just a moment too long. But this? This was a different level.

Her dice sat in her hand, forgotten, as she pondered the way Denise Ellery nervously stared at other women during booster club events, and remembered the girls who hung around the gym after practice. Maybe Ruth's "nothing" wasn't nothing at all.

"Ava?" Esther's voice pulled her back.

She forced a smile and rolled, the dice tumbling across the felt. They came up mismatched, but her mind wasn't on the score. She was already thinking about who she needed to talk to next.

And if there was truth to what Mabel was saying, that he'd been investigated and that Denise had sought legal advice, then Spruce Cove might have hired itself a sex predator.

The Bunco game continued, but Ava barely noticed the dice in her hands.

When Esther finally reclaimed her seat, Ava stood, brushing crumbs from her sweater. "I should get going."

"Take a cookie for the road," Mabel said.

"Price of information," Ida added.

Ava slipped one into her pocket, pulling her coat back on. Outside, the snow crunched under her boots as she headed toward the paper, the gossip replaying in her head like a headline she couldn't quite write yet.

***

The snow was picking up. Not a blizzard, but the kind of steady, sideways fall that stuck to her eyelashes and found every gap in her scarf. She'd skipped lunch without even realizing it, her stomach grumbling as she crunched down the path toward town.

The gossip sat in her chest like a hot coal. She could feel it wanting to be tossed to someone who'd know exactly what to do with it and in Spruce Cove, that someone was Liz. Ava adjusted her pace, boots crunching against the packed snow. The wind off the bay carried the smell of salt and something faintly fishy, and she found herself half-smiling at how this town managed to be cozy and sharp-edged at the same time.

The *Spruce Cove Gazette* office came into view, its front window crowded with fliers: the winter festival, a lost mitten ("green, child-sized, sentimental value"), and an ad for a woodstove cleaning service that featured a cartoon chimney sweep who looked suspiciously like the mayor.

She swung open the door and was hit with the familiar warmth and the sight of Ryan leaning against Liz's desk, both of them grinning like they'd been caught mid-punchline. Liz was holding a stapler like it was a microphone and leaning back in her chair, smirking.

"... and that's when I told him, 'If you think I'm buying day-old doughnuts, you've got another think coming,'" Liz was saying.

"Your commitment to fresh pastries is admirable," Ryan said, deadpan.

Liz spotted Ava and brightened. "Hey! You missed the part where I single-handedly defended the integrity of the town's bakery."

Ryan glanced at Ava. "She's very brave. We're considering giving her a medal."

"I'll settle for free croissants," Liz said, leaning toward Ryan.

"You two should take this act on the road," Ava said, unbuttoning her coat. "We could sell tickets with proceeds going to the 'Donuts for Cops' fund."

"I'd donate," Liz said.

Ryan smirked. "Why do I feel like this fund would be mismanaged?"

"Because Liz would insist on paying herself in croissants," Ava said, hanging her coat.

"Untrue," Liz said. "I'd insist on paying *you* in croissants so you'd stop stealing mine and never ask for a raise."

Ava slid into the empty chair beside Liz. "I didn't steal. I relocated them."

Ryan chuckled, shaking his head. "And to think, I walked into this place assuming newspaper people were respectable. Instead, I've encountered a crime scene."

"That's where you went wrong," Liz said. "Anyway, what's up? You've got that 'I've been holding onto a juicy one' look."

Ava leaned forward, elbows on her knees. "I just came from Grandma's Bunco game."

Liz's face lit. "And?"

"And I heard something you might want to know. About Coach Ellery."

Ryan's smirk faded slightly. "Go on."

"Mabel says her niece in Juneau heard there was a whole situation before they moved here," Ava said. "The kind where the high school coach gets too close to one of the senior girls. School didn't renew his contract. And then he quietly takes a job in Spruce Cove."

Liz whistled low. "Our Coach Ellery? Mr. Perfect Hair?"

"Apparently. And Ruth says Denise talked to Carter Haines a few months ago. No filings, so maybe it was property stuff. Or maybe not."

Ava sat back. "But if that rumor's true, we might have a man with a history that Juneau decided to quietly ship out of town."

Liz tapped her pen against her notepad. "That's not just gossip. That's a story." She turned to Ryan, widening her eyes just enough to be dangerous. "Want to do us a favor? Check the court records. See if anything pops up from Juneau."

"I'll buy you a beer," Liz said. "Two, if you get me something good."

He raised an eyebrow. "Do they come with plausible deniability?"

"Absolutely. I'll even write 'This is in no way related to a records search' on the bar tab."

Ava shook her head. "You know she's going to pester you until you do it."

Ryan sighed, pulling out his phone. "Fine. But if I get fired for defaming the basketball coach, I'm blaming you both."

"Understood," Liz said, already scribbling something in her notebook.

***

Ryan slid his phone into his pocket, grabbed his jacket, and gave them both a pointed look. "Remember …"

"You didn't hear it from us. Or, more specifically, the Bunco Mafia," Ava said.

"Exactly." He opened the door, letting a cold draft spill in. "I'll call if I find something."

The door clicked shut behind him, and the office settled back into the hum of the old heater. Liz was still staring at the door, pen spinning between her fingers.

"You're plotting," Ava said.

Liz swiveled toward her, a slow smile spreading. "Just thinking we never did hear back from Denise Ellery about that bookkeeping quote."

Ava crossed her arms. "You also didn't need the quote in the first place."

"Minor detail," Liz said. "Clients do follow-up visits all the time. Totally normal. And if she happens to drop something interesting while we're there ..." She trailed off, her grin turning sly.

Ava tilted her head. "You're thinking this could be more than a check-in."

"I'm thinking she's cagey enough to make me curious," Liz said. "And you know I can't leave a curiosity alone."

Ava sighed, though a corner of her mouth curved. "Fine. I'm bringing coffee."

Liz smirked. "Perfect. We'll look friendly, but alert."

Chapter 13

By the time Liz pulled her Subaru into a parking spot across from Denise Ellery's office, Ava had already said, "I don't know about this" three times.

"You're overthinking it," Liz said, tugging her keys out of the ignition. "We're not breaking into Fort Knox. We're following up on a business quote."

Ava turned to look at her. "You don't think she's going to notice you suddenly developing an intense interest in bookkeeping after years of doing your own taxes with no more than a shoebox and a pen?"

"I could be reformed," Liz said. "People change."

"People don't change into someone who alphabetizes expense reports," Ava said. "That's not a personality shift. That's a brain transplant."

Liz smirked and unbuckled. "You coming or you want to sit in the car and imagine me crashing and burning?"

"Tempting," Ava said, grabbing her bag. "But I'd rather be there to see it firsthand."

The bell above Denise Ellery's office door gave the same polite little ding as last time, though to Ava it sounded less like a greeting and more like a warning.

Inside, the space was the kind of spotless that made Ava instantly aware of her own boot prints. The reception counter gleamed, the window blinds hung in perfect symmetry, and even the potted plant in the corner stood upright like it had taken a posture class. Every file on Denise's desk was squared to the edge, every pen aligned like soldiers at inspection.

Denise looked up from behind her immaculate desk, her smile just as polished as the pencil cup and perfectly squared stack of files beside it. "Liz, Ava. What a surprise."

Liz stepped in like she'd been expected all along, unwinding her scarf with the breezy confidence of someone who'd never in her life been turned away at a bake sale table. "Hey, Denise. I realized I never heard back from you about that bookkeeping quote we talked about. Thought I'd follow up in person. Sometimes emails just get lost, you know?"

Ava trailed in behind her, shutting the door against the wind. The warmth in the office was instant but oddly impersonal, like stepping into a hotel lobby where everything looked perfect but didn't belong to anyone.

"Oh, right," Denise said, just a hair too smoothly. "Yes, it's been busy. I was meaning to."

"Totally understand," Liz cut in, dropping into the chair opposite the desk like she'd booked it weeks in advance. "And while I'm here, I have a couple of other tax-related questions. Hypotheticals."

One of Denise's brows lifted. "All right."

"Like, say a person claimed their dog as a dependent because it emotionally supports their home business. That's a deduction, right?"

Denise blinked. "No."

"What about snacks? If I buy a bag of trail mix to prevent a meltdown during a stressful day, that's a business expense?"

"No," Denise said again, though this time the corner of her mouth twitched.

"Okay, but what if the meltdown would have been in front of a paying client?" Liz pressed.

Ava bit back a smile, sinking into her chair. Liz's tax questions were like bad magic tricks. Just distracting enough to keep people from noticing the other hand rifling through their wallet.

"What if," Liz continued, "I rented a cabin for a weekend to brainstorm marketing ideas, but also to escape a neighbor who treats sunrise like an invitation to fire up the lawn mower?"

"That's creative," Denise said, smoothing the hem of her cardigan. "But no."

Liz tilted her head. "What if I rented the same cabin and accidentally got snowed in with a potential client? Do those emergency meals count?"

Denise let out a small breath that might have been a laugh. "Liz."

"I'm just saying," Liz said, eyes wide with mock sincerity, "the IRS doesn't *specifically* say 'no' to frozen lasagna."

Denise shook her head, amused despite herself. "Why don't you tell me what you actually need help with?"

"Well," Liz said, leaning forward, "I've been thinking about travel deductions. Let's say I needed to go to Juneau for work."

"What kind of work?" Ava asked, playing along.

Liz didn't miss a beat. "Important investigative journalism into latte foam art trends."

Ava smirked. "Naturally."

"Anyway," Liz went on, "I was wondering about the write-offs. Flights, hotels, maybe the occasional artisanal muffin?"

Denise reached for a folder but paused halfway, her shoulders tightening just enough for Ava to catch. "You're planning to travel to Juneau?"

"Not yet. Just curious." Liz tilted her head. "You used to live there, right?"

Denise nodded once, brief and businesslike.

"Do you still keep in touch?"

A flicker of hesitation crossed Denise's face before she looked down at her desk. "Here and there. I've been busy since we moved."

Liz nodded like it was the most ordinary answer in the world. "Sure. New place, new routines. Totally get it."

Liz kept her tone casual. "I've heard rumblings about the new coach up there. You know him?"

Denise's eyes flickered up, then back down. "Not personally."

"Shame. I heard the program went downhill fast after your husband left," Liz said, smiling like it was friendly gossip. "Not that Spruce Cove minds, half the town treats a Juneau loss like it's a national holiday."

That earned a tight little smile from Denise, the kind that said she understood the joke but had no interest in joining in. "Small towns," she said. "People always have opinions."

"True," Liz agreed, leaning back in her chair. "And they don't mind sharing them."

For a moment, the air in the office felt too still, like the pause between a question and the answer you're not going to get. Ava could almost hear the unspoken *and we're not going to talk about it.*

Denise cleared her throat and steered them back toward monthly retainer packages, speaking a little faster now, as if she could outpace the shift in conversation. Ava half-listened, watching Denise's hands move over the papers. They were steady now, but there had been that one moment, right after Juneau came up, when they'd gone completely still.

Liz wrapped it up with a vague "I'll think it over" and a promise to be in touch. Denise smiled, but it didn't reach her eyes.

They stepped back into the cold, the wind knifing across Ava's cheeks. She shoved her hands into her coat pockets.

Liz glanced back at the office window. "She's definitely hiding something."

Ava followed her gaze. Denise was standing there, just behind the glass, watching them walk away.

"Maybe she's hiding something," Ava said. "Or maybe she's just an entirely lame accountant who refuses to entertain questionable write-offs, no matter how charmingly they're presented."

They crunched down the icy sidewalk toward Liz's car.

"She answered everything until Juneau came up," Liz said. "Then she went full politician in cover-up mode. Short answers, eyes down, and suddenly obsessed with quarterly reports."

"She also never said she didn't keep in touch," Ava said. "She said 'here and there.' That's code for 'only with the people who didn't hate me when I left.'"

Liz grinned as they reached the car. "I like it when you get cynical."

"I'm not cynical," Ava said, climbing in. "I'm observant."

"Same thing, different business cards." Liz started the engine.

By the time they got back to the office, the conversation about Denise had been replaced by the usual pre-deadline scramble. Liz dove into layout edits while Ava fielded calls about classified ads and a last-minute obituary that somehow needed to run on page one.

They were in the middle of arguing over whether the headline for the salmon bake fundraiser was punchy enough when Liz's phone buzzed. She glanced at the screen, then mouthed *Ryan* to Ava before answering.

"Hey," she said, turning away from her desk. "Yeah? Now? Sure, we can do that." She hung up and grabbed her coat.

Ava raised an eyebrow. "Emergency?"

"Pie emergency," Liz corrected. "Ryan wants to meet at Annie's. Says he's got something we'll want to hear."

***

Annie's Café was doing its usual mid-afternoon impression of a snow globe, big front windows frosted just enough to blur the street, flakes swirling outside in a steady, hypnotic drift. Ava pushed the door open and was hit with the jingle of the bell, the clink of cutlery, and the low murmur of conversation.

Ryan was already in their usual corner booth, gloves on the table, looking like a man who'd just stepped out of a "life in Alaska" postcard. He stood when they came in, gentlemanly, but not before sneaking another forkful of the pie in front of him.

Liz pointed at the fork. "Starting without us?"

Ryan grinned. "Recon mission. Needed to make sure the pie was up to code before I dragged you two here."

"Up to code?" Ava slid into the booth. "Is there a pie code now?"

"There's a pie code," Ryan said gravely, reclaiming his seat. "It's unwritten, but I enforce it."

Annie herself appeared like she'd been listening from three tables away. She slid a slice of apple in front of Ava, something decadent and chocolate in front of Liz. "You three look like you're plotting something," she said.

"Always," Liz said, already reaching for her fork.

"That explains why you haven't been in all week," Annie replied. "Too busy stirring trouble."

"Stirring coffee," Ava corrected.

"Same thing," Annie said, moving off toward the counter.

Ryan waited until she was out of earshot, cradling his coffee mug in both hands. "So how was your day?"

Liz arched an eyebrow. "You first. You're the one who called the meeting."

"I was being polite," Ryan said. "Small talk before dropping bombshells."

Ava forked a bite of pie. "We don't need polite. We need results."

"You two are terrible at suspense," Ryan said, though the smirk on his face said he didn't mind the back-and-forth.

"Suspense is overrated when you're on deadline," Liz said. "Besides, you lured us here with the promise of information and pie. We've got the pie so spill."

Ryan took his sweet time sipping coffee. "You're sure you want to ruin perfectly good dessert with bad news?"

Liz stabbed her fork into the chocolate like it had insulted her. "If I choke trying to drag the truth out of you, I'm haunting you."

That got him laughing. "Fine. But first, fun fact, there's a guy on Harbor Street building a snow sculpture of a bear. Says he's entering it in some online contest."

Liz narrowed her eyes. "If this is your idea of foreplay before giving us real intel?"

Ava raised her brows. "Foreplay?"

"Figure of speech," Liz said with a dismissive wave.

Ryan smirked. "Sure. But now I know how you think."

Before Liz could volley back, Annie reappeared with a fresh pot of coffee. "Top-off?" she asked, already reaching for Ryan's mug. "And don't forget about the bachelor auction next weekend. We need more entries."

Liz's eyes lit up instantly. "Oh, I think we just found one."

Ryan froze with his fork halfway to his mouth. "Absolutely not."

"Come on," Annie said, grinning. "It's for charity. You'll go for at least seventy-five bucks."

"That's insulting," Liz said. "He's worth at least a hundred."

"Not the point," Ryan muttered, but his ears were already pink.

She left them with steaming mugs and the vague threat of seeing Ryan on stage next weekend.

Ryan set his coffee down and finally leaned forward. "All right. I checked the court records like you asked and nothing. Not a single filing in Juneau under Ellery's name. So, I called a buddy in the Juneau PD."

Liz's expression brightened. "Good boy."

"He said there *was* an investigation. They were building a case against coach. Then the girl stopped cooperating. Wouldn't talk, wouldn't press charges. Without her, they had nothing."

Ava froze mid-bite. "What kind of case?"

Ryan gave her a pointed look. "The kind that gets a teacher fired and a school board scrambling for a replacement. And my guy said there were rumblings this wasn't the only girl. Nothing they could prove, but enough to make people uncomfortable."

Liz's mouth tightened. "And that's when he 'resigned.'"

"Right," Ryan said. "District made a statement, thanked him for his service, wished him well, and he was gone. Moved here within the month."

Ava leaned back, her fork forgotten. "So the case went cold because she wouldn't talk."

"Exactly," Ryan said. "And officially, it's dead. Unofficially …" He let the pause hang.

Liz met Ava's gaze. "Unofficially, it's a story."

"Unofficially," Ryan agreed, "it's trouble. Which is why you two need to be careful. You can't afford a lawsuit."

"Careful is my middle name," Liz said.

Ava smirked. "Pretty sure it's not."

Ryan eyed her. "What's your middle name?"

"Irrelevant." Ava reached for her coffee.

"Weird middle name," Ryan said with a smirk.

The table went quiet for a second before Liz leaned back, drumming her fingers against her mug. "Well. That's one more reason to keep her on our list."

Ryan gave her a look. "You mean your imaginary list of people to annoy?"

"It's called a source list," Liz said primly. "And it's printed on very nice stationery."

Ryan shook his head. "One day, you're going to land on someone else's list, and then what?"

Liz smiled sweetly. "Depends. Do they bring handcuffs to their interrogations?"

Ava smirked into her coffee. "She's joking."

Liz tilted her head. "Am I?"

Ryan groaned. "You two are going to be the death of me."

"Please," Ava said. "You love it."

Ryan opened his mouth like he was going to deny it, then closed it again, choosing pie instead.

Ava pushed her plate away, eyeing the snowflakes spiraling past the window. "For now, we keep our heads down. We watch. We wait."

Liz raised her coffee cup. "And we order dessert first next time. You know, just in case we get banned."

The cabin was dark when Ava got home, a faint orange glow coming from the woodstove in the corner. Esther's Bunco sweater hung over a chair, George's recliner sat empty, and the only sound was the slow tick of the kitchen clock.

She should've been tired. Instead, her mind was still racing. Juneau, Coach Ellery, the girl who wouldn't cooperate, the fact that a man with that kind of rumor trailing behind him was coaching teenagers here. And the way Denise's face had flickered when Liz brought up Juneau.

Ava sat at the table, her coat still on, phone in hand. Her thumb hovered over William's name longer than it should have before she hit call.

"Hey, stranger," he said when he picked up. His voice was warm and just a little surprised, like he'd been halfway through a book and found a note tucked between the pages. "Everything okay?"

"Define okay," Ava said, leaning back in her chair.

"That's never a good start," William replied. "What happened? You sound, I don't know. Wired."

She exhaled, watching her breath fog in the cool air drifting from the window. "I haven't really told you everything that's been going on."

"Then tell me."

So, she did. She started with Chap's arrest, with how the chief had all but declared him guilty before the ink was dry on the paperwork. She told him about Liz, and the way the two of them had been quietly, and not-so-quietly, poking holes in the official version of events. She told him about Denise Ellery, about the Bunco gossip, about Coach and Juneau, and Ryan's investigation.

There were a few pauses, here and there. Moments where she realized she'd never said some of these details out loud, and doing so made them sound heavier.

When she finished, William was quiet for a moment. Then: "Ava, this isn't just writing about the town council. You're digging into something that could blow back on you."

"I know," she said.

"Do you?" he asked gently. "Because what I'm hearing is there's a potential murderer out there, a high school coach with a shady past, a wife who may or may not know more than she's saying, and you and Liz are poking at all of it without a badge or backup. That's not a puff piece for the lifestyle section, Ava. That's walking straight into the middle of something dangerous."

She smiled faintly, even though he couldn't see it. "It's not like I'm going undercover with a wire."

"That's not the point. You're putting yourself between the truth and people who might not want it told."

"That's kind of my job William," she said.

"And how many of those people also had a murder investigation hanging over them?" William countered.

She opened her mouth to argue, but nothing came out.

"I'm not saying stop," he said finally. "I'm saying be smart. Please. Don't do this alone. And don't underestimate the kind of trouble you can stir up without meaning to."

"I've got Liz," Ava said. "And Ryan. And while I'm not exactly high on the chief's Christmas card list, he wouldn't let someone kill me. I think."

There was a sigh on the other end of the line. "You're trying to make me feel better, but all I'm hearing is you and your friend are chasing stories that could get you hurt."

Ava stared at the wood grain in the table, the little nicks and dents where Esther had chopped vegetables directly on it over the years. "We'll be fine," she said softly.

"You'd tell me if you weren't?"

She hesitated. "Probably. Eventually."

That got a low chuckle from him, but it didn't hide the worry in his voice. "You're a terrible liar."

"I prefer 'selective truth-teller,'" she said.

For a few seconds, neither of them spoke. Then William said, "Call me when you get your next lead. Even if it's just to say you're fine. I don't want to find out what's happening to you because it made the evening news."

"Fine," Ava said.

"Good." He hesitated again, then: "And Ava?"

"Yeah?"

"Watch your back."

When they hung up, the cabin felt even quieter than before. Ava slipped her phone into her pocket, but the weight of the call lingered. Outside, the snow kept falling, slow, steady, relentless. She had the sense that the truth was buried out there somewhere, and she wasn't going to find it by sitting still.

Chapter 14

The Spruce Cove Gazette office always smelled like coffee that had opinions. Today's opinion was "burnt."

Liz was deep into a stack of agenda items from the town council meeting, highlighting with the grim satisfaction of a woman who knew exactly which elected officials misused the words "action item." The heater made its usual death rattle. The fichus in the corner, rescued from the library's discard table and now regretting it, slumped like a martyr.

Ava stood in the doorway with her notebook and her best "I'm not about to ask you for something big" smile.

Liz barely looked up. "You're smiling like a raccoon that found the good trash."

"I have an idea for a series," Ava said, putting her notebook down on Liz's desk like it was a truce flag. Or a grenade.

Liz capped her highlighter, meeting Ava's eyes. "Is it budget-friendly, legally sound, and only mildly likely to alienate paying subscribers?"

"Two out of three," Ava said. "Which is, incidentally, how you described your last boyfriend."

"RIP, Kyle," Liz murmured. "Taken from us too soon by his CrossFit cult. Alright, hit me."

Ava inhaled. "A big school feature. A series, actually. Day-in-the-life stuff. The theater teacher building a set out of cardboard and tears. The cafeteria worker who can smell a food fight before it starts. The AP history class that never has enough textbooks. The coach's practice schedule, the pep rallies, the way the gym smells like ambition and gym socks. A look at what makes the school a community hub."

Liz blinked. "Community hub?"

"People love heartwarming," Ava said. "They share heartwarming. It's catnip for advertisers. Also, it's actual journalism about a place that affects every family in town."

"And," Liz said slowly, "this has nothing to do with you wanting a closer look at Coach Ellery."

Ava didn't flinch. Not externally. "I mean, he's part of the school. He runs a very successful basketball program."

"Uh-huh," Liz said. "And Amelia?"

Ava's stomach dipped. She kept her voice even. "She'd gotten involved with the booster club. I think that world's important to understand. We've told the town the facts of her death. We haven't really told them about her life. Not the part she chose lately, anyway."

Liz twirled her pen, a small smile pulling at one corner of her mouth. "So, this is a noble, agenda-free profile of a small-town American high school. Starring Coach 'abs like a stack of cutting boards' Ellery. With a cameo by the booster moms who color-code their family calendars and compete in the unspoken sport of out-momming each other."

Ava swallowed a laugh. "I'm not hunting for scandal."

"Thank God," Liz said. "If we run one more story that makes the school board lawyer call me 'Elizabeth' in that tone, I'll start charging him by the syllable."

"No scandal," Ava said. "I swear. It's more like show. The theater of small-town prestige. Who gets thanked on the loudspeaker. Who gets their name on the banner. Why Amelia wanted in."

Liz's brows rose. "Amelia didn't exactly scream 'volunteer hours.' She may have been saying 'I can make this look better.'"

"Exactly," Ava said, relieved to have the words on someone else's tongue. "She had ideas. She was big on polish. Events. Branding. I want to know why that mattered so much to her. And to everyone."

Liz studied her for a long beat, as if the air between them were a glass of water she could read tea leaves in. "And Chap?"

The name hit like a skipped heartbeat. Ava let out a breath she pretended she'd been holding for the heater's sake. "I know he's innocent," she said softly. "But that isn't the story. The job is to look everywhere the story lives. The school is one of those places."

Liz leaned back in her chair and propped her boots on the file cabinet like a woman auditioning for the role of "cool editor in a Netflix show about journalism." "You know what I love about you, McCormick?"

"My encyclopedic knowledge of cafeteria pizza?"

"The way you can say 'this is about community' while your pupils literally dilate at the words 'Coach practice schedule.'" She tapped her pen against her bottom lip. "I'm not against it. I'm protective. Of you. Of the paper. Of the fragile peace we have with the PTA after I called their auction basket 'feral.'"

"It was a taxidermy otter holding a wine opener," Ava said. "You were gentle."

"I am always gentle," Liz said primly, then cracked a grin. "Okay. A series. Four parts? Five if you can get the lunch lady to give up her lemon bar recipe."

"I'll take what I can get," Ava said.

Liz spun to her computer, fingers already flying. "We'll package it with little pull quotes and photos. People love the faces. We'll do a sidebar explaining what a booster club actually does, and we'll use small words so the internet doesn't call us elitist."

"Can we call the series 'School Spirits' and pair it with coffee shop coupons?" Ava asked.

Liz paused, considering. "Tempting. But this town takes the word 'spirits' and runs toward the liquor store."

"True," Ava said. "How about 'All the Little Hometowns Under One Roof'?"

"That sounds like a Hallmark movie starring Candace Cameron and an extremely handsome custodian who can waltz."

"Okay, first, I would absolutely watch that," Ava said. "Second, I was thinking 'Between the Bells.'"

Liz pointed her pen like a wand. "There she is. Between the Bells. Done."

They sat for a moment in the warmth of a shared idea. Outside, someone banged a car door. The heater coughed up a final clank like it was offended to be left out of the brainstorming.

Liz's eyes softened. "You sure you're ready for this? Spending half your week practically in Coach Ellery's pocket?"

Ava flipped her notebook closed. "If that's where the truth is, I'll just try not to sit on his keys."

Liz arched a brow. "Keys, sure. But maybe keep an eye on what it does to your heart."

"My heart's fine. It's my patience that's about to take a beating."

"Uh-huh." Liz clicked open her email. "I'll call Principal Wetherbee. I'll be charming, which is a sacrifice I'm willing to make for journalism. You go buy a fresh pen, tuck your hair behind your ear like you're a serious reporter on an HBO limited series, and try not to trip over a pom-pom."

Ava stood, shouldering her bag. "Any other instructions?"

"Don't get thrown out," Liz said. "If the drama teacher corners you about the understudy scandal, pretend you're late for a mammogram. And if you see the booster moms, hold your ground. They can smell insecurity."

"I'm not interviewing them for gossip," Ava said. "I want their version. Why this matters."

"Oh, their version will come with a buttercream frosting border," Liz said. "But sure. Ask about mission over metrics. Ask about how recognition gets handed out. Ask what Amelia brought besides a Pinterest board and highlighter pens."

Liz pointed at her with the pen again, but this time it felt like a benediction. "Yes. Now go ask too many questions at the school until someone threatens to email me."

Ava nearly made it out the door before Liz called after her, "And McCormick?"

Ava turned. "Yeah?"

"If Coach winks at you, make a note."

Ava rolled her eyes. "I'm immune to winks."

"Sure," Liz said. "And I only drink coffee for the antioxidants."

Ava stepped into the front office air, which carried the familiar smells of printer toner and hope. Her phone buzzed. Esther sending a photo of George scowling at a tangled fishing net with the caption, "Your grandfather's losing another round to that net." Ava grinned and texted back a heart. Proud that Esther finally learned to text.

***

The Gazette door swung open again as Liz stuck her head out. "I almost forgot," she stage-whispered. "If you can get the janitor for a quote about the glitter situation after pep rallies, I'll buy you a muffin the size of your head."

"I thought this wasn't about scandal," Ava said.

"It's not," Liz said solemnly. "It's about truth. Glitter is forever."

Ava laughed, the sound surprising her with how close it was to happy. "Between the Bells," she said, testing the title out loud. It tasted like possibility and a little bit like danger.

"Between the Bells," Liz echoed. "Bring me a story."

Ava tightened her scarf and headed toward the high school, notebook ready, heartbeat steady-ish. She told herself she was going for the kids and the teachers and the theater of small-town pride. She told herself she was going because she was a reporter.

She did not tell herself she was going because she could not stand the idea of everyone else writing the story of Chap and Amelia and Coach without her hands on the keyboard.

Some truths didn't need the loudspeaker. They needed the work.

She pushed open the Gazette's glass door and stepped into the cold. The sky was a shade of gray that promised snow if you squinted and had an active imagination. She did. She also had good boots and a stubborn streak and a title.

Between the Bells. Start with the bell.

She smiled into the wind and walked.

***

The front office smelled faintly of copier toner and cinnamon gum. A motivational poster about "Soaring Like an Eagle" drooped slightly on one side, as if even it had accepted the limits of a Tuesday.

Mrs. Keating, the secretary, looked up from her desk with the kind of smile that could welcome you or gut you, depending on your tone. "You're the reporter," she said, as if Ava had been delivered by courier.

"Guilty," Ava said, flashing her ID. "I'm doing a feature series on the school. The whole place, not just the basketball team." She said this as if Mrs. Keating had been planning to hand her over to the nearest whistle-blower in a tracksuit.

Mrs. Keating buzzed her in with a wave. "Principal Wetherbee's in a meeting with the band teacher. Something about a trombone emergency. You can wander until he's done. Stay away from the chemistry lab if you value your eyebrows."

Ava stepped into the hallway and was hit with the familiar smell of pencil shavings, floor wax, and whatever air freshener the janitorial staff had settled on in 1998. A bulletin board announced Spirit Week. The sophomore hallway seemed to be going with a loose "farm chic" theme: overalls, plaid, and one kid in a full chicken suit who nodded politely as he passed.

150

She pulled out her notebook. Today's plan:

- Cafeteria lunch shift.
- Stop by the theater wing.
- Swing past the gym to watch part of practice.
- Find at least three excuses to say Amelia's name without sounding like she was trying.

First stop: cafeteria.

The lunch ladies, who introduced themselves as Sharon and "Just Call Me Peach," ran the line with military precision. Peach, who could probably deadlift a vending machine, gave Ava a tour of the industrial kitchen while sliding plastic trays of chicken nuggets onto the line without missing a beat.

"Kids know we're watching," Peach said. "We can spot a food fight before the first French fry flies." She squinted at a group of football players. "Those three? Gonna spill chocolate milk in under five minutes. Mark my words."

Ava jotted it down.

She slid in a question, light as a feather: "Did you know Amelia Colburn?"

Sharon, spooning mashed potatoes, glanced up. "Boosters Amelia? Sure. She was trying to get better uniforms for the cafeteria staff. Said we deserved to look professional. I told her I'm not wearing polyester slacks, but she meant well."

File that under: image matters.

Theater wing, next.

Mr. Taylor, the drama teacher, greeted her with a paintbrush in one hand and a script in the other. The set for the spring musical looked like it was held together by optimism and duct tape.

"We're doing *Guys and Dolls*," he said, gesturing grandly. "With a budget smaller than a bake sale. Speaking of bake sales, did you know Amelia tried to convince the boosters to host a casino night? Said it was 'on brand.'"

Ava chuckled. "Did they?"

"God, no. This is Spruce Cove. We call Bingo a gateway drug."

She scribbled notes, pretending not to notice how her pulse picked up when she saw movement through the window. The gym was just across the hall.

Practice.

Coach Ellery's voice carried before she reached the door, crisp, controlled, but with that edge of charm that made people lean in.

She lingered in the doorway. The team was running drills, sneakers squeaking on polished wood. Ellery barked a play, then casually jogged to midcourt. He didn't look up, but Ava still felt a strange awareness settle in her chest. Like he'd clocked her presence without showing it.

"Can I help you?"

She turned to find Assistant Coach Morales, clipboard in hand.

"Doing a school series. Just here to observe," Ava said.

Morales nodded. "Long as you stay off the court. And no quoting me when I say half these boys couldn't run a clean pick if it came with free pizza."

She smiled. "Noted."

After a few minutes, she tossed Amelia into the conversation. "Did Amelia ever help with the team?"

Morales shrugged. "Boosters handled travel gear. Amelia pushed for embroidered warm-ups. Said it'd 'make us look like winners.' I told her we just needed to play like winners."

The whistle blew. Coach Ellery glanced toward the door, eyes meeting hers for a fraction of a second before he turned back to the team. It was nothing. And, also, something.

By the end of the day, Ava's notebook was a tangle of quotes, arrows, and question marks. No smoking gun. No breadcrumb trail. Just tiny, telling details about Amelia's quest for polish.

Back at the Gazette, the warm, over-caffeinated air hit her like a hug. Liz was at her desk and across from her, leaning one hip against the file cabinet like he'd been born there, was Deputy Hale.

"You look like someone who needs a lead," Hale said.

Ava dropped into the chair opposite Liz. "Got details, no direction."

Hale's grin was all easy charm. "Talk to the janitor. Sam's been here longer than the paint. Police always start with the janitor. They see everything, and nobody notices them."

Liz nodded. "And bring him donuts. I swear half your job is snack-based bribery."

"Works every time," Hale said.

***

The parking lot was still mostly empty when Ava pulled in, her coffee sloshing dangerously in its travel mug. The sun was barely over the rooftops, turning the frost on the baseball field into a glittering sheet. She'd always forgotten how different a school felt before the chaos began, like it was holding its breath.

Inside, the only sound was the low squeak of a floor buffer and the faint hiss of radiators. Sam was in the main hallway, pushing the buffer with one hand and sipping from a battered thermos with the other.

"I heard you're doing some kind of series on the school," he said, spotting her. "Figured it was only a matter of time before you hunted me down."

Ava held up a white paper bag. "And I come with gifts. Glazed, maple, and one Bavarian cream in case you like surprises."

He took the bag like it was a signed contract. "Smart. Food works better than coffee if you want people to talk."

She fell into step beside him as he moved down the hall. "You've been here a while, right?"

"Since Clinton was in office," he said. "First term. Which makes me either part of the décor or a haunting, depending on who you ask."

They passed the trophy case, gold letters catching the new light. Ava waited until they'd reached the intersection by the gym before sliding Amelia's name into the conversation. "You remember Amelia Colburn?"

Sam nodded, chewing. "Boosters Amelia. Always had a tote bag big enough to smuggle the pep band."

"She was involved," Ava said, keeping it casual. "I'm trying to understand how."

Sam slowed, leaning on the buffer handle. "She stayed late. Later than the rest of them, most nights. Meetings would end, the other moms would be halfway home, but Amelia? She'd hang around. In the gym, sometimes the front office. Always had 'something to finish.'"

Ava jotted a note. "Alone?"

"Sometimes Coach was still here, doing whatever coaches do when the team's gone. Sometimes just her. I'd be locking up and she'd wave like she owned the place."

Ava raised a brow. "Seem odd?"

He shook his head. "Didn't feel shady. More like she wanted to be here."

"Why?" she asked.

He grinned around a bite of donut. "You're the reporter. I just keep the floors clean."

Ava thanked him and stepped back into the crisp morning air. The first bell rang, a bright chime that spilled through the open doors and down the steps. Students began to stream past her, laughter and sneaker squeaks filling the quiet Sam had left behind.

She turned toward her car, but in her mind the hallway was still empty, the echo of footsteps stretched long after they should've faded. Amelia's footsteps. Staying late, long after the coffee cooled and the lights dimmed.

Not sneaky. Not rushed. Just choosing to be there.

And Ava knew she'd need to find out why.

Chapter 15

Ava woke to the insistent buzz of her phone doing a jittery tap dance against the wooden nightstand. For a second she thought it was the baseboard heater complaining again. Then she saw the name on the screen and bolted upright as if someone had just yelled "free pie."

Chap.

Her voice came out sleep-raspy and hopeful enough to make her mad at herself. "Hey."

There was a scrape of air, like he'd moved closer to the receiver. When he spoke, the words were steady but thinned-out, like they'd been stretched too far. "Morning Red."

No one called her that except him and one ill-fated Sephora clerk. It landed like a hand on her sternum.

"What's wrong?" Ava asked, kicking free of the quilt. The room was cold; Spruce Cove liked to be dramatic in the mornings. White fog blanketed the windowpanes. The sound of seagulls carried, impatient.

"They're transferring me," he said.

The word skimmed along her skin and then sank. "Transferring where?"

"Lemon Creek. Juneau." A pause. "Today."

She swung her legs to the floor, toes hunting for the slippers she never wore until she needed them. Lemon Creek. The name felt like a storm gathering, far-off, but carrying weight and direction. "When?"

"Soon as they finish the paperwork and pretend to look for the keys." He tried for light and missed by a mile. "A couple of hours."

Ava pressed the phone tighter to her ear, as if proximity could change logistics. "Have you … did your lawyer …"

"He knows." A breath that wasn't a laugh. "He said, 'This is standard.' Like it's a discount oil change."

Her heart slammed hard enough to feel juvenile. "Okay," she said, the word a tiny lifeboat in rough water. "Okay. I'll be there before they move you."

"Ava." The way he said her name made her stop moving. "You don't have to come. It's just another set of doors."

"I can do doors," she said, finding jeans from the chair and hop-wriggling into them like a woman with purpose and questionable balance. "I'm practically bilingual in doors."

"Don't make me laugh," he murmured. "It hurts."

She stilled. "You're hurt?"

"No." It was honest enough to sting. "Not like that."

The house creaked around her, the familiar morning symphony: Esther's low hum in the kitchen, the hiss of the kettle, George's footsteps above the garage like slow thunder. Normalcy made her want to scream into a pillow.

"What do you need?" Ava asked Chap. "And don't say 'nothing.' Clothes? Books? The crossword where Grandpa cheated on seventeen-down?"

There was a pause long enough for her to hear a door clang in the background.

"You can't bring anything," he said gently. "Except your face. I wouldn't mind that."

Her throat went tight. She groped for humor because that's what she did when feelings got loud. "Tragic, considering I slept on it."

"I like you lopsided," he said, and she could hear the ghost of his smile. "Makes you human."

She went quiet, hand braced on the dresser, forehead leaning into the cold window glass. Outside, the channel was a sheet of dull pewter, the sky the same. Two cormorants arrowed low over the water, black punctuation marks.

"Are you scared?" she asked, barely above a whisper.

The kind of silence followed that you taste. "I don't know what I am," he said finally. "I keep trying to pick one thing and my brain's like, nope, sampler platter."

Her laugh cracked. "I hate this."

"I know."

"I hate that I'm here and you're there and there's …" she gestured at the wall like he could see it "… this stupid phone between us."

"I know."

"I hate that Lemon Creek sounds like a brand of herbal tea and is, in fact, the opposite."

That tug of a smile again. "Save that line for when you visit. The guards love comedy."

Ava shoved her notebook into her tote, grabbed the sweater that made her look like a responsible citizen and not a woman whose insides were Velcroed together. "I'm coming now."

"Ava, listen."

"I'm listening."

"Don't miss a day of your life over me." He said it softly, as if he'd practiced the sentence and didn't like how it felt in his mouth. "You're allowed to have a good morning, even if mine isn't."

She stared at the long crack in the paint by her door, the one George swore he'd fix and then declared "historical." "I don't do good mornings without you being okay."

"That's not the deal," he said, a little rougher. "You promised that you'd keep going."

"I didn't promise I'd do it cheerfully," she shot back, finding her boots, jamming heel to neoprene. "Besides, you're the one about to ride a ferry in handcuffs. At least let me be dramatic."

"Taking a floatplane, not the ferry," he said. "Though the ferry has great soft serve ice cream."

She felt the tears come and didn't move to stop them. They weren't the hot, chaotic ones. These were quiet and adult, like the weeping equivalent of paying taxes. "Chap."

"Yeah."

"I'll see you before you go."

A long breath. "Yeah."

"And when you get there, call me when you can. Or have someone call me. I don't care if it's a carrier pigeon with a tiny ankle monitor."

"I'll find a way," he said. "You know me. Resourceful. Irritating."

"My favorite combination."

She could hear voices in the background now, firm and male, the cadence of routine. He heard them too.

"I have to …"

"I know."

"Tell Esther I think about her pie every day."

"I will."

"And tell George … no, don't tell George anything. He scares me more than prison."

She smiled wetly. "He'll be delighted to hear it."

"Ava?"

"Yeah?"

"Don't come up here angry," he said, his voice dropping into something she felt in her ribs. "Come as you. It's the only thing that doesn't make this place feel like a bad dream."

Her fingers tightened around the phone. "I don't know how to be anything else with you."

A soft exhale. "Lucky me."

Someone said his name on the other end, sharper this time. Chap's answer was low and respectful.

"Go," she said, before they could tear him away mid-sentence and leave her talking to air. "I'm on my way."

"Drive safe."

"You, too," she blurted, then rolled her eyes at herself. "You know what I mean."

"I do."

The line went quiet. She stared at the black screen for a moment, then pressed it to her heart like she was twelve and still believed in love songs.

Esther knocked once and pushed the door open with her hip, wielding a mug of coffee that smelled like competence. She clocked Ava's face in one glance and didn't ask a single stupid question.

"When?" Esther said.

"Today," Ava managed. "Lemon Creek."

Esther's jaw set. "Finish your coffee. I'll warm a cinnamon roll for the road, don't argue. George will bring the truck around."

"I was going to take my car."

"You'll drive something with more metal than that. Some idiot salted the road like they're flavoring popcorn," Esther said, already moving, already arranging the world so it felt less impossible. "Boots. Phone. Chap's coat that you keep pretending isn't Chap's coat."

Ava looked down at the flannel draped over her desk chair, the one she'd "borrowed" and never returned. "It smells like his boat," she said, half to herself.

"Then it'll keep him close 'til you get there." Esther reached over and swept a strand of hair behind Ava's ear with a tenderness that made Ava's knees consider buckling. "We are with you."

"I know." Ava cleared her throat. "I'm fine."

"You're not," Esther said. "But you will be."

Downstairs, George opened the front door and called up in his no-nonsense voice, "Let's move, kiddo. Road's slick and rules of the road don't count for much today."

Ava slung the tote over her shoulder, grabbed the coat that wasn't hers, and followed the sound of her family.

Outside, the cold bit at her nose. The bay was iron-gray and stubborn and alive. Somewhere under that flat sky, another truck would head toward a place with a gentle name and hard edges.

She shut the door gently behind her and walked toward the truck.

***

George drove like he owned the road and everyone else was trespassing. Both hands on the wheel, jaw tight, eyes locked ahead. The old truck smelled faintly of chainsaw grease, cedar shavings and the coffee he'd spilled on the passenger seat sometime last spring.

"You don't have to come with me," Ava said, watching spruce trees whip past in blurs of dark green.

George snorted. "And leave you to walk into that place alone? Not happening."

"I've been to the jail before."

"Yeah. This is different." He flicked his eyes toward her. "This is your guy, or whatever he is, being shipped off to prison. Forgive me if I want to stand next to you in case someone says something stupid."

Ava managed a thin smile. "You think I can't handle stupid?"

"I think you can handle it," George said. "I also think I can handle it louder."

They drove in silence for a moment, the tires hissing over a patch of slush. Her hand was wrapped tight around Chap's flannel in her lap, the fabric soft from years of wear.

"You really believe he didn't do it," George said, not as a question.

"Yes."

"That's a lot of weight to carry."

"Not as much as he's carrying." She kept her gaze out the window, watching the channel flash silver in breaks between the trees.

George nodded, then cleared his throat. "When we get there, don't let the Chief get in your head. He likes to drop little barbs and watch people bleed themselves out."

160

"Good pep talk."

"I'm serious, Ava. Go in there, say what you need to say to Chap, and walk out without giving that man a damn thing."

"Except maybe a dirty look?"

George smiled faintly. "That's free."

The jail loomed into view a few minutes later, squat and gray against the pale sky. George pulled into the lot and cut the engine. For a moment they sat in the quiet cab, breath clouding in the cold air.

"You ready?" he asked.

"No," Ava said. "But I'm going in anyway."

"That's my girl."

***

The guard's key ring clanged against his belt as he led Ava down the narrow hallway. Each heavy door shut behind them with a final, echoing thud.

Room three was small, concrete-walled, with a single metal table bolted to the floor. Chap was already there, sitting straight-backed, his hands shackled in front of him. The fluorescent lights turned the shadows under his eyes darker.

"Hey," he said, standing as she entered.

She hated the shackles. She hated that she had to pretend she didn't notice them. "Hey."

He sat back down, and for a moment they just looked at each other. Twenty minutes felt like twenty seconds waiting to run out.

"They say I'm going in a couple of hours," he said.

"I know." She folded her hands on the table so she wouldn't reach for him and break a rule. "I came to tell you something before you go."

His eyes searched hers. "What?"

"I'm certain I am going to find out who killed Amelia." Her voice was quiet, deliberate. "Not just for you. For her."

A muscle in his jaw twitched. "Ava …"

"No." She leaned in, voice tightening. "Someone did this, and it wasn't you. I'm not letting them get away with it."

A shadow moved in the doorway. "No need to look far, Ms. McCormick."

Ava turned. The Chief was leaning against the frame, arms crossed, his expression smug enough to get him punched in the right Alaska bar. "You're looking at him."

Her stomach dropped. Chap's face hardened, but he didn't say a word.

"Classy," Ava said flatly. "Dropping accusations like that during a jailhouse visit. Is that before or after the donut break in your training manual?"

The Chief's smile was thin. "Just thought you should know where to focus your attention."

"Funny," she said. "I thought my attention was my business."

The guard at the door shifted uncomfortably. "Time's almost up."

The Chief stepped back, giving her a little salute before disappearing down the hall.

Ava turned back to Chap, her pulse still hammering. "Don't listen to him."

"I don't," Chap said. "But you do. I saw your face."

She swallowed hard. "It doesn't matter what he says. I know the truth."

His mouth softened. "That's all I need to hear."

The guard cleared his throat again, and this time it was final. Ava stood, the weight of the moment pressing into her shoulders.

"I'll call when I can," Chap said.

"You'd better," she replied, managing a shaky smile. "And if you can't, send that carrier pigeon I mentioned."

"Deal."

She left without looking back, because if she did, she might not be able to walk out at all.

Ava pushed through the outer doors and into a gust of cold air sharp enough to sting her cheeks. The sky was the flat gray of unpolished steel, and her breath came out in quick, angry clouds.

She spotted George leaning against the truck, arms crossed, scanning the lot like he was sizing up everyone's worthiness to breathe oxygen. A few spaces over, a familiar figure in a police jacket leaned against his cruiser.

"Hi Ava," Deputy Hale called, straightening as she approached.

Ava stopped, still holding onto the heat and claustrophobia of the visiting room. "What are you doing here? I thought you were off today."

"Dropping off a report," Ryan said, nodding toward the building. "And maybe hoping for a donut if the kitchen gods are generous."

George opened the truck door for her, but she didn't move. Hale's gaze flicked over her face, reading the mood like a weather report.

"Chap holding up?" he asked.

"As much as you can when you're about to be moved away in shackles."

Ryan winced. "Yeah. Lemon Creek's not exactly the Ritz."

"You've been?" Ava asked.

He shook his head. "No, but I've been in enough places like it. You learn quick that survival is more about who you talk to than what you eat."

"Comforting," she said dryly.

"I'm saying he'll figure it out," Hale replied, softer. "Chap's smart. And he's got you in his corner. That counts."

Ava let out a breath that wanted to be a laugh. "Sometimes I think I'm making it worse for him. Drawing attention. Riling up the Chief."

"That man's riled up by a strong wind," Hale said. "Don't flatter yourself."

George chuckled in approval.

Hale stepped closer, lowering his voice. "If you want my two cents, go home today. Eat something warm. Remind yourself that you're still allowed to have a life outside this mess."

"That sounds suspiciously like you're telling me to take a mental health day."

"That's exactly what I'm telling you," Hale said. "And if you won't do it for yourself, do it so you've got the stamina to keep poking the bear."

Ava studied him for a moment. "You're surprisingly good at pep talks."

"I've been told my bedside manner is wasted on small-town law enforcement," he said, flashing a crooked grin. "Don't make me start quoting inspirational posters."

"That's my cue to leave," George muttered, climbing into the driver's seat.

Ava smiled faintly at Ryan. "Thanks."

"Anytime," he said, stepping back. "And Ava, Chap's tough. He'll be okay."

She nodded, even though her chest still felt heavy. "I'll hold you to that."

As she climbed into the truck, Ryan shot her a knowing nod. George pulled out of the lot, and Ava kept her eyes on the side mirror until the jail disappeared from view.

***

By the time George's truck slid into the driveway, the clouds had thinned into streaks of silver and blush. The air smelled faintly of salt and woodsmoke, and Ava felt some of the tight coil in her chest start to loosen.

After Chap was gone, she had dragged herself upstairs, curled under the quilt, and stared at the ceiling until sleep finally came. When she woke again it was late afternoon. The television murmured in the background where she had left it on, and the comforting sounds of Esther moving around downstairs tugged her out of bed.

In the kitchen, Esther's apron was already dusted with flour. "Clams are soaking in the sink," she announced. "We're making chowder."

"You're on onion duty. George harvested the clams on the beach in front. Said they were practically volunteering to come home with him."

"They were fat and happy," George grunted. "Now they're soup."

Ava arched a brow. "That's dark."

"Life's dark," George said, already rummaging for the stockpot. "Soup helps."

They worked in companionable rhythm. Esther chopped celery with the precision of a surgeon; Ava diced onions until her eyes watered. George tended the stockpot, stirring in milk and potatoes, humming some old tune that wandered in and out of key.

As the chowder thickened, the kitchen filled with the briny-sweet smell of clams and butter. Esther passed Ava a spoon. "Taste."

Ava blew on it, took a sip, and closed her eyes. "That could fix most of my problems."

"Good," Esther said. "It'll go nicely with bread." She slid a loaf from the oven, crust golden and crackling.

They ate at the small kitchen table, bowls steaming, the only sounds the clink of spoons and the occasional appreciative sigh. Outside, the late-afternoon light softened to gold.

George glanced out the window mid-bite. "Whale," he said.

Ava turned in time to see it breach, a sleek dark shape rising from the channel with water cascading off its back in silver sheets before it disappeared again.

They all watched the ripples widen. No one spoke until Esther said quietly, "No matter how bad the storm, there's still beauty in the water."

Ava looked at her, then back at the channel, where the surface was smooth again. She thought of Chap on his way to Lemon Creek, of the Chief's smirk, and the growing list of unanswered questions surrounding

Amelia's death. She exhaled and for the first time all day, the weight in her chest eased just enough to let hope in.

Chapter 16

The Gaff Hook was loud with laughter and the low hum of 80s rock ballads, but Ava barely heard it over the swirling thoughts in her head. A neon Bud Light sign flickered behind the bar, casting a blue haze across the worn floorboards. The heater clicked and hummed from somewhere in the rafters, fighting a losing battle against the Alaskan chill that seeped in every time someone opened the door.

She sat across from Liz in what was starting to become their usual booth. It was tucked in the corner beneath a mounted deer head and an old framed photo of Ruby's grandfather holding a giant king salmon. Both were nursing a half-empty bottle of Amber Tide and staring down at the crumpled sticky note between them.

"It's just numbers," Ava said, tapping the note with her index finger. "Four sad, lonely numbers."

Liz squinted at it. "Could be a locker combo. Or a phone PIN. Or my cholesterol levels from last year."

Ava cracked a tired smile. "You think Amelia was worried about your LDL?"

"I think if she knew what was coming, she'd have left more than four damn digits," Liz muttered. "There's gotta be something we're missing."

Ruby, the bartender and unofficial town therapist, wandered by their table with a tray of empty glasses balanced in one hand. She glanced down at the sticky note.

"You two trying to crack the Da Vinci Code?"

Liz didn't look up. "Trying to solve a murder, thank you very much."

Ruby didn't miss a beat. "Well, make sure you put in a good word for me when Netflix comes knocking. You want another round?"

Ava nodded. "Amber Tide. And whatever deep-fried regret you've got going on in the back."

"Coming up," Ruby said, already heading to the bar.

Just then, Deputy Ryan Hale walked in. He was off-duty, in jeans and a fleece, looking far too relaxed for someone who carried a badge during the day. He shook snow from his hair and scanned the room until he spotted them. With an easy smile, he made his way over.

"How did I know that I would find the two of you scheming on a Tuesday night," he asked, leaning down to kiss Liz on the cheek before sliding in beside her.

Liz lifted her beer. "We're not scheming. We're hypothetically decoding."

Ryan raised an eyebrow. "Uh-huh. Should I be worried?"

Ava handed him the sticky note. "Four numbers. That's all Amelia left behind, far as we know. Caroline found it in her things."

He glanced at it, then shrugged. "Could be a lot of things. But that's the right length for a door code."

Liz blinked. "Like a keypad?"

Ryan nodded, reaching across the table to take a sip of Liz's beer before she could protest. "Yeah. Most new electronic locks use four-digit entries."

The idea landed with a quiet, echoing thud between them.

Ava leaned back, fingers tightening around the bottle, and looked out the window at the red building across the street with peeling paint and mismatched signage. A sign above the door read "Wellspring Office Suites," but half the letters were missing. The whole place looked like it had been slapped together by a committee of blindfolded volunteers.

"So, we know that she was seen entering that building in the days before she died," Ava murmured. "I personally saw her slipping inside. It looked like she didn't want anyone to notice."

Liz followed her gaze. "And Denise's office is in there."

Ava nodded slowly. "She's got that keypad lock on her door."

Liz raised an eyebrow. "You think Amelia was given the code for some reason?"

Ava didn't answer right away, just tapped the sticky note with slow deliberation.

"Possibly."

Ryan's eyes narrowed. "I'm going to pretend I didn't hear any of that. And if either of you ends up calling me from a holding cell tonight, I'm bringing popcorn."

He tipped an imaginary hat and wandered back toward the bar, just as Ruby returned with fresh drinks and a steaming plate of French fries.

"Don't do anything I wouldn't do," she warned, setting them down.

"So, nothing illegal or interesting?" Liz asked.

Ruby winked. "Exactly."

Ava and Liz sat in silence for a second, the sticky note now weighted with meaning.

Then Liz grinned. "We're totally breaking in, aren't we?"

Ava raised her bottle in toast. "To our future criminal records."

They clinked bottles.

And just like that, the plan was hatched.

***

The second round of Amber Tide had gone down easier than the first. Ava blamed the warmth in her chest and the slight blurring at the edge of her caution on the beer and maybe a little on the thrill creeping into her bloodstream. That familiar buzz of doing something mildly reckless, like the time she and a college friend crashed a wedding in Portland just for the cake.

Liz leaned in, elbows on the scarred wooden table, her gold hoop earrings catching the light. Her eyes sparkled with something between mischief and madness. "Okay, say it is a door code. What's our next move?"

Ava arched an eyebrow. "Our move? You're saying we're actually going through with this?"

Liz gave her a look. The one that said, *"do you really need to ask?"*

"Oh, please. You just stared out that window like you were plotting a heist. Don't pretend you're not already picking out a black hoodie in your head."

"I don't even own a black hoodie."

"You own like three," Liz deadpanned. "One says 'Coffee First, Then Chaos.'"

Ava laughed, tipping her head back. "Touché."

She ran her finger over the condensation on her bottle. Her heart was tapping a faster rhythm now, her thoughts suddenly sharper despite the alcohol. Or maybe because of it.

"Fine. But I'm not doing this sober."

"You're not doing this sober now," Liz pointed out, lifting her bottle like it was a microphone and she was giving an acceptance speech. "To questionable decisions and adrenaline."

They clinked bottles and drank. The sticky note sat between them like a fourth conspirator, its ink slightly smudged from their fingers and condensation.

Liz twirled her bottle and squinted toward the window. "We'll wait until the building closes up for the night. Denise will have to go home and cook dinner. The taxidermy place is hardly ever open. It'll be dead."

Ava winced. "Bad choice of words."

"Fair," Liz said. "It'll be unattended. How's that?"

"Better."

Ava nodded slowly, the plan stitching itself together faster than she could believe. "We'll go through the back. Less chance of being seen."

"I've got a flashlight in my glove box. And look at that." Liz lifted her foot, wiggling her sneaker, "I wore my quiet sneakers."

"Did you plan for this?"

"Of course not. But I've seen enough Dateline to know that rubber soles and plausible deniability are key."

Ava let out another laugh, but it caught in her throat this time. The humor had carried them through so much, but underneath it was something sharp and heavy. Amelia was gone. Chap was behind bars. And here they were, about to break into an office because nothing made sense anymore.

"Yeah," she said softly. "My late-night adventures usually involved heartbreak and tequila, not breaking and entering."

"Well," Liz said, scooting out from the booth and throwing some crumpled bills on the table, "tonight, we do both."

Ava stared at the sticky note again. Four numbers. A door. A secret. Maybe a truth they weren't ready for.

She grabbed her coat. "Let's go find out what Amelia was hiding."

***

The red building didn't look like much from the street, tired paint curling like sunburned skin, windows that hadn't been washed since Friends was still on TV. But in the dark alley behind it, it loomed in a way that made Ava's skin prickle. The peeling sign for "Wellspring Office Suites" hung crooked, a few letters missing so it read "Well ring," which felt like a bad omen.

"Tell me again why we're not home with wine and Netflix?" Ava whispered, crouching beside Liz behind a dented garbage bin.

Liz was kneeling with the focus of a jewel thief, unzipping a small black pouch. "Because Amelia left us a clue. Because you saw her go into this building like she was dodging paparazzi. And because if we don't follow the lead, we'll hate ourselves in the morning."

She dug around in the pouch. "Gloves, flashlight, backup batteries and gum."

Ava frowned. "Gum?"

"You want to be the girl with beer breath when we get arrested?" Liz unwrapped a stick and popped it in her mouth.

The keypad by the back door glowed faintly, four tiny green dots waiting for someone to confess a number. Ava pulled the sticky note from her coat pocket, the ink smudged from their earlier scheming at The Gaff Hook.

"You want me to do it?" Liz asked, trying to sound casual but eyeing the keypad like it might bite.

"You've had two beers and you're talking to your flashlight like it's a cat. I'll do it."

Ava pressed the first number. The keypad gave a muted beep. Second number. Third. Fourth.

A soft green light blinked. *Click.*

Liz's eyebrows shot up. "Well, crap. That actually worked."

The door groaned on its hinges when Ava pushed it open, the sound ricocheting down the narrow hallway beyond. They froze, listening for footsteps, alarms, shouts, anything.

Nothing.

Inside, the air was a stale cocktail of dust, lavender cleaning spray, and something faintly metallic. The corridor stretched ahead, lined with mismatched office doors labeled in peeling gold. Somewhere, a vending machine hummed like a low warning.

Too easy, Ava thought, and not in a good way.

The office was *perfect*. Pens lined up like soldiers, papers squared into perfect stacks, a single framed family Christmas photo centered on the desk.

"Creepy neat," Liz whispered. "Like she's hiding the chaos in a closet somewhere."

"You take the desk," Ava said. "I'll check the cabinet."

They split up. Ava eased open the top drawer: Booster Club Budget, Concessions Orders, PTA Minutes. She flipped through anyway, pretending a hot dog vendor invoice might contain a confession.

Behind her, Liz murmured, "Wow. She really does have color-coded folders. Either she's hiding something or she's the only person in Spruce Cove who actually enjoys tax season."

The filing cabinet squealed when Liz tugged it open. They both froze. Somewhere in the building, something went *thunk*.

Liz's eyes widened. "That was a door. Tell me that was not a door."

They waited. The sound didn't repeat. The heating unit kicked on with a metallic *ping*, making them both jump.

"Jesus," Liz breathed. "We're going to give ourselves heart attacks."

Ten minutes later, Ava was still finding nothing but bake sale receipts. Liz unearthed stale peppermints and paper doilies.

"High crimes," Liz whispered, holding up the mints.

Ava crouched to tug at the bottom drawer. It resisted, stuck on something. She reached underneath, fingers brushing something cold and smooth. She nudged it free and caught it before it hit the floor.

A single earring. Blue teardrop.

The air went thin. Ava brought it into the flashlight beam.

Liz crouched beside her, face pale. "That …"

"Matches the one in Amelia's room." Ava's voice was barely sound.

She slipped it into her coat pocket and pulled the drawer open the rest of the way. That's when she saw the unmarked manila folder wedged behind a stack of ledgers.

She pulled it free and opened it.

STATE OF ALASKA IN THE SUPERIOR COURT FOR THE FIRST JUDICIAL DISTRICT

DENISE ELLERY, Plaintiff

v.

CONNER ELLERY, Defendant

Complaint for Dissolution of Marriage

Liz leaned closer. "Well. That's one way to spice up Booster Club gossip."

"Shh." Ava pointed to handwriting in the margin, Denise's looping cursive pressed so hard it nearly tore the paper:

Not again. He promised it was over after Juneau. I won't protect him anymore.

The building creaked.

Liz whispered, "That was footsteps."

"It's an old building," Ava said but her voice lacked conviction.

She turned another page. A draft letter to an attorney, half-filled out.

I thought I could forgive him. But then, Amelia.

Liz's breath caught. "Amelia?"

"It was him," Ava's voice scraped her throat.

From somewhere down the hall came a low, dragging sound, like something heavy being moved. They both stared at the frosted glass of the office door.

A shadow passed across it. Paused. Moved on.

Liz mouthed: *Nope. Nope. Nope.*

Ava flipped to the next sheet, a typed witness statement:

EXHIBIT C – Statement of Witness

Date: [Blank]

Name: [Blank]

Subject states Mr. Ellery met with Amelia the week before her death.

Meeting took place at Wellspring Office Suites, Room 3B.

Entry believed to be made via keypad.

Witness observed elevated voices. Words included: "ruin," "baby," and "not again."

The words swam in Ava's vision.

Liz pointed at the page. "Mr. Ellery, as in …"

"Coach," Ava whispered. The word tasted bitter.

Another sound, closer this time. Not a creak. Not a heater ping. Something like the muffled *click* of a door latch.

Liz whispered, "We have to go. Now."

Ava hesitated, folder in her hands. "We can't just …"

"Grab it or leave it, McCormick, but I am not ending up as Exhibit D."

They moved fast. Liz killed the flashlight, plunging them into darkness. They navigated by muscle memory, each step a soft scrape against the carpet.

Out in the hallway, the exit sign glowed faintly, throwing orange light over their faces. The air felt heavier, as if someone else's breath was in it.

Halfway to the back door, something clattered in the lobby.

"Don't run," Liz whispered. "Running makes you look guilty."

"Breaking into an office makes you look guilty," Ava hissed.

"Good point."

The keypad at the exit blinked like an impatient eye. Ava's hands shook as she punched in the numbers. Green light. Soft *click*.

They slipped outside into the alley, breath clouding in the freezing air. Ava clutched the folder to her chest like it was the only thing keeping her upright.

Liz let out a shaky laugh. "We're either heroes or complete idiots."

Ava didn't answer. She kept walking, ears straining for footsteps behind them certain that if she turned around, she'd see a figure in the dark.

Chapter 17

Ava's phone was ringing before she was fully awake.

She squinted at the screen, the morning light slicing across her pillow in that smug way only Alaskan sunrises could manage. Too early, too bright, and far too judgmental for someone who'd gone to bed at 3 a.m.

William.

Her stomach did a little flip, equal parts reflex and regret. She swiped to answer before she could talk herself out of it.

"Hey," she croaked. Her voice sounded like gravel and tea.

"You sound like death warmed over," William said, his tone halfway between teasing and worry. "Are you okay?"

"Define okay," she said, sitting up against the headboard. "If you mean 'breathing,' then yes. If you mean 'making good life choices'" She let the sentence trail off.

There was a pause. The kind where she could practically hear him pressing a hand to his forehead. "Ava. What did you do?"

She pulled her knees up, resting her chin on them. "Technically, Liz and I didn't *do* anything illegal. Not really."

"That's a lie I can tell you've rehearsed," William said.

She sighed. "Fine. We might have done a little research."

"Research," he repeated, flat. "The kind where you what? You ask a few harmless questions?"

Ava hesitated just long enough for him to notice. "Something like that."

There was a beat of silence, the sound of him exhaling sharply through his nose. "Ava. What aren't you telling me?"

She twisted the edge of the quilt between her fingers. "It was field research."

His voice sharpened. "Field research?"

"Mm-hmm."

"As in you were actually *where*?"

"Hypothetically," she said.

Another pause. Longer this time. "Hypothetically *where*?"

She winced. "Inside a building we maybe didn't have permission to be in."

He groaned. "You told me last week you were just asking questions, Ava. Not breaking and entering."

"Breaking *into*," she corrected. "And we didn't take anything, so there's that."

"Congratulations, you're a law-abiding citizen," he shot back. "Except for the part where you could have gotten arrested. Or worse."

She could picture him pacing, the way his brow furrowed when he was trying to decide if he should keep arguing or just strangle her through the phone.

"I'm fine," she said, softening her voice. "It wasn't dangerous."

"Ava, everything about this is dangerous. You're digging into a murder investigation in a town where everyone knows everyone, and now you're what? Playing cat burglar?"

She tried for levity. "We're more like raccoons. Clever, resourceful, adorable."

"That's not funny." His voice was low now, the edge of genuine fear threading through it. "You could get hurt."

Her chest pinched at the sound. "I know."

"I'm not there to," he stopped himself. Took a breath. "Promise me you'll be careful."

"Careful is relative," she said.

"Ava."

"Fine," she relented. "I promise I'll be less reckless."

"That's not the same thing."

"It's the best you're going to get."

There was a beat of silence, then his tone shifted softer, familiar. "You have a way of doing this to me, you know. Make me half-crazy with worry and then talk me down like it's no big deal."

She smiled despite herself. "Maybe you're just easy to talk down."

"No," he said, and she could hear the smile in his voice now. "You're just good at getting under my skin."

"Are you trying to flirt with me Mr. Hudson?"

"Maybe I am."

Her cheeks warmed, which annoyed her because she hadn't planned on enjoying this call. "You aren't mad at me?"

"Oh, I am," he said. "I'm furious. But it doesn't cancel out the fact that I miss you."

The words landed in her chest like a stone dropped in water, ripples spreading before she could stop them.

"That's unfair," she murmured.

"Life's unfair," he said lightly. "Especially when you make a habit of breaking into places."

She sighed. "You're never letting this go, are you?"

"Not a chance. And if you're smart, you'll use that Yale degree of yours to figure out how to avoid jail time."

"Maybe I'll charm my way out."

"Ava, you're gorgeous, but even you can't flirt your way past that chief of yours from the sounds of it."

"Please. Harrow talks tough, but he still owes me for that time I saved him from giving a press conference with spinach in his teeth."

William laughed, a real laugh that was warm and unguarded, and for a moment, it was like nothing had changed between them. Like they were still in New Haven, curled up on a couch together, plotting out a life they thought they wanted.

"Just don't make me get on a plane," he said finally. "Because I will."

Her throat tightened. "I'll be fine."

"You'd better be."

They lingered there for a breath or two, neither hanging up first.

When she finally did, Ava set the phone down on the quilt and stared at the ceiling. She hated that he could still get to her. Hated that he still cared enough to call and that some part of her was glad he did.

The worst part? He wasn't wrong.

She *had* gotten in over her head. And there was no climbing back out now.

***

By the time Liz's dented Subaru pulled into the cracked asphalt lot behind the school, the late-morning sun had burned away most of the coastal fog. The building loomed in that utilitarian way small-town schools always did, no frills, no modern glass atriums, just beige paint and a faint whiff of industrial cleaner drifting from the vents.

"This is where the magic happens," Liz said, cutting the engine. "And by magic, I mean long staff meetings and budget cuts."

Ava glanced at the back door they were headed for. "Your friend's okay meeting us here?"

"She's got a prep period. Nobody's going to question us if we look like we belong." Liz reached into the back seat and tossed Ava a faded visitor lanyard. "Here. Instant legitimacy. Just act like this is part of your series."

Inside, Liz led them down a short hall and into a cramped office lined with motivational posters that looked like they'd been here since the 90s.

Marcie Brenner was already waiting, mid-thirties, glasses smudged, a coffee mug in one hand and a stack of graded papers in the other. She shut the door behind them with her hip.

"You've got ten minutes before I have to pretend I know algebra again," Marcie said, setting the papers down.

Liz grinned. "That's nine more than I need."

Marcie shot her a look. "You said this was important."

"It is," Liz said, leaning on the desk. "We're trying to get clarity on Coach Ellery's past. Specifically, Juneau. You said you had heard things."

Marcie's lips pressed together, and for a moment Ava thought she might shut down the conversation entirely. But then she glanced at the door, lowered her voice, and said, "It wasn't just inappropriate behavior. There was a girl."

Ava's stomach tightened. "A student?"

Marcie nodded once. "Sixteen, maybe seventeen. She got pregnant."

The hum of the overhead light seemed to get louder.

Marcie went on, fingers worrying at the chipped edge of her mug. "Last year, I was teaching over in Sitka, and we went to a reading conference in Juneau. The kind where the coffee's horrible, the handouts are useless, and everyone's counting down until lunch."

Liz smirked. "Ah yes, professional development, where good teachers go to die of boredom."

Marcie's mouth twitched. "Exactly. So, a few of us from Sitka ducked into the staff lounge. Some Juneau teachers were there. You could tell they'd been dying to talk about something all morning. They never said his name at first, but I picked up on it. They meant a coach. Charismatic, popular with the students, the sort of guy who gets invited to too many graduation parties." She lowered her voice. "The kind everyone swears is harmless until he's not."

Ava leaned in. "And that's when the pregnancy came up?"

Marcie nodded. "One of the PE teachers said it. A junior left school mid-year after finding out she was pregnant. She never named the father, but she'd been spending a lot of time with the basketball coach. It was one of those moments where everyone goes still, but no one's actually shocked."

"And Denise?" Ava asked.

"That's when it got strange," Marcie said. "One of the secretaries said Denise stopped showing up to any of the school events she used to attend. The games, fundraisers, even the booster auction. Spent all her time at her accounting office instead. Like she knew the walls were closing in, but she was busy shoring them up instead of looking for the exit."

Liz tapped her pen against the desk. "So, Denise goes silent, the girl disappears, and Coach 'resigns for personal reasons.'"

Marcie gave a humorless laugh. "Exactly. And then, right after the school year ends, I hear he took the coaching job in Spruce Cove. I thought it was just gossip until I saw Denise at the grocery store here. I nearly dropped my basket."

For a moment, no one spoke. The weight of it hung between them. The idea of a scandal neatly swept away, and two adults still in positions of authority.

Marcie's eyes darted to the hallway. "I shouldn't even be talking about this. People who stick their nose into other people's business around here usually end up wishing they hadn't."

Liz leaned back in her chair, crossing her arms. "Lucky for us, we're more into answers than popularity contests."

That earned the smallest twitch of a smile from Marcie. "Just, be careful. I don't think Denise is dangerous. But she's smart. And she's the kind of loyal that's fine when you're on her side and terrifying when you're not."

The bell rang, sharp and shrill. Marcie gathered her papers. "That's my cue. Don't mention my name if this gets out."

"Wouldn't dream of it," Liz said.

Out in the hallway, the noise of shuffling feet and slamming lockers was almost jarring after the low murmur of that office. Ava followed Liz toward the exit, her mind turning over the new information like a coin she didn't want to spend.

"So," Liz said as they stepped back into the bright air, "we've got a teenage girl, a possible pregnancy, and a coach who skips town before anyone can make it official." She shook her head. "Typical. A grown man who thinks he's God's gift to women but can't figure out that birth control isn't just a rumor."

Ava gave her a look. "Charming."

Liz slid behind the wheel. "Don't blame me. I didn't come up with the cliché. He just auditioned for it."

"And we have a wife who might have helped him erase the problem," Ava added.

Liz unlocked the car. "So, remind me why we're not already parked outside Denise's office with coffee?"

Ava slid into the passenger seat. "We are heading that way. We just needed the context first."

Liz grinned. "Perfect. Nothing like a little live theater before lunch."

***

Liz's idea of a stakeout involved coffee, a box of donuts, and a pair of plastic binoculars she swore were "vintage" but looked like they came from the toy aisle.

"This is how the pros do it," she said, handing Ava the binoculars and settling in behind the wheel of her parked Subaru, angled just enough to see the front of Denise's accounting office.

Ava peered through the cloudy lenses. "I think these were made for a six-year-old."

"Or by a six-year-old," Liz admitted, ripping into a maple bar. "But it's the thought that counts. Besides, they came with a free whistle." She pulled the tiny plastic whistle out of the glove box and blew on it. It made a wheezy, dying-bird sound.

Ava winced. "Please tell me that's not part of your surveillance strategy."

"Relax. It's for emergencies. Or seagulls."

They'd been parked for twenty minutes, sipping coffee and watching the door. The most exciting thing so far had been a delivery guy dropping off a stack of printer paper and looking at them like he knew exactly what they were doing.

"This is thrilling," Ava said, blowing on her coffee.

"Stakeouts are ninety percent boredom, ten percent action," Liz replied. "We're just in the ninety."

A silver SUV slowed as it passed them, the driver craning their neck to look at the Subaru. Ava ducked instinctively, nearly spilling her drink.

"Smooth," Liz said. "Nothing says 'we're not spying' like disappearing into your hoodie."

"They looked suspicious," Ava hissed.

"They looked like Mrs. Greene from the library."

"She's nosy."

"She's eighty-four."

"Exactly."

Liz tore off another piece of maple bar and offered it to Ava. "Eat something. You're jumpy. And cranky. You're cranky-jumpy."

Ava was mid-bite when the office door opened.

Denise stepped out, folders clutched to her chest like she was bracing for wind. Except there was no wind, only the flat stillness of a Tuesday morning. She scanned the street quickly, eyes darting over parked cars before landing somewhere far away, like she was listening for something only she could hear. Her neat gray cardigan hung too loose, as though she'd lost weight, and the way her shoulders hunched made her look smaller than Ava remembered.

"She looks tense," Ava murmured.

Liz adjusted the binoculars like she was dialing in a sniper shot. "Or constipated. Hard to say from here."

A man emerged behind her, tall, broad-shouldered, moving with the easy authority of someone who'd never had to hurry in his life. He laid a hand on her shoulder.

Denise flinched. Not the kind of polite recoil you give a stranger in your personal space. This was sharp, full-bodied, almost like the touch burned. Half her folders slipped from her arms and fanned out across the sidewalk.

He bent to help, but she snatched them up herself in jerky, defensive movements, not even glancing at him. She turned back toward the office, nearly catching the door with her hip in her haste to get inside.

"You see that," Ava asked.

Liz lowered the binoculars. "Oh, I saw it. Question is, was that fear or fury?"

Before Ava could answer, a sudden, *violent* knock on Liz's window made both of them scream. Ava's coffee sloshed over her jeans, Liz dropped the binoculars, and the donut hole in Ava's mouth shot forward like a tragic pastry cannonball, hitting the dashboard, bouncing, and rolling under the seat.

"Jesus!" Ava gasped, clutching her chest.

Liz swatted at her jeans like she could brush off the fright. "If I die of a heart attack, you're paying for my funeral."

Ryan stood there, one eyebrow raised, looking far too pleased with himself.

Liz fumbled for the window button, muttering, "Why are you like this?" as it rolled down two inches.

"You want to tell me why you're parked here like a couple of teenagers on prom night?" Ryan asked, smirk firmly in place.

Ava, still blotting coffee off her thigh, blurted, "We're birdwatching."

Ryan's eyes flicked to the empty donut box. "What kind of bird eats maple bars?"

"The uh, Spruce Cove sugar gull," Liz said, her voice deadly serious.

Ryan tilted his head. "Not a thing."

"It could be," Liz offered brightly.

He glanced toward Denise's office, then back at them. "Look, I don't know what you two are up to but maybe don't do it in front of half the town. People talk."

"People talk no matter what we do," Ava muttered.

"True," Ryan said. "But you make it easy."

Liz saluted him with her coffee cup. "Noted, Deputy."

He shook his head and walked back to his patrol car, muttering something about "trouble magnets."

As soon as he was out of earshot, Liz exhaled dramatically. "See? Even Ryan admits we're interesting."

"Pretty sure that wasn't a compliment," Ava said.

"Details."

They turned back to the office just in time to see Denise closing the blinds.

Ava frowned. "Wait … that guy who was with her."

Liz's hand froze on the gearshift. "Tall, broad shoulders, walked like he's never been late to anything in his life?"

"Yeah."

Liz's eyebrows lifted. "Coach."

Ava felt her pulse tick up. "Which means whatever that flinch was, it wasn't a friendly office visit."

They both stared at the blinds for a beat, like maybe they'd open again and give them one more piece of the puzzle.

"Guess the show's over," Liz said finally, starting the car. "But I'd say we've got enough for an intermission snack."

Ava smirked. "You mean lunch?"

Liz pulled out of the parking spot. "Tomato, tomahto."

***

The Subaru rattled over a pothole big enough to swallow a small dog. Liz swerved around the next one with practiced ease, one hand on the wheel, the other fishing for the rogue donut hole that had rolled under the seat during Ryan's surprise visit.

"So," she said, "team meeting. Who's our prime suspect now? Coach, with the possible history of seducing and abandoning teenage girls? Or Denise, who might be one bad day away from snapping?"

Ava stared out the passenger window at the string of weathered storefronts sliding past. "If Denise was jealous enough to kill Amelia, why flinch from her own husband's touch? That didn't look like a woman clinging to her marriage."

"Or it's an act," Liz countered. "Classic misdirection. Cry in public, keep the murder weapon in your desk drawer."

Ava turned to her. "You think she's that good?"

"I think," Liz said, finally retrieving the squashed donut hole and examining it like evidence, "she's married to a guy who can walk away from a mess without looking back. That kind of skill rubs off."

Ava shook her head. "My money's on Coach. He's arrogant, creepy, and he has a history of terribly bad and illegal decisions."

"Fine. I'll take Denise." Liz popped the mangled donut in her mouth. "Whoever wins buys the other lunch for a year."

Ava smirked. "Hope you like making sandwiches."

Liz grinned, accelerating toward the main road. "Hope you like losing."

Chapter 18

The night before, Liz had declared they were "absolutely not" walking into the Ellery's house without a plan.

Ava had pictured a legal pad with bullet points, maybe a printed list of questions. Liz had other methods: a tray of nachos, a bottle of wine, and three seasons of *Interrogation Room: Special Crimes Unit*.

"Best training tool out there," Liz said, settling in on Ava's couch and hitting play. "Watch how Detective Morales leans in. That's dominance. People spill their guts when you lean."

Ava eyed the screen. "Or because there's a boom mic over their heads and a script in their hands."

"Minor details," Liz said, shoving a loaded chip into her mouth.

For two hours they studied techniques: eyebrow raises, long silences, walking slowly around the room like a shark. Liz took notes. Ava poured more wine.

By the time Morales had extracted a tearful confession from a jewel thief in a too-tight dress, Liz had a plan.

"You'll be the good cop," she told Ava. "All sympathetic smiles and soft voice. I'll be the bad cop. Blunt, suspicious, ready to call out a lie when I hear it."

"I thought you said we're just asking questions."

"Questions are interrogation," Liz said. "It's just like the show, except without the dramatic music."

"And the commercial breaks."

"Exactly," Liz said. "Which means we bring our own snacks and our own plot twists."

Ava laughed, though her stomach was still a fist. "And I agreed to this because?"

"Because you love me," Liz said, hitting play.

***

Now, sitting in Liz's Subaru outside the Ellerys' home, Ava was starting to think they'd leaned too hard on television for strategy.

The two-story house was neat in the way small-town houses get before winter, fresh coat of paint, a few flowerpots stubbornly hanging on against the chill, a cheerful red door. But Ava noticed the crack in the front step, the gutter pulling loose from the roofline. Little flaws that were invisible unless you were looking.

Liz checked her watch. "If Coach is home, this'll get messy. We need Denise alone."

"How do we even know if he's here?" Ava asked.

"Observation." Liz pointed to the driveway. "One car. He drives a black F-150. This is a Ford Explorer. Denise's."

"Or he's inside watching TV."

"Then we improvise," Liz said, and for a moment she looked exactly like Detective Morales before the commercial break.

They watched the windows for five long minutes. No movement. Somewhere down the street, a lawn mower droned, cut out, and sputtered to life again.

Finally Liz unbuckled. "Game time."

Ava's heart thudded harder than a conversation about taxes should warrant. At their feet, a doormat read *Bless This Mess* in cheery cursive, like the house was in on its own secrets. Ava read and reread *Bless This Mess* wondering if the map was trying to warn them with a joke.

Liz pressed the bell, then slid half a step to the side like they'd practiced, forcing a wider door crack.

When it opened, Denise stood framed in the doorway, polite but tight, like a woman bracing for a tornado warning she wanted to pretend was a drill. Jeans, cream sweater, sleeves shoved to the elbows. Hair pulled back, not styled. She glanced at each of them quickly, as if counting witnesses.

"Liz," she said, then, "Ava. What's going on? If this is about bookkeeping, it can wait until business hours."

"It's not about bookkeeping," Liz said, her smile more geometry than warmth. "We were hoping to talk. Just a few questions."

"I'm on my way out." Denise began, shifting, but Liz planted the edge of her boot against the jamb, not hard enough to be a threat, just definite enough to be a boundary.

"Won't take long," Liz said, casual, steel under cotton.

Ava softened. "We're not here to cause trouble, Denise. We just think you might know something important."

For a second, Denise's gaze slid past them to the quiet street. Her fingers curled around the door like she might close it and lock it forever. Then she stepped back. "Fine. But make it quick."

***

Inside was lemon-cleaner bright and airless, like the room had been wiped down and sealed. The living room was more theory than life: pillows at perfect diagonals, a throw folded into a museum-grade rectangle, a tray with a candle that had never seen flame and a travel magazine splayed to *Seven Days to a New You*. No family photos. No shoes kicked off. No coffee-ring ghosts on the table.

Liz sat, perching like she owned the couch and the moment. "How long have you been in Spruce Cove?" she asked, casual as weather. "Year? Year and change?"

"Just about," Denise said. Her eyes flicked toward the hallway. A small sound, fridge hum, maybe rose and faded.

"And before that?" Liz asked, the cat before the pounce.

"Juneau," Denise said. She said it like it might bite.

"Right." Liz crossed a leg; her ankle bounced once. "Busy town. Good schools. Lots of extracurriculars." She let the word sit and sharpen.

Ava shot her a too-soon look, but Liz just smoothed her sleeve and waited.

"What is this?" Denise asked. She didn't raise her voice, but her hands tightened, knuckles blanching. "I told the police what I know."

"Which wasn't much," Liz said, sweet as poison. "We're wondering if there's more now than there was then."

Ava leaned in, elbows on knees, the good cop without pretending. "We're not your enemy, Denise. We're trying to understand what happened to Amelia. Sometimes things feel small in the moment and only later you realize they were the hinge."

Denise swallowed, a motion that didn't land. "I don't know anything. I do numbers. I go to work. I come home. I'm a mom. I don't …" She stopped, reset. "What do you want from me?"

"Clarity," Liz said. "Juneau. The move. What you've seen here. Anything off about Amelia. Anything off about your husband."

A muscle in Denise's cheek twitched. "People gossip," she said. "They always have enough pieces to build a story they like."

"Stories can be true," Liz said. "Or useful. Sometimes both."

A soft electronic chirp came from down the hall. Denise flinched, barely, and smoothed it away by adjusting her cuff. Ava's gaze snagged on a faint yellow bruise just at the edge of the wrist bone, old enough to be fading, shaped like a thumbprint that had waited out a week of long sleeves.

Ava lowered her voice. "Are you okay?"

Denise lifted her chin. "I'm fine."

Silence stretched, the kind that makes you aware of your own breath. In the kitchen, a wall clock clicked from 11:59 to 12:00. Somewhere beyond the fence, the mower droned again.

Ava let the quiet do some work. Detective Morales had leaned on silence like it was a tool; you could make a person need to fill it. "You have an immaculate house," she said finally, soft enough to be an invitation. "It looks like a photograph. Beautiful. Untouched."

"I like things neat," Denise said, mouth pressed flat.

"Neat is one thing," Liz said, eyeing vacuum tracks. "Exhibition-grade is another."

"I had a client over," Denise said too fast. Her fingers laced and unlaced, again, again. "What do you want to ask me?"

"Let's start with something simple," Liz said. "When did you meet Amelia?"

"At the booster auction," Denise said after a beat. "She bid on a basket. Movie tickets, a blanket." Her gaze hovered around their shoulders, not quite landing. She wasn't remembering so much as selecting. "She was friendly."

"Friendly how?" Liz asked.

"Charming. The kind of girl people notice."

Ava watched the way she said *girl*, like the word tasted wrong. "Did she ever come to your office?"

"No." Immediate. Then, smaller: "Not that I remember."

"And your husband?" Liz asked lightly, like weather again. "Big community guy. Teams. Raffles. Pep talks. Spirit wear."

Denise's fingers twisted like she was wringing water from them. "He's dedicated."

"To his job," Liz said, nodding. "To his athletes. To his wife?"

Something flashed offense, fear, anger with a lid screwed tight. "This is intrusive."

"Probably," Liz said, cheery as a bell. "Intrusive gets answers."

A phone vibrated on the end table, skittering once against the wood. Denise jerked, snatched it up, set it facedown without looking. Ava caught the flash of the screen: Coach. No first name. No emoji. Just a title like a rank that didn't need defending.

"Do you want to grab that?" Ava asked.

"No," Denise said. Quieter: "He's at practice."

"Is he?" Liz asked, mild.

Denise's lips parted and closed. The phone buzzed again, insistently, then stilled. She set it on the table like a live thing she'd prefer not to handle.

Ava leaned into the soft place. "Pressure makes people do weird things. You know that better than anyone. But if Amelia was in trouble, if someone pushed her into it, keeping quiet won't save you. It won't save anyone."

Denise's laugh came out too sharp, a slip of metal. "Save me," she said, mocking with a thread of panic. "From what? The rumor mill? Your amateur detective routine? You don't know what you're talking about."

"Then help us know," Ava said. "Tell us what you're afraid of."

Liz leaned forward, voice calm with an edge. "Because right now, Denise, you look a lot less like a bystander and a lot more like a suspect."

The word hit the room like dropped glass. Denise's folded hands tightened until the knuckles went white.

"I had nothing to do with what happened to her," she said, each word clipped, like cutting the air might make them truer.

"Then tell us who did," Liz said.

"I'm not …" Denise started. Stopped. Her shoulders drew up and collapsed a fraction. "You're wasting your time."

"Juneau," Liz said, abrupt now, like a hand slamming the table. "He left fast. No school makes it that easy unless they're thrilled to see someone go."

Go seemed to echo. Denise's gaze slipped toward the hallway again, toward whichever appliance was chirping, toward whichever fear was louder. "We moved for a fresh start," she said.

"Fresh starts come with boxes," Liz said, scanning the immaculate surfaces. "Photos. Souvenirs. History. Where's yours?"

"In storage," Denise said.

"All of it?"

"Most."

Ava softened the edges again. "Fresh starts work best when you're not dragging a secret like an anchor."

192

A quick blink, betrayal of something under the varnish. Her fingers stilled. "I run a business," she said, as if that sentence could keep the world in order. "People count on me."

"People count on you to keep their books," Liz said. "Not cover up their crimes."

A different kind of quiet fell, aware of itself. Ava could feel the pivot, the door easing open a quarter inch in a dark room.

From the hallway: a click, a whir. Denise straightened. "We're done," she said, brittle again. "I have a one o'clock appointment."

"It's twelve-oh-four," Liz said, glancing at the clock. "Just a couple more minutes."

"One last thing," Ava said gently. "Yesterday, outside your office, was that your husband?"

Denise swallowed. "Yes."

"He touched your shoulder. You recoiled." Ava kept her tone clinical and kind, like naming a symptom could help. "Why?"

Denise's brows drew together. "Wait. You were watching me?"

"Stakeout," Liz said, like it was a perfectly reasonable hobby. "We had donuts."

Denise's mouth pressed into a line. "That's highly unsettling."

"Only if you've got something to hide," Liz said lightly.

"He startled me," Denise said at last.

"Or?" Liz prompted.

"Or nothing," Denise snapped, a crack at the edge of the word. She drew a steadying breath. "I've told you what I know. Amelia was a nice girl. Tragic. That's all."

"Is that really all?" Ava asked softly.

For a second, Denise's eyes flashed. They were there and gone, like a lighthouse. "You should go," she said. "Please go."

Liz didn't move. "We will. And next time, it probably won't just be us. Once they prove Chap wasn't the father, the police will have questions. The kind you can't ignore." She let the pause stretch just long enough to land. "And we both know which man's name is going to come up."

On cue, the facedown phone buzzed. Denise's head turned. She didn't touch it.

Ava stood slowly, careful not to spook whatever invisible animal had wandered into the room. "Thank you for your time," she said. It wasn't the right phrase, but it was the only one that fit inside the brittle shape of this conversation.

At the door, Denise set her hand on the glossy red knob. The paint gleamed, unmarred. "We're done," she said, voice flat. "And don't come back."

"And if what we need is the truth?" Liz asked.

Denise looked at her, really looked, like a person choosing a path she couldn't undo. "Then stop asking questions you don't want answers to," she said, and opened the door.

Outside, the air felt colder. Ava exhaled a breath she hadn't noticed she was holding. Beside her, Liz rolled her shoulders, eyes locked on the red door.

"Well," Liz said, starting down the walk, "now I really want the answers."

***

They'd made it halfway to the Subaru when the door hinges creaked again.

"Wait," Denise said.

She stood with one hand still on the door, the other fisted into the hem of her sweater like she needed fabric to keep her standing. She glanced over her shoulder into the house, then stepped back, universal language for: *Fine. Come in. But I'm not the only one who's going to regret it.*

The lemon-cleaner air hadn't changed, but Denise had. She sat this time, perched on the edge of the couch as if the cushions might swallow her. Her hands worried the hem: twist, untwist.

"Whatever you think you know," she said, "it's worse."

Liz didn't sit. She leaned against the arm of the couch, arms crossed. Ava took the chair opposite, knees angled toward Denise.

"In Juneau," Denise said, "he was fired. Didn't 'resign.' No 'mutual agreement.' He was fired." She swallowed. "They called it misconduct. Said they couldn't keep him on with the situation."

Ava's voice was quiet. "What situation?"

"A girl on the team," Denise said. "Sixteen. Rumors she was pregnant." Her voice cracked on the last word. "She disappeared before it could be confirmed. Family moved her out of state. The school kept it quiet. He told me it was all lies, kids making trouble. But I heard things. I decided to trust him, pretended I believed him."

Her hands twisted harder. "It was working. Then one afternoon, I came home early. His truck was in the driveway. Amelia's car was parked a few houses down, like she didn't want anyone to see it here." She closed her eyes for a couple of seconds. "My stomach dropped so fast I had to hold the doorframe. I told myself maybe she was dropping something off. Maybe they were talking about the team. But when she left, she wouldn't look at me. Not even a quick wave. She kept walking like she was guilty."

Her eyes met Ava's. Guilt and dread, equal measures. "A week later, Amelia showed up at my office. Didn't sit. Just stood there. I thought she was going to tell me they were having an affair. Instead, she said she knew about Juneau. That she wasn't going to let it happen again. And she looked at me like I was part of the problem. Like I'd picked a side."

"Did you pick a side?" Liz asked.

"I picked survival," Denise said, and the words landed like a confession she'd rehearsed alone. "I asked her not to do it. I told her it would blow up our whole family. The kids, everything. I told her to be careful. That around here, people don't always thank you for telling the truth."

"And your husband?" Liz said, voice sharp now.

"He said he would 'take care of it.'" Denise's mouth twisted. "Like I'd asked about a broken appliance, not a girl's life. He said I 'didn't want to know more.'" She mimed the air quotes like they still burned. "God, I hated him in that moment. And then I hated myself for letting it go."

Ava's stomach tightened. "And you didn't ask?"

Denise shook her head, a small, jerky motion. "I've been careful. For years. I learned not to push. Not to give him a reason." She looked down at her hands. "He controls the bank accounts, the passwords. If I go out, he wants to know where I am, who I'm with. He'll humiliate me in front of people if I step out of line. Take the keys if I'm late. Tell 'jokes' that aren't jokes." She swallowed. "After Amelia, I thought if I poke at this, he'll do worse."

A tear slid over her cheek, followed by another she didn't catch in time. "I don't know what happened that night. I swear. I just know she was going to say something. And then she was gone." Her voice dropped. "And every time I look at him now, I wonder if he's thinking about her."

A long, quiet minute. The lemon scent was suddenly too much.

"You've been living with all of this, alone," Ava said.

Denise let out a sound that might have been a laugh if it weren't so tired. "Not alone. Following his rules."

Liz straightened. The steel was still there but softened at the edges. "You just told us more than you think."

Denise shook her head. "You wanted the truth. That's it. I'm not proud of what I've done. Or haven't done. But I can't change it now."

"You just started to," Ava said. She wasn't trying for a line; it came out like a fact.

Denise's gaze moved to the doorway, to the path out, like she might take it and keep going. Then she closed her eyes and opened them again, the decision to keep breathing. "You should go," she said. "Please."

They didn't argue.

196

Outside, the noon light felt too clean for what they were carrying. A crow screeched. Somewhere, a chainsaw gave a final cough and fell quiet.

Liz stopped at the doormat and looked down. *Bless This Mess* stared back at them, cheerful and oblivious.

"Accurate," she said.

Ava let out a breath that wasn't quite a laugh. "Understatement."

Chapter 19

Ava's phone buzzed violently against the nightstand, dragging her from a dreamless sleep. The room was still dark, the kind of cold blue silence just before sunrise.

Disoriented, she blinked at the glowing screen.

Unknown Caller – Juneau, AK

Her stomach dropped.

She reached for it, heart already racing, and swiped to answer.

A flat, mechanical voice clicked on.

"This is a collect call from Chap Fisher, an inmate at Lemon Creek Correctional Center.

This call is subject to monitoring and recording. Press one to accept."

Her finger jabbed at the screen.

A beat of silence.

Then "Ava?"

His voice was rough, gravel-etched, and edged with something unfamiliar. Fear, maybe.

Or worse clarity.

"I'm here," she said, sitting up straighter. "What is it? Are you okay?"

"No. I mean, not really. But I remembered something."

She swung her legs over the edge of the bed. "Talk to me."

"I was talking to this guy in here. Older guy, kind of a know-it-all, but not a bad one. He's in for some white-collar mess, I don't know. But we were talking about basketball. Random, right? And he mentions that his kid used to play for Juneau. Said Ellery was his coach."

Ava's pulse picked up. "He knew Coach?"

"Knew about him," Chap said. "Said Ellery was run out of town. Quietly. Not on paper. There was some incident at the school. Something the administration covered up. His son told him Ellery got caught sending texts to a student."

Ava's stomach turned. "Texts like inappropriate?"

"Yeah. You don't mistake that tone. The way he said 'messages to a student' it was clear. And the worst part? The school buried it. Didn't want the scandal."

She swallowed, trying to keep her voice level. "Did he give you the girl's name?"

"Yeah. Rachel Tripp."

Ava said it out loud, testing it in the air like a puzzle piece. "Rachel Tripp."

"That conversation, it triggered something in me. Something I didn't want to remember."

She held her breath.

"Back at The Gaff Hook. That night."

Ava's chest tightened.

"I remember what Amelia said to me that night. Not that she was pregnant. I already knew that. She told me Ellery was the father."

A silence stretched between them, dense and charged.

"Said he wasn't the man we all thought he was. That she couldn't talk to anyone else about it because no one else knew about the pregnancy. Just me. She was rattled. Not because she was pregnant. But because she realized what kind of man he really was."

"And you confronted him."

"Yeah," Chap said, his voice thick with shame. "I did. I was already drunk, but I went up to him at the bar and told him to stay away from her. I didn't say her name, at least I don't think I did. I wasn't loud, but I was stupid. No one else knew what it was about."

Ava ran a hand through her hair. The pieces were locking into place, one agonizing click at a time.

"Then Earl started creeping on her. Same night. She was trying to get away from him and I stepped in again. Outside, it got heated. I said something, I didn't mean to, but it slipped. I made a comment that tipped Earl off that she was pregnant."

"And Earl just turned on her. Called her something like damaged goods. When Amelia found out I said something to Earl, she looked at me like I broke something in her. I tried to say I didn't mean it, but it was too late. She yelled at me and walked away. I kept drinking. The rest of the night is still blank ever since."

"But now you remember something."

"I do. Because of that student. That's what I think Amelia found out. She knew about Coach's past. About what he did in Juneau. That's why she said he wasn't who she thought. And now, I think, maybe he found out she knew."

Ava's voice dropped. "You think he silenced her."

Chap went quiet for a moment. Ava waited, hearing only the faint hum of prison air behind him.

Then he said it, soft and strangled: "I don't know what else makes sense. I didn't kill her, Ava. But I might've been the last person she trusted. And I ..."

A breath. A pause.

"I threw that trust away. Like it meant nothing. Like she meant nothing. And now she's gone and I can't take any of it back."

Ava pressed her hand against her chest, trying to calm the growing ache.

"I'll talk to Liz," she said. "We'll find Rachel. We're going to find the truth."

He didn't say thank you. He just exhaled, like maybe that was the only thread of hope he had left.

They said goodbye in the awkward, abrupt way prison calls end. No goodbyes, just a dead line.

Ava set the phone down and stared into the early gray light curling around the window.

She could've told him about Denise Ellery. About how long she'd known, how long she'd stayed quiet.

But Ava hadn't. And she wouldn't. Not yet.

She told herself it was kindness. That Chap needed the truth, yes, but not hope. Not yet. Not the kind that rose too fast, too easily, and left you shattered when it fell apart.

Still, the omission sat heavy in her chest, a pebble of guilt she couldn't quite swallow.

Maybe she wasn't protecting him. Maybe she was protecting herself from seeing what it would do to him if this all turned out to mean nothing.

She stood and started toward the kitchen, already knowing what she had to do next.

***

Ava tugged her sleeves over her hands and kicked the space heater with her heel, trying to coax it into doing more than grumbling. The McCormick shop had once been George's sacred space. Part workshop, part nautical junkyard, the walls still lined with old floats and rusted hooks.

Now, it was their war room with a crime board. It was their best shot.

The wind creaked through the weather-warped wood doors, and a thin draft whispered under the eaves like a secret.

She was already pacing in front of the whiteboard when Liz and Ryan arrived. They looked like they hadn't slept. Liz with her hair in a bun so tight it radiated tension, and Ryan cradling a travel mug like it was the only thing tethering him to consciousness.

"No muffins?" Liz asked, eyeing the counter.

"Esther's bringing scones. You'll survive," Ava said. "We've got movement."

Ryan leaned against the old counter. "You talked to Chap?"

She nodded. "He called this morning. His cellmate at Lemon Creek, turns out the guy's son played for Coach Ellery back in Juneau."

That got their attention.

"Yeah, yeah. We knew about the affair," Liz said. "And the pregnancy."

"And the buried investigation," Ryan added. "Nothing ever stuck."

"Right," Ava said. "But now we've got a name. Rachel Tripp."

Liz's eyebrows rose. "That's new."

"Exactly. The inmate told Chap her name. Also, Chap is starting to remember that night."

The room stilled.

"He remembers Amelia telling him that Coach was the father. That he wasn't who she thought he was." Ava's voice was low. "She trusted Chap with that. Because she hadn't told anyone else she was pregnant."

Ryan swore quietly.

Ava continued, her tone growing more certain as she spoke. "Chap was really drunk. He confronted Coach Ellery. Told him to stay away from her."

Liz grimaced. "That must've gone well."

"It didn't. Then Earl started hitting on Amelia. Chap stepped in again. Drunk, pissed, trying to play hero." She hesitated. "He let it slip. About the pregnancy."

"Earl turned nasty. Basically, told Amelia he wasn't interested in a pregnant woman. Like he had a chance in the first place. She was furious. Said it wasn't Chap's secret to share."

Ryan gave a slow nod. "That tracks. The yelling, the crying outside the bar. That's what witnesses said."

"Until this morning, Chap didn't remember any of it. It was all blank. But now, it's starting to come back."

"Chap said it himself," Ava murmured. "He might've been the last person Amelia trusted. And he let her down."

Liz crossed her arms. "So, what's our next move?"

"We find Rachel," Ava said. "If there's a pattern, it didn't start with Amelia. Rachel might be able to confirm that."

Ryan pulled out his phone. "I'll dig through DMV records, school transfers. We'll get a number."

"We keep this quiet," Ava said. "No uniforms. No badges. Just us."

"You tell Chap we'd find her?" Liz asked.

"I did." Ava's voice caught. "But I didn't tell him about Denise."

Ryan looked up, frowning. "Why not?"

"Because Denise didn't know the whole story. She didn't even know Amelia was pregnant. And I'm not giving Chap hope until we have something solid."

She could've told him. About Denise's voice cracking. About her guilt. But Ava hadn't.

And she wouldn't. Not yet.

Chap needed the truth. But he didn't need hope. Not until they had something to build it on.

Liz gave a small nod. "If Rachel won't talk?"

"Then we tell her that Amelia's dead," Ava said. "And that silence never protected the right people."

The space heater hissed in the corner. The anchor lamp above them swayed gently in the draft.

Ryan slipped his phone back into his pocket. "I'll head to the station and start digging. Let's keep this quiet. Harrow stays out of it."

Ava nodded. "Good."

Liz tapped a red marker against the whiteboard. "Alright, McCormick," she said. "Let's figure out our next move."

***

Esther stepped in, bundled in one of George's oversized flannels, holding three steaming mugs that smelled suspiciously like the cinnamon-vanilla blend she hoarded for special occasions.

"Any news?" she asked, setting the mugs down on the old counter.

"Not yet," Ava said, curling her fingers around the warmth. "Ryan said he'd text if he found anything."

Liz took a mug, blew on it, then glanced at Esther. "We should probably fill you in while we wait."

So, they did. In low voices, over the hiss of the space heater, they told her about Denise Ellery. About the way her voice cracked when she admitted she'd known her husband had been involved with a student in Juneau. About the buried whispers, the texts, and the name, Rachel Tripp, finally pulled from the shadows by one of Chap's fellow inmates.

By the time they finished, Esther's eyebrows had climbed higher, her jaw set like stone.

"So let me get this straight. You're telling me the same man Amelia was mixed up with has also chased after some poor kid?"

"More or less," Ava said. "Chap's cellmate remembered whispers about inappropriate texts. Said the coach got quietly fired from Juneau. But no official record."

"Because of course not," Esther muttered. "God forbid a man's career suffer the consequences of his actions."

Liz gave a short, humorless laugh. "Guess they figured better to ship him off than deal with the mess."

Esther shook her head slowly. "If Chap's right, and this Rachel Tripp can prove it, I hope they roast him. Slow."

Ava almost smiled. "You and me both."

The heater clanked in the corner, spitting out a weak puff of warmth. Outside, the wind pressed hard against the walls, as if even the weather was listening in.

***

Ava's phone buzzed on the bench beside her. She lunged for it like it might scurry away.

Ryan: *Found her.*

Ava: *Rachel?*

Ryan: *Rachel Tripp. Moved to Pendleton, Oregon, about the time Ellery left Juneau.*

Ava: *You get a number?*

Three dots blinked, disappeared, blinked again. Ava could almost see him at his desk, glancing over his shoulder to make sure Harrow wasn't lurking.

Ryan: *Working on it. Not exactly in the phone book.*

Liz leaned closer, trying to read upside down. "Well?"

"He's got her in Pendleton," Ava said, pulse quickening. "Looking for a number."

Esther's eyebrows shot up. "Pendleton? That's a long way to run."

Another buzz.

Ryan: *Got it. Cell phone. Unlisted.*

He pasted the digits into the thread, along with a final note: Careful. Harrow cannot know I pulled this.

Ava stared at the screen, the weight of it settling in her chest.

Liz met her gaze. "We calling now?"

"Give me a minute," Ava said. "We only get one chance to do this right."

Esther huffed, but there was no mistaking the spark in her eyes. "Just make sure, when you do, she knows she's not alone."

Ava set the phone down like it was a live wire, the numbers still glowing in her mind.

Liz tapped the whiteboard with the back of the red marker, leaving a smudge. "We can't just cold call her. Not if she thinks this is some rumor mill garbage."

"She won't," Ava said. "But if she's built a life in Pendleton, she's not going to want to dig this up. We need her to see the connection to Amelia … and to Coach."

Esther leaned forward, elbows on her knees, coffee mug cradled in both hands. "Then you tell her. Flat out. Who you are, what happened, and why she's the only one who can help. No circling the drain."

Liz gave a short nod. "We go at it like we're already on the same side. Make her feel like she's helping us, helping herself."

Ava's gaze flicked to her phone again. "If she hangs up, that's it. One shot."

"Then you make it count," Esther said, her voice steady, eyes bright.

Ava drew in a breath. "Alright. Let's call her."

The heater clanked, sending up a weak puff of warmth as Liz pulled her own phone closer, ready to hit speaker. Outside, the wind rattled the warped doors like it was impatient to hear what Rachel Tripp might say.

***

Ava stared at the number Ryan had texted, her thumb hovering over the green call button.

Liz tipped her chin toward the phone. "We're not going to get more ready."

"Maybe," Ava said. "But we're doing it anyway." She hit call and set the phone on speaker. One ring. Two. "Hello?" The voice was young, guarded, but not hardened.

"Hi. Is this Rachel Tripp?" Ava kept her voice gentle, almost casual.

"Who's asking?"

"My name's Ava McCormick. I'm here with Liz Walker. We're calling from Spruce Cove, Alaska. We know this is unexpected, but it's about Coach Ellery."

Silence, long enough Ava thought she might hang up. Then: "I don't want anything to do with him."

"I get that," Ava said quickly. "We wouldn't be calling unless it was important. There's an ongoing murder investigation here. We think Coach Ellery could be involved."

"I don't know anything about a murder," Rachel said, but her voice had thinned.

Liz leaned toward the phone, voice low and steady. "We're not saying you do. But what happened to you in Juneau. It may be linked to what happened here. It could help us understand what he's capable of."

A sharp inhale on the other end.

Ava's tone softened. "You were still in high school. There were messages. More than messages."

Rachel's reply was a whisper. "I was seventeen. He told me he loved me. And then, I got pregnant."

Ava's throat tightened. Liz went still beside her.

"My parents made me leave before anyone found out," Rachel continued. "We came to Oregon so it wouldn't ruin my future. I didn't get a choice. I had the baby in secret. Signed adoption papers. Went back to school like nothing happened."

Her voice wavered, but she pushed on. "And he just stayed there. Like he hadn't done anything wrong. I heard he left later."

"He's here now," Ava said quietly. "A woman named Amelia Colburn is dead. She wasn't a student, she was an adult, but we think she found out about you. That could be why she's gone."

Rachel was silent for a moment. "I don't know her. But if she knew, yeah. He'd want to shut her up."

"Will you talk to the police?" Liz asked.

"No." The word was fast, firm. "I can't go through that again. My parents would lose it. And what if he comes after me?"

Ava started to speak, but the line clicked dead.

The War Room felt colder. Outside, the wind pressed against the weathered boards, the sound like a long, slow exhale.

Liz looked at Ava. "She gave us enough to prove he's scum."

Ava nodded. "But not enough to prove he's a killer."

***

Ava stared at the phone a second longer, as if willing it to ring back. It didn't. Esther's voice broke the silence. "Come up to the house," she said, standing in the doorway with her hands tucked into George's flannel. "I've got a bottle of Pinot we've been saving for something good. This isn't good, exactly, but it feels important."

Fifteen minutes later, the three of them sat around Esther's worn kitchen table, glasses in hand. The wine was smooth, the conversation anything but. They spoke of Amelia, bright and complicated. Of Denise, haunted by a marriage built on lies. Of Rachel, still carrying scars she didn't ask for. And of Chap, who'd been tangled in Coach's wreckage more ways than one.

"I can't believe I ever doubted him," Esther said, her eyes glassy.

Liz let out a slow breath. "You're not alone. I did too."

Then Esther turned to Ava and gave a small, knowing smile. "But not you. Not really."

The wind rattled the windowpanes, the sound like the sigh of the whole town. They drank to Amelia. To the truth. And, silently, to the man they still believed they could save.

Chapter 20

Caroline's text had three rules: park two houses down, side gate, don't ring anything. It read like a heist note written by someone who irons their pajamas.

The gate stuck the way old wood does in winter; Ava eased it with her hip while Liz performed the gentle "don't break your tailbone" hover she reserved for black ice and Ava's life choices. The porch swing out front creaked once in the wind and then decided it wasn't getting involved.

The back door opened before either of them touched it. Caroline, quilted jacket, hair in a no-nonsense knot, stood in the crack like a bouncer. Warm air slipped out carrying the Colburn house's signature scent: citrus cleaner over older notes of wood and dust. A runner rug tracked a line straight enough to pass a sobriety test. School portraits marched up the staircase like tiny soldiers who had all learned to tuck in their shirts.

"Hi," Ava said softly.

Caroline's nod managed hello and goodbye in a single, precise dip. From a cubby, she produced a holiday gift bag still shouting JOY in slightly scuffed glitter. Excellent camouflage in a house where seasonal spirit had an inventory system. Inside the bag there was a scuffed laptop, a slim external drive with blue painter's tape labeled AM BACKUP, and a wrinkled Post-it with four faded characters. No commentary, no explanations. Only the things she could pass across a threshold without adding them to her family's vocabulary.

"Present," Caroline murmured.

Liz lifted the bakery sack like a decoy. "If your mom materializes, we love maple bars and refuse to leave until she takes two."

"Commit to the bit," Caroline said, deadpan, and pressed the bakery sack back into Liz's hands. "If my father appears, you're fundraising for the basketball boosters. You take checks."

"Excellent," Liz said. "Suggested donation?"

"Silence," Caroline said. "Worth every penny."

They slip-walked back along the path, boots whispering. The swing kept its counsel. At the gate, Liz exhaled. "That was the most stressful game of pass-the-laptop ever."

"It's your first," Ava said.

"And I'm undefeated," Liz replied, buckling the JOY bag into the back seat like a toddler they weren't ready to explain to anyone.

***

By the time the JOY bag stopped crackling and the heater remembered how to work, they were at Liz's house.

The house smelled like coffee and an aggressively scented candle, *Skate Date*. The table was an ecosystem: legal pads; a mason jar with two stubborn carnations refusing to admit it was February; a ring light leaning like a tired flamingo; three pens that had lost their caps to a better life; and, now, Amelia's laptop at the center like an altar.

"Ground rules," Liz said, propping her phone on a small stand and tapping record. "Camera's rolling. Read-only. If we find anything, we wait for Ryan to log and export it."

Ava set the faded Post-it near the window. The ink had gone soft gray, the corners rubbed by a thumb and a hard week. "A hint, maybe. Not a key."

Liz opened the laptop. It woke with a chime and an attitude. The login box waited like a bouncer who loved saying no.

"Attempt one," Liz announced, wiggling her fingers. She typed the Post-it digits.

Shake. Wrong.

"Could have been too literal." She tried the reverse.

Shake. Wrong.

"Third time's the charm is propaganda," Ava said. "What about the 'add one' trick? An exclamation mark?"

"That's for people who enjoy chaos," Liz said.

Shake. Wrong.

A polite warning slid onto the screen: 1 attempt remaining.

Liz leaned back as if the laptop had hissed. "Lockout timer. No hero moves."

Ava's stomach did that small elevator drop. She grabbed her phone and, with the urgency of someone trying to defuse a soufflé, started typing: *how to get into a mac if you forgot the password and also the universe is watching.*

Search results stacked up like bad options at midnight.

"This one says, 'Ask the owner,'" she reported. "Helpful."

"Technically, we did," Liz said. "The owner is not taking calls."

"Okay, 'Top 5 Mac Unlock Tools (No Password!).' That feels like a virus wearing a fake mustache." Ava scrolled. "Here's a forum guy who says you can boot into 'single-user mode' and type very intimidating things into Terminal."

"That's for older machines," Liz said, eyes on the screen. "Also known as: a great way to brick someone's laptop on a Tuesday."

"'Reset with Apple ID?'" Ava tried, pointing at the grayed-out link. "Why is it ghosting us?"

"Because we're offline and because if her Apple ID routes to a family email, we've just started a group chat we can't explain," Liz said. "Step away from the last try. We're not frying the logic board out of enthusiasm."

Ava skimmed another result. "This article suggests 'erase Mac and restore from backup.'"

"Which is the plot of a horror movie," Liz said. "We're not erasing anything. Read-only or nothing."

"Fine," Ava sighed, thumbs still flying. "What about Disk Utility? Can we, I don't know, peek?"

"We can confirm the backup mounts," Liz said, already reaching for the external drive. "If Time Machine isn't encrypted, we can open Mail from the backup without touching the login. No saves. No exports. When we find something, Ryan does the export."

Ava lowered the phone like it had talked her out of a tattoo. "Scout's honor," she said. "And for the record, the internet just tried to sell me a $29.99 'Miracle Unlocker.'"

"Put it on your Christmas list," Liz said, deadpan, and plugged in the drive.

Liz pointed to the grayed-out link. "Unavailable offline. Also, if her Apple ID routes to a family email, we create more problems than answers."

"Copy. We like answers."

"Attempt nothing," Liz decided. "We wait out the one-minute lockout like civilized people and try a human guess."

They waited. Ava tore the bakery bag, exposing a maple bar that looked like it had survived a war and was ready to talk to a reporter. Liz used the minute to build a suspect list of Password Personality Types on a legal pad: *Birthday Person, Pet Name Person, Lazy Genius (last four of phone)*.

"Which was Amelia?" Ava asked.

"Secret fourth type: 'Whatever is easiest until it bites me,'" Liz said. "The Post-it is the tell."

The lockout lifted. Liz hovered, then pulled her hands back. "No. We're done playing with the login. We don't need the front door if the back door is open."

Ava arched a brow. "Metaphor game strong."

"External drive," Liz said, tapping AM BACKUP. "If Time Machine isn't encrypted, Mail drafts can be browsed without logging in. Read-only."

"Fine," Ava said. "Kindergarten rules, don't touch."

"Put that on my tombstone," Liz replied. "*Elizabeth Walker, 1989– Don't Touch.*"

Liz plugged in the drive. It mounted with a cheerful icon that did not respect the mood. No password prompt, which meant no encryption. She gave the camera a crisp narration, fingers moving slowly, deliberately: Backups.backupdb ▸ Amelia-MacBook ▸ Latest ▸ Users ▸ Amelia ▸ Library ▸ Mail.

"Which version?" Ava asked.

"V10," Liz said. "She updated macOS at some point. Mail Data. Drafts." A folder bloomed. A column populated with unsent messages. Apologies, reminders, a draft labeled *Dentist?* That put a quiet fist through the middle of Ava's chest.

In the center sat a subject line that looked like it had been waiting with its coat on:

This man is doing it again.

Ava's stomach dropped two floors. Liz opened the draft.

The email was short. The kind of short that happens when fear edits you:

To whom it may concern,

I am writing because this is happening again. Last year, reports about Coach Conner Ellery were handled "internally," and he was allowed to resign. He is now at Spruce Cove High. I have reason to believe the same behavior has continued here.

If you had acted last year, he wouldn't be here.

Sincerely,

Amelia Colburn, Concerned Citizen

Below sat a checklist Amelia had typed to herself.

Attachments to add: practice_roster_Sep3.pdf

SC_student_statement_redacted.pdf

records_request_last_year.docx

No names. No explicit accusation.

"There it is," Ava said, keeping her voice even. "A pattern."

"She wasn't just mad," Liz said, nodding at the checklist. "She was organized: roster for proximity; a redacted Spruce Cove student statement for 'here and now'; and a records request to pry Juneau open."

"Read-only until Ryan," Ava reminded, because saying it out loud kept hands from wandering.

"Copy that." Liz intentionally parked the cursor away from Save, then highlighted the Finder path for the camera: Backups.backupdb ▸ … ▸ MailData ▸ Drafts.

"Check the files," Ava said.

The roster opened as a tidy list with names, numbers, positions. The sort of document that puts a coach inside kids' lives in a way that looks like leadership until it doesn't.

Next: SC_student_statement_redacted.pdf. Black bars masked a name; initials anchored the top corner; a November date. The content was laid out the pattern: texts; "extra reps" after hours; a ride home "not my direction"; a hand that stayed on a shoulder too long; a request to keep "our workouts" private so others wouldn't "get jealous." At the bottom: "This is for the record. I don't want my parents to know yet. I want it to stop."

Liz didn't swear. She'd run out of word for that weeks ago. "That last line."

Ava swallowed. "Records request."

"Records_request_last_year.docx" opened on a clean single page. The language was clipped, confident: A demand for all materials related to Ellery's internal handling last year. Complaint, witness statements, emails, separation agreement, referrals and any non-disparagement clauses or recommendations issued to future employers. Alaska Open Records Act citations stood like guardrails.

"She was going to try to pry Juneau's file loose," Ava said. "Then line it up beside this statement. That's a pattern the police can't ignore."

The wind chime made of old keys clinked once on Liz's porch.

214

"Call him," Liz said.

Ryan answered on the first ring. "Tell me you're sitting still."

"We are at Liz's and have Amelia's laptop with a Time Machine backup," Ava said. "Screen recording is running. We haven't copied anything. There's an unsent draft to the Juneau School Board with the subject 'This man is doing it again.' There's a checklist for a practice roster, a redacted Spruce Cove student statement, and a drafted records request for the Juneau School District. Can you come log it and do the export?"

"I'll be right there," Ryan said. Paper rustled on his end. "Don't touch another thing. Don't destroy the evidence. And please lock your door."

"Understood."

The call ended. Silence returned, the kind that made the candle's tiny hiss sound bossy.

Ava's phone lit with No Caller ID. Two rings, then it dropped. No voicemail, just the kind of nothing that pretends to be accidental.

Liz's porch cam chimed a motion alert a moment later. On the screen, a blue SUV idled at the curb, paused for a moment too long, then eased on. The image froze on a salt-flecked bumper and half a plate.

"Document it," Liz said.

Ava snapped the porch-cam still and the missed-call screen, then sent both to Ryan with a single line: Possible tail. Time-stamped.

Liz lifted the curtain an inch, seeing the street in slices. "Could be a neighbor."

They locked the back door. Just in case.

Ava grabbed screenshots of the laptop screen with the draft open, timestamps and file path visible, and queued them for Ryan as well. "Captured. I'll send these, too."

"Good," Liz said.

The room went quiet. The kind of quiet that makes a house sound louder. A moment later the porch-cam pinged again. Both of them froze, then exhaled when the clip showed only the wind pushing the chimes.

"The camera needs to stop auditioning for haunted house," Liz muttered.

Ryan arrived three minutes early, wearing his I-am-both-responsible-and-worried jacket. He took a slow lap, filming the setup with his phone, then opened a battered notebook and wrote the date like it mattered.

"Walk me through it," he said.

Liz narrated, the cursor slow and deliberate: backup mounted; path to MailData/Drafts; draft opened. Ryan read the subject, the body, the checklist, then spent longer on the redacted student statement than on anything else. The deputy part of his face stayed in charge; the human behind it peeked out.

"This helps," he said. "It's not the whole case, but it helps." He photographed the missed-call log and the porch-cam stills, then dictated a department address and had Ava forward the files. "If that number calls again, let it go to voicemail and save it. Do not engage."

"Wasn't planning to," Ava said.

"I know," he replied. "Saying it anyway."

He sat for the export, logging each step like he was placing flat stones for the rest of the world to follow without falling in. The .eml, the two PDFs, the records-request doc, bagged and tagged digitally and on paper. When he closed his notebook, he didn't move.

"Harrow needs to be looped in," he said, lifting a hand before Liz could deploy a sentence as a weapon. "If this moves, he has to think it moved *his* way."

"Tell him we got our hands on the backup," Liz said. "No need to specify by whom."

"I'll say exactly that." He paused at the door and turned to Liz. "Stay away from Ellery. Text me when you lock up. Liz, you're sleeping at my place tonight. Not a debate."

Liz lifted a brow. "Bossy."

"Correct," he said, soft enough to count as affection. "Doors locked. If anyone tails you, go straight to the station, not here."

The look they traded had the quick shorthand of people who knew each other's spare keys. Liz nodded once. "Okay."

Ryan touched the doorjamb like a man making a promise and left with the carefulness of someone carrying a match through dry grass.

***

The house resumed being a place where coffee cooled and a candle did its best. Liz set both palms on the table as if blessing it.

"We could wait," she said.

"We could," Ava agreed. Neither moved.

"Or," Liz continued, "we start a draft. Clean and careful."

"*Unsent email to Juneau exists. Redacted student statement exists. District allowed a quiet resignation last year. Pattern alleged.* End with: *Requests for comment have been sent to Coach Ellery and to Juneau.*"

"Add month names," Ava said. "Last year is a feeling; November is a fact."

Liz's mouth tilted. "Look at us being boringly brave."

"Your sweatshirt is doing the heavy lifting," Ava said, eyeing the giant beer-drinking moose. "It radiates courage."

"So which Lord invented coffee?" Liz asked, raising her mug in a small benediction.

"Whichever one answers emails," Ava said.

They opened blank documents like swimmers bracing for cold water. Words began to behave. The room warmed by an inch.

As Ava typed, her phone buzzed with a group text from Esther and the Bunco Mafia, dropping gossip about who'd used a fake name to buy rhubarb at the winter market. Liz answered with three knives and a pie emoji; Ava added a heart and silenced the thread. Breathing mattered. So did not losing their minds.

"Headline?" Liz asked.

"'Handled Internally,'" Ava said, and wrote it before either of them could flinch. "Subhead: *Last year in Juneau, a coach leaves quietly. This winter in Spruce Cove, the pattern doesn't.*"

"Add: *Documents reviewed by the Gazette include a draft email, a redacted student statement, and a prepared public-records request,*" Liz said. "And please thank my sweatshirt in the acknowledgments."

"The sweatshirt receives a medal," Ava said. "For services rendered. Morale."

They wrote. They fact-checked each other in the fussy way learned in newsrooms and families. Liz command-F'd for every "seems" and "appears" and made Ava earn them; Ava swapped out "silence" for "quiet handling," which was uglier and therefore more accurate. They argued for three minutes about whether "last year" needed the actual month; they added it. Ava cut a sentence she loved because it made the student sound poetic when all the student wanted was an adult to act like one.

When the draft was saved, a new quiet entered the room. The sound of a page turning.

"Send to Ryan for his file?" Liz asked.

"Send," Ava said. "OK. Let's send our own public records request and see what happens."

Liz opened the district's web form. "Name, outlet, dates, specifics. Give me the language."

Ava dictated from Amelia's draft, tightening a phrase here, softening a land mine there. When Liz hit submit, a ding arrived a heartbeat later:

Juneau School Board Autoresponder: *We have received your public-records request. Estimated response time: 5-10 business days.*

"Paperwork that isn't boring," Liz said, toasting the air.

Another ping. Not the autoresponder this time, the porch-cam. Same blue SUV, same slow roll, same too-long pause before it eased on. Ava grabbed the still, caught a partial plate, and texted it to Ryan: Second pass. Time-stamped, plate partial attached.

"Could still be a neighbor," Liz said, light on purpose.

"Maybe," Ava said, locking the back door anyway. "Or a neighbor whose errands got curious."

Liz flipped on the kitchen light and let the curtain fall. "Back to work."

Ava set the phone face down and reopened the draft. The room found that careful quiet again. The kind that makes a house sound louder.

"Note: we're not special," Liz said, voice light by decision. "We are two women with a candle, and a pastry."

"Now," Ava said, "we make copies of our notes, text Esther that we're alive, and attempt to behave like the kind of people who can keep a lid on this."

Liz laughed. "We are objectively not those people. Our job description is 'make noise.'"

"Fine," Ava said. "Quiet-adjacent. We don't publish, we wait for Ryan, and we prepare to be very tidy and very loud later."

"So an embargo on our impulses," Liz said.

"Whispering with documentation," Ava agreed.

Outside, February considered snow and withheld it just to keep everyone humble. Inside, the candle's flame leaned once and steadied. The JOY bag slumped on a chair like it had done enough for today. The phones lay face-down, but the messages inside them had weight.

They didn't have the ending yet, endings are arrogant that way. What they had was the word that mattered and the work to match it. A pattern. A path. A deputy with a notebook. A district with a clock that had just started.

Ava glanced at the window. A faint smear of blue, maybe the same bumper or maybe not, slid out of frame like a thought deciding not to be said. She breathed once, twice, then reached for the keyboard.

Chapter 21

George's shop smelled like what happened when a storm passed through a lumberyard and stopped to make friends with the harbor. Sawdust clung to the edges of the workbench. The salt on the high panes had dried into delicate lace, the kind that made you wonder how long it had been there and whether George ever noticed. A pegboard covered the back wall, every hook and tool arranged in a way that made perfect sense to him and almost no one else. If you squinted, you could see the pattern; if you asked, he'd say, *"There's a pattern, you just haven't learned it yet."*

Recently, he'd stood in this very spot, watching Ava and Liz turn the adjacent wall into a war room. He'd allowed it under one condition: "Tape on paint, not on wood." That was George, boundaries delivered. Now, the wall obeyed. It had columns, cards, red thread looping like someone had handed geometry to a poet. It looked orderly. It felt like a heartbeat.

Ava stood in front of it and made herself breathe in for a count of five. It was the same breathing she used when a dentist told her to relax or a live interview started in three, two, one. She counted to five again, just to be sure.

Behind her, Liz walked a perfect six-step loop across the concrete. Turn. Six steps back. It wasn't pacing if you kept the count exactly, or so she claimed. The rhythm made the shop feel like it had its own metronome.

"Elevator pitch," Liz said, stopping beneath a header card that read *Juneau → Spruce Cove*. "Except he hates elevators."

"Stair pitch," Ava answered. "He likes rules. And stairs."

"Two handrails," Liz said, squaring a card by less than a millimeter. "And a landing halfway up, so he feels safe."

"That's almost sweet."

"That's almost strategy," Liz replied.

The side door opened without a knock. Esther slipped in, carrying a stack of blank index cards. She set them on the workbench and squared the top one with the kind of precision you only get from a lifetime of folding fitted sheets correctly.

"No dramatics. Facts only," Esther said. "Quiet."

"We can do quiet," Liz said.

"You can do volume control," Esther said. "I'm requesting silence."

"Copy."

George followed behind Esther, February still on his shoulders like a coat he hadn't taken off yet. His knit hat was in his hand. He took in Liz and Ava's wall with the steady appraisal of someone who knew where every tool lived in his world, literal and otherwise. He didn't admire the string. He checked its balance.

"If he asks for three things," George said, "give him two and a question he can't ignore."

"Settle for credible," Ava offered.

"Always," he agreed, with the finality of someone who thought charm was for people who didn't have facts.

The door slowly squeaked open. Ryan came in first, coat unzipped, like he'd left in a hurry but hadn't decided whether it was worth zipping up again. The Chief followed, stillness rolling off him like a change in weather.

He looked at faces before he looked at string. Ava respected the choice and, just a little, resented it.

"Afternoon," the Chief said. Not warm, not cold. Functional, the way a gavel is functional. "Ryan says you've got something besides yarn."

"Have a seat," Esther said, and chairs appeared as if she'd willed them into being.

The Chief and Ryan sat on one side of the bench; Ava and Liz on the other. George leaned against the tool chest like the person you wanted in the room if something wobbled. The space heater ticked twice, keeping time with Liz's shoe against the concrete.

"Five minutes," the Chief said. A pace, not a threat.

Liz started, because Liz believed she could land a plane. "We didn't break into anything to get these," she said. "We found things. We talked to people. We'll tell you exactly what we touched and where we stopped."

Ava pointed her capped pen at a card labeled *Amelia's Journal*. The handwriting on it was Liz's: small, square, legible enough to be carved in stone. "She wrote about earrings he gave her," Ava said. "She called them a 'peace offering.' Said they were beautiful, subtle, expensive, grown-up."

Liz lifted a small Ziploc bag from the tray beside her. Inside, a delicate blue teardrop earring caught the light like it was trying to behave. "This was in Amelia's jewelry box," she said. "A single earring. No match in the house."

She set it down, picked up a second bag.

"And this one was in Denise Ellery's desk drawer," Liz said. "Same style. We found it during a ..." her mouth curved, just barely "... questionably advisable after-hours visit. We documented it, then stopped. Ryan has it logged."

Ryan placed a folder on the bench, stamped "Official Property."

"Chain of custody starts with me," he said.

The Chief's eyes narrowed, his attention snapping back to Liz. "And how exactly did you get into Ms. Ellery's office after hours?"

"Unlocked door," Liz said. "Wrong place, right time. We didn't go looking for trouble, just answers."

Ava added, "And we stopped the second we knew what we were looking at. Called Ryan. Hands off since."

The Chief's expression didn't change, but his eyes stayed on them a half-second longer than polite. Then he shifted his gaze to Ava. "Keep going."

Ava glanced at the thread running from *Amelia's Journal* to the next card: *Denise Ellery*. The red line had a slight dip in the middle, like it had sagged under the weight of what was on it.

"We spoke with Denise Ellery," Ava said. Her voice came out level, but inside she was still hearing Denise's words from two days ago, clipped, tired, brittle in the way that made you wonder if she'd once been warm and had learned better.

"She told us," Ava went on, "that in Juneau, Coach was fired, and she did not say 'resigned,' for misconduct. There was a teenage girl on his team. Rumors of a pregnancy. She said it was handled quietly, and she chose survival." Ava didn't need to glance at Liz; she could feel her standing straighter.

Liz's turn: "She also told us she'd given police her statement, but with us, she said the quiet parts out loud."

George shifted behind them.

Ava tapped the next card: *Civil Filing: Denise Ellery v. Conner Ellery*. "We found this in her desk. Irreconcilable differences. Not a verdict but confirms marital issues."

The Chief didn't blink, which was its own kind of listening. His gaze slid to *Rachel Tripp, phone*.

Liz caught the handoff. "Rachel's the girl in question from Juneau. She's in Oregon now. She told us she was seventeen when Coach said he loved her. She got pregnant. Her parents moved her to avoid the shame. She had the baby, signed adoption papers, and went back to school like nothing happened." Liz's voice didn't waver, but her thumb traced the edge of the evidence bag on the bench.

Ava added, "When we asked if she'd talk to police, she said, 'No,' and hung up." She kept her tone even. "We have the call logs. She's a source. Not a witness. Not yet."

Ryan slid a yellow Post-it across the bench. Time. Partial number. Oregon underlined twice.

The Chief shifted his weight. Not impatient, exactly, but aware of clocks.

Ryan angled the evidence bags so they didn't catch light. "The earrings tie the Ellerys to Amelia," he said quietly. "One in her room, one in Mrs. Ellery's desk. Add the journal calling them a peace offering, that's edging toward motive. Not proof. Motion."

The Chief's gaze landed on Ava. "One sentence, Ms. McCormick."

"Last year in Juneau, a coach's affair with a student was handled quietly," Ava said. "This year he's here. He and Amelia started an affair. She got pregnant. We're assuming the baby was his and at some point, she realized he was also involved with another girl here in Spruce Cove. She began building a record with journal entries, a kept gift, names she wouldn't yet write. The Ellery marriage was already breaking. Our suspect is Coach Ellery. We believe Mrs. Ellery has material information and should be questioned on the record."

The heater clicked once. Outside, a seagull gave a single irritated cry.

***

The Chief didn't answer right away. He let Ava's sentence hang there like a freshly posted notice on the town hall board, something you might stop to read twice just to be sure you'd seen it right. His gaze moved from Ava, to Liz, to the wall. The red thread caught the overhead light in a single, sharp glint.

Then, finally, he stood.

Ryan stood with him, not because he had anything else to add, but because some things were pure muscle memory. Ava didn't move. Staying seated was her own kind of statement.

"We'll do this properly," the Chief said. His voice had the cadence of someone who had explained this before and didn't mind explaining it again, but only once. "No heroics. Ryan, you start the paperwork. I'll brief the DA. Ms. Colburn's family hears before anyone else. Bring Mrs. Ellery in for a recorded statement. Primary suspect: Coach Ellery."

He let the weight of those words land before continuing. "Ms. McCormick, Liz: hands off. If anything changes, you call Deputy Hale. Not your readers. Not your friends."

Ava opened her mouth, not to argue, but to confirm, when Liz's heel gave a deliberate little tap on the floor. One crisp syllable in Morse code: Do not ruin this.

"Understood," Ava said.

"Got it," Liz echoed, and she managed to make it sound like she'd been agreeing with police directives her entire life.

The Chief's eyes softened just enough that you could call it almost a smile if you were generous.

"Good," he said. Then he looked past them to George, like the only person in the room he might actually thank for keeping the space from tilting. "Appreciate the room."

George gave a half-shrug. "Bring back something worth pinning to the board," he said.

It wasn't a joke, not exactly, but it wasn't a command either. More like a shared understanding.

The Chief inclined his head, that almost-smile still flickering, and turned toward the door. Ryan followed, pausing just long enough to aim one last look at the evidence wall. It was the kind of look you gave something you weren't sure you'd see again in quite the same state.

The door wedged closed.

The shop breathed out.

"That," Esther said softly, "was a yes with conditions."

***

The door swung back open. A sound that made Ava's head come up.

Liz stilled mid-step in her six-count pacing loop. Esther's hand froze on the index cards like she was about to deal a hand no one wanted.

Ryan appeared in the doorway first, a flush of wind on his cheeks. His coat was still unzipped, his gloves shoved into one pocket like he'd decided halfway here that there wasn't time to dress for it. The look on his face was half business, half something else. The sort of thing that made Ava's chest tighten before he even opened his mouth.

"Quick," he said, voice low but carrying. His eyes did a fast inventory: Ava, Liz, the wall, George before locking back on Ava. "We're meeting with the judge at three. Case is reopening. The Chief wants to bring Denise Ellery in for a recorded statement before dinner."

For a second, the words didn't move in her head. Like she'd heard them but couldn't get them into the right order. Then it hit.

The investigation is reopened.

Ava's ribs expanded in that unhelpful, too-big way hope had, as if her lungs were trying to make more room before she'd even decided if she could handle what was coming. "Thank you," she said. The words felt too small for the space they had to fill.

Ryan's gaze slid to the evidence wall. He didn't linger long, but he didn't have to. The map of cards and string had a gravitational pull. "Don't touch it," he said, tilting his chin toward it. It wasn't an order so much as the thing you said to a dog you loved and a woman you trusted. He didn't quite trust to leave a puzzle unsolved.

Then his attention shifted to Liz. His tone softened in a way Ava couldn't help but notice.

"Text me your ETA. Spare key's still under the …"

"I know," Liz cut in, her mouth twitching like there was an inside joke neither of them was willing to explain.

He gave her a quick nod, like that was all the reassurance he needed, and stepped back into the cold. The door swung shut behind him, leaving the smell of his coat in the room for a few seconds after he'd gone.

They all listened to the sound of his footsteps on the gravel, the crunch fading until it was swallowed by the general hush of the harbor.

Only then did the shop breathe again.

The heater ticked twice, steady as a clock. The cards on the wall stayed where they were.

Liz was the first to speak. "Well." She didn't look at Ava when she said it; she kept her eyes on the thread between Juneau and Spruce Cove, like it might start vibrating if she stared long enough.

Ava let herself look at Liz scan the wall. The same wall the Chief had stood in front of earlier, unreadable. It wasn't about showing it to them again. It was about keeping it exactly the same, like a cake you don't cut until the company arrives. "Now we hold," she said. "No tweaks. No rearranging. When they walk back in with the DA, I want them to see exactly what we saw."

Liz's mouth tilted, like she was picturing herself straightening one crooked card just to see Ava twitch. "Fine," she said. "We'll leave it. Even if it's killing me."

Esther made a small approving sound, the same one she used when a batch of dough hit the exact right rise. George shifted his weight against the tool chest but didn't speak, which for George was about as loud as support got.

They didn't move toward the wall, didn't straighten a single card. It stood there in its full, unsmiling glory, part map, part dare, part truth waiting to be pinned down officially.

***

Esther broke the quiet first. "You all need feeding," she said, like it was an indisputable fact. "And not just because I've seen the way your hands shake when you forget to eat. Kitchen. Now."

George nodded toward the wall, his cap in his hand. "Leave it. Let it breathe."

Liz reached up and flicked off the task lamp. Without its warm cone of light, the cards and thread faded into a softer outline, like a photograph going still. The war-room wall could stand on its own for a while.

Ava followed the others across the shop, their footsteps echoing off the wooden floorboards. February wind met them halfway across the yard, sharp and salt-edged, pushing them the rest of the way into the kitchen's golden warmth. George claimed the kettle without ceremony. Esther dug into the shortbread tin, muttering about rationing. Liz leaned against the counter, scrolling her phone with the air of someone half-expecting bad news and pretending otherwise.

Ava stood in the doorway, watching the domestic choreography. The clink of mugs, the low hum of conversation. As if she were looking through a window. It was comfort, but not the kind she could sink into right now.

She slipped upstairs before anyone noticed, closing her bedroom door behind her.

The quiet was different here, less shared air, more her own heartbeat. She sat on the edge of the bed and pulled her phone from her pocket, staring at the contact she didn't need to look up.

The prison's main line answered after the third ring. She gave her name, clear and steady, and waited through the hold. In the background, she caught the faraway sounds she'd learned to picture without wanting to. Metal doors, an indistinct shout, footsteps that echoed too long.

Then, the click.

"McCormick," Chap said. That careful neutral tone, polite enough to keep a caller talking, guarded enough to keep everything else behind the walls.

"It's good news," she said, skipping any lead-in.

A pause, and she could hear the faint shift of him leaning forward. "Go on."

"The investigation is reopened."

Silence. She pictured his face, trying not to hope too hard. "Say that again."

"Reopened. The Chief came to see us. We walked him through everything Liz and I have been doing. He didn't argue. Denise Ellery's

228

giving a recorded statement at 3. Coach Ellery is now the primary suspect."

On the other end, a measured breath.

"I didn't want to give you crumbs, Chap. No half-stories. We've been busy. We've been building a case to prove you didn't kill Amelia. Not guesses. Evidence."

She told him, piece by piece. Amelia's journal. The blue teardrop earrings, one from her room, one from Denise's desk. The civil filing for divorce. Denise's story about Juneau, the student, the pregnancy no one wanted to acknowledge. Rachel Tripp in Oregon, and the silence on the line after her "no" to police.

When she stopped, the quiet between them felt heavier than the hold music had been.

"You've been sitting on this?"

"Not sitting," she said. "Holding until it was solid. Until the Chief would have to do something. Now we have movement."

Another slow exhale. "And you think this clears me?"

"I think it's the first real crack in the wall," she said. "And we're not stopping now."

A second passed, and his voice softened, just enough for her to hear the man, not the inmate. "Thank you, Ava."

She leaned back, feeling the bed frame catch her shoulders. "Hold on, Chap. We're just getting started."

Chapter 22

The chairs outside Spruce Cove's sole interrogation room were the kind a town ordered by the hundreds when the school needed more seating for graduation. They were metal with legs that squeaked if anyone dared shift their weight. Ava sat and tried not to move. Across from her, the vending machine barely hummed.

Ryan passed with a yellow legal pad and two pens behind his ear like he was storing optimism there. He didn't stop, but he tilted the pad toward her like a secret handshake. Translation: *we're rolling; please don't get me fired.*

The Chief followed, expression neutral the way Midwestern casseroles were: there was salt in there somewhere, hiding behind kindness. His look said, *you're press; I'm police. You are in my hallway.* Ava could behave. She had a brain and a mother who had taught her how to wait without making it about herself.

She kept her phone facedown because she didn't trust herself not to refresh into oblivion. Behind the door: Denise, her lawyer, Ryan and the Chief. The recorder that clicked when someone breathed too hard. It was the kind of door that turned juicy sound into respectable muffling. No words, just cadence. Question, pause, paper rustle. Chair scrape. She jotted the sounds as if they were reportable facts: Cadence steady. Chair scrape at 6:28. Recorder clack at 6:32.

The door opened once, just the front desk clerk with a bottle of water. False alarm. Ava flopped back down, the chair protesting under her. Somewhere behind those closed doors, Denise Ellery was taking her husband down. Somewhere in this town, another woman was sliding a pie into the oven. Honestly, Ava would take either: legal freedom or dessert. Preferably both.

When the door finally opened for real, the recorder's red light still glowed. The Chief exited first, followed by the lawyer wearing a blazer with shoulder pads and then Denise. Her eyes were that raw pink you only got from crying in stop-and-starts. She kept her hands in her coat pockets like she was holding in the words she hadn't said.

Ava stood, because standing felt like a compromise between professionalism and a heart beating too loud. She didn't speak. She didn't have it in her to further press a woman who had just done a terrifying thing. There was dignity in not making her job the main character.

Denise glanced at her anyway. No glare, no thank-you, just acknowledgment. The human version of clicking *I have read the terms and conditions* even though she hadn't. Ava nodded back, a whisper of a motion, and the Chief swept them past.

Out in the lot, the sky turned the moody blue that made you want a sweater and a therapist. The station light hummed like it was a living thing. A moth kept trying to headbutt it into submission.

"Interviewing Coach next?" she asked the Chief's shoulder as it moved by.

"If we can find him," he said, not stopping.

The words were simple. The meaning landed like a dropped bowling ball. Not at home. Not at school. Not on a track with teenagers who thought stretching was optional because they were made of rubber and bad choices. *If we can find him.*

She texted Liz one word: "Unavailable." Three dots appeared, and then: "Ping if anything you can print. I'm in a meeting with an advertiser who calls me 'kiddo.'"

"Condolences," she sent, and tucked the phone away like it might bite if she kept holding it.

***

She did a lap around the block to bleed off the itch in her muscles. Her phone buzzed in her palm. William.

"Hey," he said when she answered, his voice threaded through with airport noise of an espresso machine shrieking, a gate-change announcement swallowing vowels, a suitcase rolling. "Is this a bad time?"

"I'm loitering at the moment," she said. "Excellent lighting, terrible chairs. What's with the public-address symphony?"

"Travel day," he said, which covered a world of sins. "Sorry it's loud. I just wanted to hear you. Are you okay?"

She started pacing the hallway and whispered, "I'm fine."

"Ava." He managed to put concern into a single syllable and make it sound like a seatbelt. "You don't have to be brave with me. Are you safe?"

"As safe as a person who is spending her time stalking uniformed police officers," she said. "I'm not alone."

"Good," he said, relief audible under the word. "Is it moving? The case?"

She picked at a thumbnail, then stopped herself. "We think we've figured out who it is." She kept her voice even. "It isn't the person they've been holding."

A burst of feedback swallowed his inhale. "If he's out there, that's … Ava, please tell me you're not doing the intrepid-reporter thing solo."

"I'm doing the stand-here-and-take-notes thing," she said. "Deputy Hale's orbiting. The Chief is doing his job, finally."

He exhaled; somewhere a metal grate rattled down. "Humor me. No empty lots. No walking to your car with both earbuds in. Keys in your hand like a small, tasteful weapon. Big flashlight. Bigger friend."

"I don't own a big flashlight," she said. "I do own a salty grandmother."

232

"That counts," he said, and she could hear the smile he didn't have time to make. "Text me when you get home. One word. *Alive*. Don't make me …"

"Get on a plane?" she teased. "You would hate our small planes."

"I hate not knowing you're okay," he said, and the line went quiet enough that she heard her own breath. A cart beeped an apology at a crowd of feet on his end. "I'm proud of you, but I'm worried."

"Got it."

"Where are you right now?" he asked. "Exactly."

"At the corner of *don't push me* and *I promise*," she said, then softened it. "At the police station. Plenty of company."

"Okay," he said. "Okay. I have to … they're … I'll call when I can. Text me *alive*."

"I will."

"Ava?"

"Yeah?"

"Good job," he said, gently, and then the call dissolved into boarding passes and bad acoustics.

***

She slipped the phone back into her pocket and promptly ignored his request. She went for a walk alone. The thrift store had three prom dresses pressed flat against the window like debutantes in a hostage photo. The bakery was so closed the croissants looked like fossils. By the time she circled back, the hallway smelled like Lysol.

Ryan caught her at the door.

"Anything I can put on the record?"

"Not yet," he said. "Hands off. If Harrow gives me a crumb to give you, I'll call."

"You're a delight when you're bossy."

"I'm hangry," he said. "Go home. You can say police want to talk to him. No color, no guesses."

"Bone-dry?"

"Like pilot bread." He started toward the lot, then glanced back. "And, Ava? Let the cops do the cop part."

"I would never," she said, knowing he didn't buy it and knowing he was right.

On her way to the car, her phone buzzed again.

Caroline: *Can we talk? Not at the station.*

Ava stood with her hand on the car door and felt the streetlight outline her knuckles like a children's tracing.

Ava: *Church kitchen? Ten minutes?*

Caroline: *Thank you.*

Two words could unclench a chest if the syntax was right.

***

The church kitchen smelled like spaghetti from last night's Bible study. The corkboard above the sink offered sign-up sheets with tidy columns for name and phone number and the promise that order could solve anything.

Caroline was already there when Ava pushed through the swinging door, hands wrapped around a Styrofoam cup, nails short not because she liked them that way but because worry had eaten them.

"Thank you for coming," Caroline said.

"Of course," Ava said. She kept her bag on her shoulder like armor. "I can stay a few minutes."

Caroline glanced at the door, then lowered her voice. "I shouldn't be bothering you tonight. I know a lot is going on. I just need to know."

"I never thought it was Chap," Caroline said, the words landing like something she'd been holding between her teeth. "My parents are still wrapping their heads around what has happened. Chap's guilt wasn't a debate in our house, it was policy."

A movement by the coffee urn made her look up. There was Mason, shoulders squared, hands in his pockets like he didn't trust them. She hadn't realized he'd come in; he must've slipped through the side door. The last time she'd seen him, he'd been one of the loudest voices in the *Chap did it* chorus. Tonight, he just looked tired. He didn't speak; he scrubbed a hand over his jaw and stared at the corkboard, listening.

"We were so sure," he said. "I was." He gave a humorless laugh. "Pride, not proof. I need to make it right."

Caroline's fingers worried the cup's rim until it squeaked. "I dropped a pie at your place. For the house. Blueberry."

"You didn't have to do that," Ava said.

"I wanted to say thank you," Caroline said. "For how you've handled all of this. For seeing Amelia."

"Food works," Ava said. "Tell me it's the kind with the sugar on top."

Caroline managed a small smile. "Of course."

"Just so you know, I'm off the clock," Ava said. "I just wanted to see how you're holding up."

"Thank you," Caroline said.

Just as they stood up, the refrigerator gasket popped as the compressor kicked off, loud enough to make all three of them startle and then laugh, the kind that was more of a release valve than humor.

***

When Ava slid back into the car, the police scanner crackled in a low, endless drone. She didn't always listen. Tonight, she listened. "BOLO on Explorer. Trailhead near the terminal overflow parking lot." Her spine sat up like a kid at story time.

She drove tentatively, like someone who didn't want her premiums to go up. The terminal lot was wet and waking up. Yellow tape ran along the overflow like a clothesline. A Trooper she knew from zoning meetings lifted a hand.

"Evening, Ms. McCormick."

"Staying behind the tape," she said. "Look at me making good choices."

He nodded. "Let's keep it that way."

"Stay at your fifty feet," he said.

"Forty-nine would be gratuitous," she agreed.

The Explorer leaned crooked on the shoulder, one tire slipping into the grass as if the car had grown tired of holding itself up. Dew clung to the windshield, a thin glaze that made the whole thing look embalmed. Troopers were on hand to assist. One lifted a camera; another unsealed an evidence bag with a sigh too weary for evening.

"Ferry schedule," someone called for the log. The folded paper went from console to tongs to a clear evidence bag.

Ryan appeared at her elbow. "Keep the story dry."

"I'm giving the car a nickname in my story."

He winced. "You wound me."

"I'm an equal-opportunity wounder," she said. "What do we have that I can print?"

"Car here. Person not," he said. "That's it. Harrow's allergic to me today, so I'm not pushing my luck."

"He should take antihistamines," she said. "Or eat some local honey."

"Go back to your desk," he said. "Write *vehicle located near terminal* a few times until your keyboard files a complaint."

"I'll sprinkle in verbs," she promised.

"Mercy," he said, drifting back to his assigned proximity.

She made notes that wouldn't be sexy but would be true: time, location, who was doing what, what they bagged. Her hand knew how to be steady when her insides didn't. A ferry horn bellowed, a crow laughed like a man who told the same joke at every barbecue. The town did its town thing around this taped square.

She stayed all night in hopes a Trooper would pull Coach from the bushes. They didn't. By the time she went home, the light had decided to

236

be morning. The house smelled like toast with a death wish. Esther sat at the kitchen table with the crossword.

"You're up early," she said.

"I'm always up early. My dreams refuse to be compelling." Esther tapped the crossword with a pencil. "Four-letter word for 'harshly criticize.'"

"Flay," Ava said.

"Fun." Esther said with the kind of nonchalance that could win awards. "Do you want eggs, or do you want to pretend coffee is breakfast?"

"Coffee is breakfast," Ava lied.

"Toast," Esther decided. "You look like an anemic heroine from a Brontë novel."

"I don't own a moor."

"You own under-eye circles." She popped bread into the toaster. "What's the word from the land of law and order?"

"Vehicle near the terminal. Coach wasn't in it," Ava said. "Denise gave a statement. That's what I can say. I will not say the sentiments I muttered in my car."

"How very grownup."

"I know. I hate it." Ava sagged into a chair and the chair complained. "Anyone drop anything off?"

On the counter sat a blueberry pie, its lattice top still dusted with sugar. The tin was dented in one corner, as if it had lived a few lives.

"Blueberry," Esther said, pointing. "From Caroline. She said thank you."

"She didn't have to," Ava said. "I haven't fixed any of this yet."

"You're not supposed to," Esther said, sliding toast and jam her way. "All that's left is to tell the town the truth and eat some toast."

"I think that's plenty for one morning," Esther said. "Pie later."

"Thank you," Ava said, mouth already full. "I'm going to shower and then go back out."

"Blessed are the grimly functional," Esther said. "Try not to antagonize the Chief with your face."

"I thought you said it's a beautiful face."

"It has opinions," Esther said.

Upstairs, Ava peeled off yesterday and the fear that lived under her left shoulder blade. The shower did its best. When she came back through the kitchen, Esther was washing dishes, sleeves rolled, the music of Johnny Cash on low. Esther performed *normal* the way mothers did when the world was spinning out of control and a child needed calming.

"Keep me updated," Esther said without looking.

"I will," Ava answered, which was their shared euphemism for *I will send you three words at some point and you will read them like tea leaves.*

Back at the terminal, the lot was a polite mess. The tape was down. She updated their live blog with the kind of dryness that would make a saltine jealous: Coach Ellery's vehicle was located near the Dockside Trailhead adjacent to the ferry terminal. The police department is seeking to interview Mr. Ellery. She left it at that. No adjectives. If she used an adjective, she'd start being honest in ways readers would underline and send to their friends.

Ryan appeared again. "Soon," he said.

"I'm already standing," she said.

"Hold that thought. Hold your line." He tapped her elbow with a pen and disappeared. Favorite phantom.

The day wobbled forward. The ferry came and went. A man in a Coors Light hat asked a Trooper if the crime would delay his vacation. "The tide's in charge, sir," the Trooper said, and Ava bit her lip so she didn't compliment his bedside manner.

By late morning, the tow truck took the Explorer. The lot exhaled like it had been holding its stomach muscles for hours. She went back to the office and put up another live line. A colleague pinged her: Can we say "suspect"? She typed "no" in three languages and then please don't make me come down there in emoji.

When she got home, Esther and George were at the table trying to remember the name of an actor with "good eyebrows."

"Every actor has good eyebrows," Ava said, kissing George's crown. He pretended to wave her away and failed.

"Not like this one," he said, stubborn.

"Significant brow energy?" she suggested, and he pointed a finger-gun like she'd won something.

She eyed the blueberry lattice in the fridge, its sugared top glistening like it was judging her.

"So, your grandma said you spoke with Caroline and Mason." George asked.

"She and the family have a lot to deal with," Ava said. "Caroline's grateful. In Spruce Cove, gratitude comes baked in a pie."

"It sure does," Esther murmured.

**

Ava hadn't slept in more than twenty-four hours. Her body ached with it, skin tight, eyes grainy. She climbed the stairs, every step heavier than the last, and collapsed into bed, finally letting herself drift under. Moments later, her phone buzzed.

Liz: *you up?*

Liz: *please tell me you didn't sleep through your phone*

Liz: *chief's at the terminal. they're set up for a press conference.*

Ava: *awake. on my way.*

Liz: *good. basics only: car, time, location, custody y/n. no color.*

Liz: *text me when you get there so i don't have to haunt the scanner.*

"Go," Esther said when Ava grabbed her bag. "And text me. I think I like texts now. George says I'm unstoppable."

"You do?" Ava blinked.

"I also learned the thumbs-up," Esther added, lifting her phone like a trophy. "Prepare yourself."

239

***

The afternoon air was cold. The terminal lot was wet but awake. A folding podium with the town seal sat by the pay phones; a small speaker rested on a milk crate with an orange extension cord snaking off it. No TV trucks. No crowd. A town employee clipped a phone onto a wobbly tripod for the Facebook stream and taped a printer page to the podium: PRESS. Around here, "press" meant Liz and Ava.

Ava: parked. setup's ready; officers posted.

Liz: on my way. five minutes.

Liz: if they confirm custody before i get there, text me the time and where.

Ryan slid in on her left, eyes on the podium. "Chief just came in. Troopers are on the perimeter."

"I'm set," she said. Her pulse kicked under her ribs. If this held, there would be justice for Amelia. And, finally, Chap would be free. She thought of William's voice under airport noise: *Text me alive.* She would.

Ryan nodded and headed back toward the tape.

Neighbors drifted in: dog walkers with coffee, two fishermen still in boots, the bakery owner in a flour-dusted hoodie. Half the boys' basketball team showed up in school hoodies and Air Jordans, one with a ball tucked under his arm; they kept their voices low, eyes jumpy. *Is it about the coach? They found his SUV, right? What about Chap?* Phones lifted ready to record.

Chief Harrow stepped to the folding podium with the town seal, flanked by a State Trooper. He kept it short.

"At approximately 10:12 a.m., officers of the Spruce Cove Police Department, with assistance from the State Troopers, took Conner Ellery into custody near the ferry terminal," he said. "The arrest was without incident. He is being processed at the station. This remains an active investigation. We'll share more when we can. No questions."

The words landed clean and heavy. Relief hit first, sharp and bright, followed by the ache that never felt like victory. Nothing brought Amelia back. But truth had a place to stand now and Chap had a way out.

A small, collective exhale moved through the crowd. One gasp, one "knew it," one "poor Denise," and a quiet "thank God." The basketball boys shifted as a group; one muttered, "Guess practice isn't the headline," and the kid next to him elbowed him to shut up.

Ava: *confirmed custody. 10:12 a.m., north side by the pay phones.*

Liz: *posting. two minutes out. grab a quote.*

A Trooper lifted the little speaker off its milk crate. He coiled the orange extension cord. People lingered, trading theories in low voices the way towns do when they've waited too long for an answer and finally get it. Ava opened a blank note and started shaping verbs. Later, she'd text Esther and William.

No one cheered. No one cried. The police did their jobs. The town took a breath.

Chapter 23

By 2 o'clock, the *Gazette* office sounded like someone had put a coffee shop and a post office into a blender. The bell over the glass door never got the memo about pacing; it dinged like an excited cousin at a wedding. The fax machine, a beige dinosaur, purred as if it had feelings about relevance. Phones rang. Someone knocked on the front window with the kind of friendly persistence that would eventually crack a knuckle or the glass.

Ava's desk had turned into a geography of paper and cables and half a blueberry muffin she did not remember agreeing to. Her laptop blinked at her with the open live blog: Coach Ellery in Custody; PD Promises Update. The headline was accurate and boring, exactly what Liz demanded before coffee. Liz herself moved through the newsroom like a brisk wind, one hand on a to-go mug, the other distributing assignments, her brain already editing page one.

"Give me three lines for the afternoon brief: where he was picked up, 'without incident,' and 'processing at the station,'" Liz said without looking up, because her eyes were everywhere else.

"On it," Ava said, fingers already marching. "Do you want the bit about the boys' basketball team member watching with a ball like hope is a sport?"

"Not in the brief," Liz said. "Save the kids for the longer story. You're writing the story."

"Copy," Ava said, deadpan, and earned the side smile that made long days feel short.

The doorbell dinged. And dinged. And dinged again because Spruce Cove was a small town that believed in physical proximity as a customer service strategy. A fisherman with tide still on his boots leaned in, cap already in his hands because somehow the newsroom felt like a church.

"You got anything that isn't what the Chief said?" he asked, voice pitched low, the way people spoke at hospital waiting rooms and wakes.

"Not yet," Liz said kindly. "If we did, we'd be printing it. Promise."

He nodded like that was fair, then slid a brown paper bag onto the front counter. "Day-olds from the wharf," he said. "The cinnamon ones are less sad."

Behind him came a parade that could have been cast by a local director with a grudge against silence: the bakery owner with a tray of scones, the librarian with a stack of ancient microfiche boxes she'd "thought about tossing" until today, two boys from the basketball team with the resigned posture of teenagers unsure about their future. The shorter one carried a ball like it was a passport, the only ID he'd ever need. The other wore slides.

"Is it true?" Slide Kid asked, words shrinking at the last second as if they had asked for permission and not gotten it. "About Coach?"

"It's true he's in custody," Ava said, gentling her voice the way you did when you gave bad news to a good dog. "It's true the Chief said, 'without incident.' That's what we can print."

Slide Kid nodded, eyes flicking to his friend as if there were a code he was missing. "Is there practice?"

"Ask your assistant coach," Liz said, and that was when the taller boy's mouth did something that was almost laughter and almost the sound a person makes when they drop a glass.

The doorbell dinged again. Caroline stepped in with a paper grocery bag balanced on her hip like a toddler. She scanned the room and found Ava, the little relief in her shoulders like a micro-weather system that blew in and softened the air. Mason came behind her with a cardboard coffee carrier and the expression of a man who had recently learned you could be wrong without dying from it.

"I brought fruit," Caroline said, which was maybe the most Caroline sentence anyone had ever said. "And cups."

"You're a saint," Liz told her, then took the coffee like it was a life-saving device. "No halo required."

Caroline's eyes asked the question she didn't, so Ava answered with the fraction of a nod that meant: *As of ten minutes ago, same status: Chap is still in jail.* Caroline exhaled as if even that tiny certainty could be a pillow. Mason hovered by the display, eyes fixed on the photo of Coach and the boys' team grinning after regionals. One boy held the cut-down net aloft like a crown, the rest clustered around him, a blur of sweat and pride.

Inside the office, the two interns, both summer kids who had turned into one-year holdovers because nobody had the heart to send them back to campus when campus was three ferries away, took up position at the phones. One was very good at "No, we can't tell you that" and even better at saying it like a gift. The other took names for the Community Voices page Liz insisted on every month because, as she put it, "Letting the town talk keeps them from climbing into our windows."

"Mr. Frakes wants to send us a letter," Intern Two called out. "Wants the subject line to read 'I told you so' in all caps."

"Forward to opinion," Liz said. "And please remind him we have a three-exclamation-point max."

"Got it," Intern Two said, solemn.

Ava wrote quickly and cleanly, the way you do when the facts are sharp and the rest of the world is a fog bank. She filed the brief. She hit update. She took two phone calls that consisted of the exact same question from two different octaves: "How sure are you?" She said the same thing both times: "As sure as the police statement."

Her inbox lit up like a parade: ESTHER, WILLIAM (one line: *Alive?*), CLERK–SUPERIOR COURT (automatic, subject: *Docket Update*), SCPD (press release PDF), Denise Ellery (no subject; she marked it for later because kindness deserved attention, not speed).

"You hear that?" Ryan asked as he walked by, already reading a press release on his phone.

The fax sputtered out a page. Then another. Then stopped halfway through a third as if it had decided to take a union break.

"Of course," Liz said, smacking the side of the antiquated machine. "Of course you're dramatic."

Ava slid her hands into the fax the way you coaxed a stubborn drawer. "There you are," she told the paper, which, to be fair, needed encouragement to exist.

The first page was a boilerplate cover sheet from the Clerk's Office of the Superior Court. A box checked next to Courtesy Copy. The second page wore the bulk of the words: Order Granting Motion to Dismiss Without Prejudice. The third page, once it was freed from the bowels of the fax machine, carried the judge's signature and the sentence that punched louder than anything else: Defendant to be released forthwith.

A sound happened in her throat that didn't have a word. Relief, yes, but also a heat at the back of her eyes that meant her body had opinions too.

"Is that what I think it is?" Liz asked, already moving.

"It's the order," Ava said. "It's real." Her voice came out like it had been sitting on its hands and finally got to move.

Liz didn't hug in the office; she had established long ago that there would be rules or there would be lawsuits. But she leaned. Leaning in Liz-speak was the equivalent of a full-body tackle everywhere else. "We confirm?" she asked.

"Calling the clerk," Ava said. "Then live update. Then the story."

The phone call took exactly twelve words, because the woman at the clerk's desk had the kind of voice that told you she'd been preparing for this exact twenty seconds since she was young. "Yes, ma'am," the woman said. "Order signed. 'Forthwith' means 'now.' Yes, you can print that."

Ava thanked her. Then she updated the live blog, fingers steady: Court Grants Motion to Dismiss Against Chapman Fisher; "Forthwith" Release Ordered. Her screen filled with the kind of comments that were both inevitable and boring: "Finally," "About time," and "I always knew" from people who absolutely had not. She didn't read more. She didn't need to. Truth didn't ask for applause; it asked for accuracy.

Behind her, Caroline caught Mason's sleeve. "Did you hear?" she asked, too bright, too soft.

He nodded like a man told a piece of news he had practiced in his head but never quite believed would land. "I'll call Mom and Dad," he said. "We'll …" He didn't finish. He had no plan, no playbook.

Ava's phone buzzed so hard it scuttled toward the edge of her desk like a crab. She grabbed it on reflex.

"Chap?" she said, because even though the number said *Unknown*, her heart knew better.

There was noise in the background, voices bouncing off ceilings, an announcement of the M/V Columbia's arrival. Then Chap's voice, close and raw and somehow smiling. "Hey, McCormick."

She hadn't realized she'd been braced for bars in the background. The absence felt like suddenly noticing how heavy your coat had been when you took it off. "Hey."

"They handed me a paper with my name on it," he said. "I almost asked them to read it to me because my eyes were doing dumb things."

"I have the paper too," she said. "Faxed. Printed. Signed. 'Forthwith' and everything."

He laughed, the kind that hit a bruised spot and still felt good. "I'm headed home."

She pressed her palm to her sternum as if that would make the words sit properly in her body. Juneau. Headed home. "I'll meet you," she said, which was impractical and also true.

"You've got work," he said gently. "You've always got work."

"Sometimes work is driving someone home from the ferry," she said. "Sometimes work is telling the truth to the right person."

"You're good at telling the truth," he said. "Not driving."

"Don't get lippy with me sir," she said, and managed to make it light.

"I won't," he said. A pause. "And Ava?"

"Yeah?"

"Thank you," he said. Not the brittle kind of thank you people said when they wanted a debt erased. The kind that landed and made itself a chair. "For not giving up on me. Even when it looked like you should."

"You're welcome," she said, and then had to bite the inside of her cheek to keep her voice from climbing a ladder it couldn't get down from. "Text me when you're on the ferry. Grandma will make too much food."

"Wouldn't want to disappoint Esther," he said, with reverence. "See you soon."

He hung up. She stared at the phone like it had revealed a magic trick. Then she looked up and realized the newsroom had paused. Not all the way. Not dramatically. But enough that everyone within ten feet was pretending very hard to do something else.

"Release is official," she said, to the room and to herself.

Caroline's hand went to her mouth and stayed there. Mason made a tiny broken sound that was not the sound of a man breaking, but the sound of something springing back into place.

Liz clapped once, softly, like a coach who didn't want to embarrass anybody. "Okay," she said. "We work."

"Story?" Ava asked, already pulling up a blank document.

"Story," Liz said. "Start at the terminal. Jump to the order. Keep the verbs clean. Use names we can print. And Ava?"

"Mm?"

"Take a victory lap," Liz said. "In a paragraph. You get one."

Ava nodded. She wrote. She wrote fast enough to outrun the swirl of everything and slow enough not to trip. She wrote what the town had done and what the police had done and what the paper had refused to do: guess. She did not write about the precise shape of relief in her chest, because this story was not a diary. She did make one sentence that tasted like satisfaction and put Liz's name on it too.

By ten, the newsroom had turned into a nest of folding chairs someone had loaned from the community center. People drifted in and out, asking the same questions, telling the same stories, pressing the same

247

hands. Denise slipped in wearing sunglasses like armor. She placed a covered dish on the counter and said, "It's lasagna," and nobody called it a stereotype because sometimes a stereotype was love wearing sweatpants.

"Take it home," she said to Ava. "Eat it late. Or early. I don't know what time it is."

"Thank you," Ava said. "Both for the pasta and everything else."

Denise nodded once like *everything else* was a grocery item she had been on the lookout for and had finally found.

By 2 p.m., the beige fax coughed again, like it had swallowed a fly and wanted to tell someone about it. It spit out a Notice of Hearing Vacated and a Receipt of Property with a list that would someday make Ava tear up in a grocery line: 1 wallet; 1 key ring; 1 paperback (worn). She put the papers into a folder labeled Chap in a handwriting she had only used on birthday cards and articles that scared her.

By 3 p.m., the story went up. Liz wrote the headline because she trusted herself to be boring in a way that was dignified: Ellery in Custody; Court Dismisses Case Against Fisher. She changed nothing else. Which, for Liz, was the equivalent of a bouquet and a balloon.

"Go," Liz said to Ava, once the words were live. "You wrote it. Go tell your people. Bring back quotes if your people want to give them. Otherwise bring back your face."

"I think I will," Ava said, smiling.

"Take my car," Liz added, throwing over keys. "Yours still sounds like a vacuum that swallowed a coin."

Ava managed a half-smile. "I can't even argue with that." And she didn't. Liz's car had heat that worked without prayer.

As she headed for the door, the boys' basketball pair reappeared, this time with two more in tow and the new head coach, who looked like he had slept zero minutes and made peace with it. They clustered near the paper display rack, all elbows and grief.

"You going to write about us?" one asked Ava, not cocky, just curious about whether he would exist in the morning paper.

"I'm going to write about what you did right," she said. "Which is show up for each other."

He nodded like that was better than a box score.

"Tell your parents the lasagna at the Chronicle is for staff only," Liz called after them. "But that we will trade for cinnamon rolls."

"Deal," the shortest one said, because Spruce Cove understood barter.

Ava tucked the folder under her arm like it was a book she'd been waiting to read for a very long time.

***

Spruce Cove did not stop for joy. It never had. On Front Street, ravens held a meeting on the line by the cannery and sounded like they were winning. A bald eagle sat on the light pole over the harbor like a grumpy celebrity. The boardwalk was slick enough to make everyone adopt the same careful, knees-bent shuffle they used from October to May. The smell of salt and diesel and coffee from the harbor café braided themselves into the air and said *home*.

Ava drove Liz's Subaru, which had a sticker for every ferry in the fleet and a dashboard that held a knitted octopus wearing a tiny beanie. A tugboat horn sounded once, low and patient. Two fishermen in Grundens rolled a cart of totes toward the dock, arguing about herring like it was religion. A floatplane was landing the next cove over, kissing the water and taxied toward the dock.

Her phone buzzed at a light.

William: *You okay?*

She stared. Last night had been airport noise and caution. She typed with two thumbs and a thump in her chest.

Ava: *Driving. Safe. Talk later.*

William: *Good. Be careful.*

She put the phone facedown. The light turned. She took the back road because the main one had a grader blocking half a lane and she didn't have time to admire municipal perseverance.

The house looked like itself, shingles that always needed paint, a porch step that sang the same note under her left foot, bear-proof cans lined up. Salmonberry bushes along the fence had given up a month ago; they stood anyhow, tough and ready. The wind chimes hit their split-second chords and went still, which meant the breeze was honest.

A text from Esther arrived as she parked: we have pie. No capital letters. No punctuation. Proof again that Esther did, in fact, like to text now.

Ava took the path she'd taken a thousand times, hit the same singing board on the porch because habit was affection, and pushed the back door open with the shoulder that still remembered high school basketball.

"Chap's been released!" she called, because joy should not have to wait for the person carrying it.

***

The kitchen smelled like coffee and blueberry pie. Steam fogged one corner of the window above the sink where the caulk always pulled away in winter. Esther turned from the stove with a spatula like a baton. George looked up from the crossword with his reading glasses parked halfway down his nose, pencil paused over the eternal three-letter baseball era that solved everything. And at the table, holding the porcelain mug from the top shelf, the one reserved for holidays and people they intended to impress, sat William.

For a second, everything slowed down and then sharpened. He was exactly himself and not: travel hair, travel eyes, travel shoulders that had decided to stay upright until given specific permission to drop. He had the shy confidence of a man who had dashed across a continent and then remembered he might not be welcome.

"Hey," he said, standing because George had bullied manners into everyone he liked.

"Hey," Ava said. Her mouth tried to keep it breezy; her heart wasn't subtle.

"Chap?" William asked.

"In Juneau," she said. "On his way home."

"Good," William said softly.

George pushed back his chair with a small grunt and made a show of straightening a dish towel that did not need straightening. "I'll check the bird feeder," he announced to the room and the world, as if chickadees were more likely to arrive if he performed a ritual. He tucked the crossword under his arm like a football. Esther squeezed Ava's forearm, a press that said *I'm here; we're fine,* and followed George out, leaving the door ajar the way they always did. In this house, you left room for air and people.

Silence landed. Not a heavy one. A careful one. The room held coffee breath and the ticking clock above the stove that was always three minutes fast in winter because George refused to fix it on principle ("we will arrive early until the ocean learns to be on time"). A seagull complained somewhere over the cove. On the porch, a wind chime pinged like it was raising its hand.

Ava set the folder on the table and opened her mouth to fill the air with safe sentences about soup and Mrs. Tuttle's carrot cake waiting in the newsroom because that was easier than the way her chest felt at that moment. Nothing came out.

William didn't move closer. He didn't rush. He watched her the way one would watch the weather: respectfully, aware he didn't get a vote.

Her phone buzzed on the counter. Probably Liz asking for quotes. Or Chap announcing he had made the ferry. She didn't reach for it.

William's throat worked once. He placed the delicate mug back on its saucer with the kind of care you use for a thing you expect to break and don't want to help along. He met her eyes and didn't look away.

"I haven't earned it, but I'm asking for a chance."

EPILOGUE

The clouds broke just enough for him to see the mountains, jagged and endless, white with late-winter snow. The plane tilted slightly, sunlight flashing across the wing. William tightened his seatbelt and watched Alaska rise beneath him like a challenge.

This wasn't a vacation. He hadn't lied to himself that way.

He was coming for her.

Ava McCormick. The one person he had destroyed and the one who still haunted every version of his future.

He had spent the past months on the East Coast trying to focus on everything that was supposed to matter: recommendations, interviews, a future lined with bullet points. But when the noise stopped, she was still there. She cut through his defenses and became the only future he could envision. The way she looked at him the day he betrayed her had hurt more than anything she could have said.

Eventually, he stopped pretending he was ever going to get over Ava. He booked the ticket to Alaska, traced the route from Boston to Seattle to Juneau, and bought a ferry ticket the same day. He had not told his family or friends. This was not a noble gesture. No fresh-start story.

He just wanted to make things right.

The plane touched down hard, skidding briefly before finding its balance. The hum of the engines faded, replaced by the shuffle of passengers gathering their coats. William sat still for a moment, watching snow sweep across the tarmac. The mountains beyond the runway were so close they looked like they could swallow him whole.

Outside, the air was sharp enough to sting his lungs. He followed the crowd through the small Juneau airport terminal, the kind of place where everyone already looked like they belonged. He didn't. Not yet.

Hours later, the Malaspina pushed away from the dock, its deck slick with frozen mist. The lights of Juneau slipped behind him, swallowed by fog. Ahead was only darkness and sea. The engine's low rumble vibrated up through his boots, steady as a heartbeat.

He leaned against the ferry railing, wind cutting across his face. Somewhere ahead was Spruce Cove, small and stubborn, built into the edge of the world. The place she had chosen when she decided she could not stay with him.

He didn't expect her to forgive him. But she deserved to have him try like hell.

He would fight for it, for her, and for the version of himself he had buried when he betrayed her.

The ferry horn rolled across the water, low and steady. Snow began to fall, soft and certain and relentless.

William straightened, the wind biting at his face, his chest, his resolve.

"Ava," he whispered, just once, like a promise.

Then he shouldered his bag and walked toward the lights.

WOULD LOVE TO STAY
SPRUCE COVE SERIES BOOK 3

It has been less than a year since William Hudson broke Ava McCormick's heart, but it feels like forever. She left behind Yale, expectations, and the life she spent her whole life chasing. Now she is in Spruce Cove, Alaska, a place that is rough around the edges and full of people who know too much, but it is also the first place that has ever felt like it could be home.

After months of fighting to prove Chap Fisher was not guilty of murder, Ava finally helps prove his innocence. She is ready to embrace her future with Chap, who is magnetic and alive in a way that makes her forget the careful life she once thought she wanted.

Then William shows up.

The man who broke her heart is sitting in her grandparents' kitchen, looking older, softer, and sorry in a way that makes her remember what she once saw in him. William's reappearance causes Chap to pull back and start forging a life without her.

As winter thaws in Spruce Cove, Ava has to decide between two vastly different futures and the only men she has ever loved. Will she make her choice before both men give up?

Would Love to Stay is a story about the people we meet at the wrong time, the choices that shape who we become, and what it really means to stay when every instinct says to run.

Be the first to know when *Would Love to Stay* releases. Sign up at www.joyoffiction.

ACKNOWLEDGEMENTS

Writing a book takes a village. Or, in my case, one very patient husband, a superhero mom, and three amazing teenagers who bring humor, fun, and just the right amount of chaos to our household.

I'd be remiss if I didn't start with Greg, my husband and partner in everything. Thank you for holding down the fort while I had my head buried in this story, for making formatting look effortless when it absolutely isn't, and for keeping our world running with patience and love. You're the steady current that keeps everything afloat.

To my mom, who once again offered brilliant edits, and reminded me when to take a breath. Your wisdom and encouragement mean more than I can ever say.

To our kids, thank you for your laughter, your energy, and for walking the dog when I disappeared into Spruce Cove. You make every day better, noisier, and infinitely brighter.

To the readers who returned to Spruce Cove, thank you for falling in love with this town and its people. You're the reason I get to keep writing.

And finally, to the community who raised me and to the wonderfully salty people of Southeast Alaska, thank you. You gave me a sense of wonder, a deep respect for place, and a love of stories that find their truth. This book wouldn't exist without you.

Stay hooked!

ABOUT THE AUTHOR

Joy Thomas grew up in a Southeast Alaskan fishing town where boots were non-negotiable and stories were as common as rain (some of them even true). A former journalist, she writes modern fiction with heart, grit, and a splash of mystery. Her debut novel, Stay Salty, kicked off the Spruce Cove Series: a romantic mystery set in a coastal town where secrets rise like the tide and the past has a habit of washing back ashore. She lives in the Charlotte, North Carolina metro area with her family of five and a beagle named Magnolia.

VISIT JOY THOMAS ONLINE:

www.joyoffiction.com

www.ingramcontent.com/pod-product-compliance
Lightning Source LLC
Chambersburg PA
CBHW052046240626
47153CB00006B/2232